Do you watch true crime shows? Do you wish that Criminal Minds had been a wee bit sexier? Do you love a hot, alpha hero who hunts killers for fun?

Ahem, if so, this book is for you. Happy reading and happy hunting.

He didn't want a new partner, especially not *her*.

FBI Agent Gray Stone knows killers. As a top profiler at the Bureau, monsters are truly his business. So he absolutely does not need to be paired up with the infuriating—and gorgeous—Dr. Emerson Marlowe. But her mother is a senator with far too much power, and, all of a sudden, Gray finds himself on training duty, a duty that includes way too many hours and way too much temptingly close contact with Emerson.

He doesn't play well with others. In fact, he doesn't play at all.

What's he supposed to do with a sexy shadow? One who is just as good at mind games as he is? One who is smart and funny and...*dammit*. Emerson has practically no field experience, and the last thing Gray wants to do is put her in harm's way. He may not want to work with Emerson, but he will not let anyone hurt her. So when a new case goes sideways and a killer gets chillingly close, Gray has to come up with a new training plan.

New rules: She follows his orders. She does exactly what he says. And she does not get in the way.

Except Emerson can't follow orders to save her life. She does whatever she wants, and the woman is one hundred percent in his way. In his way. In his mind. In his dreams. And, maybe, just maybe, the infuriating Emerson is even working her sneaky way into his heart. But danger is growing around her, danger that doesn't seem to just be coming from their work at the FBI. A stalker has eyes on Emerson, a predator who is well-acquainted with darkness and pain. A perp who wants Emerson to suffer.

To protect his new partner, Gray will have to let his own darkness come out to hunt.

No one turns Gray's partner into prey. No one terrifies Emerson. No one hurts her. Ever. Gray stops playing the good guy, and he goes all in on protecting her. Protecting and defending—that's his way of life, but this time, the defense is personal. Emerson is *his*—uh, his partner, of course, and, hell, maybe a whole lot more. Gray has always kept his inner darkness on a tight leash, but when Emerson is threatened, his control shatters. He will claim her, he will protect her, and he will put the perp who threatens her in the ground.

Author's note: Grayson "Gray" Stone has spent far too many years playing mind games with other people. This time, he's the one who will see his life spiral out of control as he falls hard for a partner he never expected. Forced proximity, danger, desire, opposites fiercely attracting...oh, get ready for all the fun things. Did I mention the steam? Because there is plenty of it in this romance.

When He Defends

A Protector And Defender Romance
Book 4

Cynthia Eden

HOCUS POCUS PUBLISHING INC

This book is a work of fiction. Any similarities to real people, places, or events are not intentional and are purely the result of coincidence. The characters, places, and events in this story are fictional.

Published by Hocus Pocus Publishing, Inc.

Copyright © 2025 by Cindy Roussos

All rights reserved. This publication may not be reproduced, distributed, or transmitted in any form without the express written consent of the author except for the use of small quotes or excerpts used in book reviews. No part of this work may be used in the training of AI models.

If you have any problems, comments, or questions about this publication, please contact info@hocuspocuspublishing.com.

build 1

Chapter One

"What have I always wanted to do? Stop monsters."
– Emerson Marlowe

"What does she mean to you?" The tip of the screwdriver shoved beneath Emerson Marlowe's chin. Her head tipped back, and her wide, blue eyes met Gray Stone's stare as her attacker held her against his fat, sweating body.

The attacker. A prick who got off on hurting those weaker than him.

Rain pelted onto the roof of the garage. A 1988 Camaro —sporting a bright red coat of paint—waited with its wheels off on the lift to the right. A million tools and parts were scattered around the dusty garage, and the owner of that garage—the man currently shoving the tip of that screwdriver into Emerson's delicate skin—heaved out rough, gasping breaths.

Jake Waller. Age forty-seven. Divorced, three times. A loner who'd been unlucky in love and in life, thanks to the battered knee he'd got the first year he tried to play college football. Angry, jealous, disenchanted. Pissed at the world.

A man who fit the profile of the killer that Gray had been hunting to a perfect T.

One of Jake's beefy arms had locked around Emerson's waist. The other greasy hand held the screwdriver beneath her chin. If he shoved up that screwdriver, if he hurt her...

You will be a fucking dead man.

Gray had his gun out and aimed. He could pull the trigger and blow out Jake's brains right then and there. He'd prefer not to take that path. *But if you push that screwdriver up even a millimeter more, you are done, asshole.*

"What does she mean to you?" Spittle flew from Jake's mouth as he repeated his screeching question. His voice cracked on the words. He hadn't been expecting a visit from the FBI. He'd panicked as soon as Gray had introduced himself and flashed his ID.

The perp had freaked and grabbed a human shield in the form of Emerson. An Emerson who should have been waiting her sweet ass in the car. Only the woman could not follow orders for shit. Truly. She'd prissed into the garage, thrown open the door, and Jake had pounced on her.

After all, Emerson was his preferred prey. The predator always took women. Delicate builds. Pretty faces. And he left them broken and dead.

He won't be hurting my partner. But, as to the question the jerk had just posed...

Gray inclined his head slightly to Emerson before he took his gaze off her and focused completely on the threat. "Nothing."

A deep furrow appeared between Jake's brows. *I can make that furrow deeper. I can plant a bullet right between those brows.* Keeping his gun leveled at his target, Gray added, "The woman means absolutely nothing to me. Or, actually, if you want the brutal truth, she's a complete pain in my ass."

Emerson gasped.

Not because the screwdriver had moved. It hadn't. Gray would have pulled the trigger if it had. She'd gasped because he'd called her a pain in the ass.

She was one, though. Case in point, the woman was being held by a sweaty psycho who wanted to drive a screwdriver up through her chin when she should have been in the *car*.

"What?" Jake blinked his squinty eyes. He seemed to have trouble processing what Gray had just said.

So Gray said the words again. Slower. A bit more clearly. With a hint of relish as he took one gliding step forward. "She means nothing to me." Another gliding step. "She's a pain in my ass." One more step. "A partner I did not want." *Hello, yet another step.* "The current bane of my existence."

Jake blinked more. Rapidly. Confused, he began, "The bane of your—"

"But I can't let you hurt her. No one hurts her." Gray was inches away from Emerson and from Jake. "Because pain in the ass or not, she's mine." Wait, that had come out wrong. Time to clarify. "My partner." There. Way better. "And either let her go, right now, or I will put this bullet into you." Fair warning, he would be firing. Gray never bluffed. Correction, he bluffed when he played cards. He bluffed like a rock star when he was at a poker table with his former Marine buddies. But as far as the rest of his life was concerned...*I never say shit I don't mean. I will fire this gun and have zero regrets.*

The rain struck the metal roof ever harder. *Rat-tat-tat-*

tat. Thunder rumbled. The very building seemed to vibrate around them.

"I could count," Gray mused. Counting was an option. Not one he planned to take, but, still, an option. "Start at five and count my way down. Tell you if you don't let her go by the time I reach zero, I'll pull the trigger."

Jake's mouth hung open.

"But I don't feel like counting." Seriously, he was just not in the mood for that crap. Not in the mood and he did not have the patience for a countdown. "I have the shot, and I'm taking it unless you let my partner go right the hell *now.*"

Jake snapped his mouth closed. He also didn't release Emerson. A huge mistake. But Emerson used that moment to slam her right high heel down on Jake's foot as hard as she could. Jake howled.

Emerson elbowed her attacker even as her other hand tried to wrestle the screwdriver from him. She managed to get it away from her chin, and she surged to the right.

"You bitch!" Jake screamed.

Gray's jaw tightened as he pulled the trigger. The bullet blasted into his target, and a spray of blood flashed in the air as Jake fell down. The screwdriver flew from his fingers and clattered onto the cement flooring of the garage. Emerson hit the floor, too, her hands slamming against the cement as her dark hair flew around her face.

"Emerson!" Gray barked out her name as he surged toward his prey.

"I'm okay!" A quick yell back. She glanced his way, sending her hair swirling again. "I'm okay." Less strained. More controlled. More Emerson.

With his jaw locked hard, Gray closed the last bit of distance between him and Jake.

When He Defends

The fool was trying to rise, so Gray shoved his big, gleaming dress shoe onto the bullet wound—a wound in Jake's left shoulder. He hadn't sent the shot into the prick's head because at the last moment, when Emerson had gotten clear, he'd known that he didn't *have* to kill the guy.

But I sure as hell wanted to send the bullet into his brain. I wanted to destroy the bastard for threatening to hurt Emerson.

Gray ground his shoe into the wound, putting the full weight of his body into the attack. Jake howled and jerked beneath him, trying to wrench up. And when the prick wrenched up, Gray put his gun to the man's forehead. "Hi, there."

Jake froze.

"Didn't you ever learn that you aren't supposed to be rough with someone who is weaker than you? That you are supposed to watch your strength?"

Jake's breath shuddered out.

"Didn't you ever learn..." It would be so easy to pull the trigger. One little squeeze, and there would be one less twisted predator in the world. So very tempting. But Emerson was watching. Emerson who'd gotten to her feet. Who was tip-toeing closer in her red heels. Her sweet, tempting scent wrapped around him. Summer nights. Jasmine. And, somehow... innocence.

He forced his teeth to unclench. "Didn't you ever learn that you aren't supposed to put your dirty hands on things that do not belong to you?"

Jake's gaze darted toward Emerson. He tried to surge toward her. Tried to grab for the screwdriver that he'd dropped.

So Gray stomped his foot into the man's wound. Hard.

Jake screamed in agony.

"Grayson!" Emerson's shocked voice.

"Don't look at her," he barked to Jake. "Look right at me. Me!"

Jake's gaze whipped back to Gray.

"You killed those women." Three victims. Women who'd all been found, with very distinct wounds on their bodies. Some with the deep punctures made from a screwdriver. Grease and oil residue had been discovered in their wounds. The kind of grease and oil that you'd find in a car repair shop. *The kind in this garage.* "For those victims, you were their nightmare."

Jake began to smile.

"Guess what? I'm *your* nightmare." Gray pressed the muzzle of his gun a bit harder into Jake's head. "I'm going to lock you away, and I'm going to make sure that you never see the light of day again. Where you're going, you'll be the prey. Trust me on this, the other inmates will love to have their chance torturing *you*."

Fear flashed in Jake's eyes. He lost his smile.

"Kick away the screwdriver, Emerson," Gray ordered.

She kicked it away. Finally, the woman had actually followed an order. Miracle of miracles.

So he'd go for another directive. "Go outside and call for backup," he added.

Only Emerson didn't move. So much for miracles.

Gray sighed. "*Emerson.*"

"I can, uh, call for backup right here."

Can't follow orders for shit. His gaze angled toward her.

"Don't," she said before he could bark out another command.

His eyes narrowed on her.

"Don't kill him. Don't let your control break. He's not worth it."

When He Defends

Holy shit. She knows just how bad my darkness is. Because the beast that he tried so hard to keep chained inside was fighting hard to break past Gray's control. The sonofabitch on the ground had been ready to hurt Emerson, perhaps ready to kill her as he'd killed those other women.

"We don't have hard evidence yet," Emerson reminded him in her cool, calm, and collected voice.

"He just attacked you," Gray reminded her in his are-you-fucking-kidding-me voice. "That attack means we're gonna have cause to search this whole place." He glowered at the killer. "Thanks for making the whole search business easy, dumbass. Otherwise, we would have needed to do the full song and dance for a warrant, but now here I am, about to arrest your ass inside your business." A low whistle escaped him as he considered the matter. "Betting you have some mementos around here, don't you? Little trophies to remind you of your kills?" His foot lifted off Jake's shoulder. The guy's blood was everywhere. Gray was pretty sure the bullet had gone in and out of the perp. Gray was also pretty sure that his shoes were ruined. Dammit, he'd liked those shoes. Bought them less than a month ago.

Emerson really should have gone outside and made that call.

A quick glance from the corner of Gray's eye showed that she did have her phone out. She was calling from *right there*. Asking for backup. Saying they needed assistance, stat, with a violent offender who had attacked them. Then she shoved her phone back into her little black bag and fiddled with the purse strap that was—somehow, despite her scuffle—still over one delicate shoulder.

Emerson cleared her throat. Smoothed her hair back into the sleek bob that normally skimmed her shoulders. "You should move the gun away from his forehead. The suspect isn't armed any longer. He's not a lethal threat." She began to walk around the garage. "I do believe we also need to read him his rights, but I am the new one so..."

"What in the hell is she doing?" Jake wanted to know.

"Pissing me off even more," Gray snarled. Pissing him off, plus giving him orders. As if *she* was the one in command when she was the one with practically zero field experience and thus...the whole reason she'd been taken *prisoner by the perp* just moments before. But he did need to move the gun because the longer he kept it on Jake's sweaty forehead...

The more trigger happy I might become. "Jake Waller, you're under arrest."

"For what?"

Was the idiot for real? "How about for attacking a federal officer?" Gray threw back. Though, technically, Emerson wasn't an FBI agent. She was more...freelance. More... problematic.

So very problematic.

Gray hauled Jake to his feet. Read the guy his rights. Gray pulled out cuffs and began to slap them on Jake's wrists. First the right wrist.

"He would have his trophies close." Emerson's heels click-click-clicked on the cement floor. "He'd need to be able to access them anytime he wants, and this garage—well, it's his sanctuary. Makes sense to keep the trophies in his sanctuary, doesn't it?" She stopped near a shelf on the right wall. "Bingo."

Bingo? His head angled so that he could keep both Emerson and his prey in sight.

"That's a big, shiny lock on this toolbox," Emerson noted. She glanced over her shoulder and eyed Jake. "What's inside?"

"Fucking tools!" Jake bellowed. "Get away from my box! Get away!"

She did not, in fact, get away. Gray began to cuff Jake's left wrist.

Jake screamed at an ear-splitting level. "My shoulder, my shoulder! Ah! Assault, assault—" Then the sonofabitch tried to slam his head back at Gray.

Gray dodged the hit. But in that instant, Jake leapt forward, with only one wrist cuffed. He ran not for the exit, but straight for Emerson as she leaned toward the locked toolbox. His hands flew out, reaching for her.

Gray knew he was going to have to shoot the prick again. *"Freeze!"* he bellowed.

But Jake didn't get the chance to freeze because, calm as you please, Emerson lifted her hand from her little, black bag. She gripped a taser, and she immediately tased the ever-loving-hell out of Jake. His whole body shuddered, jolted, and he hit the floor. After wetting himself.

Then Emerson tipped her head back. Those plump, red lips of hers curved just the slightest bit, as if she'd enjoyed tasing the asshole. Slivers of dark hair slid over her high cheekbones, and she blinked her big, bright blue eyes at him. *Sapphire blue.* Yeah, fine, maybe he'd looked up that exact shade because her eyes were so distinct. His buddy Tyler had blue eyes, but they looked nothing like Emerson's. Emerson's eyes stared straight into your soul.

"He wasn't freezing," Emerson murmured. "So I stopped him." She frowned down at the shaking man. "Did I stop him too hard?"

Gray bounded toward her. Put himself between Emerson and the still trembling perp. Then he snapped the second cuff around Jake's left wrist even as the man bellowed and threatened and started screaming that Emerson would be next.

The hell she will, you bastard. You will never touch her again.

"You'll pay, bitch! You'll pay! I'll fill you with so many h-holes that you'll be begging me to stop. You'll cry and bleed, and I w-won't care. Just like the others—you'll end up in a shallow grave, and no one will care! I'll throw you away like the garbage that y-you are!" Some of Jake's words shook and stuttered with his trembles.

Every muscle in Gray's body locked down as he glared at the monster on the floor of that garage. *One squeeze of the trigger, and there is one less nightmare in the world.*

"Don't." For Gray's ears alone. Emerson's low, husky voice. Her soft fingers fluttered down his back and sent a weird, electric charge cascading through him in the wake of her light caress. It was a charge he felt every single time they touched. Hugely problematic.

But, then again, this *was* Emerson. Everything with her was problematic.

His breath huffed out. "You get to tase people, but I have to hold back?" In what world was that fair? Oh, wait, he knew. The world where he'd been forced to take on a partner he didn't want.

"You got to shoot him once already."

He had.

"And we both just got his confession." Her fingers fluttered over Gray's back one more time.

His teeth snapped together.

"Let's call it a win, shall we?" Emerson murmured.

His head turned toward her. He towered over Emerson, even when she wore her heels. The woman *always* seemed to wear heels. Even at the most inopportune of times. "He had a screwdriver shoved under your chin. That's not a win." Not by any definition. Anger rumbled in each word. "That's an assault."

Her eyes widened as she searched his gaze. "Grayson?"

He'd told her over and over again to call him Gray. Just Gray. "It's not a win." Flat. "It's the last mistake he'll ever make."

Gray thought she'd back away from him.

She didn't. Emerson stepped closer. "Are you okay?"

The hell, no, he wasn't. "His last mistake," Gray gritted out, "and yours, too. Consider our partnership *over*."

And, for the first time, real horror filled her gaze. She hadn't been horrified when she'd been grabbed by the serial killer. Hadn't looked horrified—or even particularly afraid when the freak had shoved that screwdriver beneath her chin but now...

Now...

Horror flashed in her incredible eyes.

So did fear.

Then she shook her head. Squared her shoulders and said, very, very definitely, "We're not over, Grayson."

"*Gray.*" Fuck. How many times did he have to tell her? *Gray*. If she called him Gray*son* and she was Emer*son*, they were too fucking sing-songy with their names. *Too coupley*. Too—ah, fuck it. "*Gray.*"

The serial killer at their feet began to whimper. Somewhere in the distance, sirens screamed. Emerson ignored everything else as she stared straight into Gray's eyes and promised him, "We're just beginning."

Chapter Two

*"Hell, no, I don't want a partner. Someone to get in my way? Slow me down? Piss me off? Someone I have to hand-hold every single minute? Sounds like hell. Thanks, but no thanks.
I work best alone. So...fuck off."*
– Gray Stone, FBI Agent

EMERSON MARLOWE PACED THE SMALL CONFINES OF her motel room. One foot in front of the other. Over and over. She reached the wall on the right, the one with the peeling paint and the slightly lopsided picture of a sunflower in the middle of it. She stared at the sunflower. Turned on her heel. Marched back across the room. Her heels made no sound as they tapped across the threadbare carpeting, but an air-conditioner—a window unit—hummed from nearby. She was in a small Tennessee town. Briar, Tennessee.

She'd helped stop a serial killer. Helped create the

profile on the man. Helped to locate him after she'd been so certain that he worked at a car repair shop. *All* of the victims had recently had repairs done to their vehicles, and, of course, add in the element that they'd also been found with oil and grease residue on their bodies...

Tied to a garage. To a mechanic. Had to be.

But the women had used different garages, so it had taken a bit of time to narrow things down. And then they'd realized that the second victim, Tara Grush, had actually broken down on the side of the road and a "Good Samaritan" had helped her to change her tire and then they'd—

A hard knock sounded at the door to her right. Emerson stopped mid-pace. Step number thirteen. Yes, she'd counted. She still counted when she was stressed, and it had been a very stressful day.

The knock hadn't come from the door that led outside of her room. Oh, no, it had come from the *connecting* door—as in, the door that connected her room to Grayson's. *Gray. Gray.* She was supposed to call him *Gray.*

Emerson turned. Stared at the door.

He knocked again. More impatient. More demanding. Typical impatience from him.

She'd known this visit would come. Night had fallen. They'd spent hours at the garage, talking with local law enforcement, collecting evidence, and making sure that nothing could be screwed up when it came to Jake Waller's case. The gleaming lock on the toolbox had been removed, and, inside, they'd found trophies from the victims. Jewelry...and thick locks of hair. Talk about something that would be an easy DNA comparison. The local cops had been shocked to discover the local man they knew was a serial killer. Most of them—and their family members—went to Jake Waller's garage for vehicle repairs.

Gray had been adamant that they keep eyes on the prisoner. Jake had been transported to a nearby hospital because of the bullet wound in his shoulder, but Gray had arranged for both a local field agent from the FBI and a police officer to stay with the perp at all times.

Gray knocked again. Even harder. "Emerson, I know you're in there." The doorknob jiggled. "Open up, or else I'll just pick the lock and come inside."

Would he? Curious, she found herself walking toward the connecting door. The lock was incredibly flimsy. A child could probably pick it.

"Emerson." A deep, rough rumble.

One that she clearly heard through the door. The doors, the walls—the *motel* was paper thin. A shiver slid over her because there was something about Gray's voice. A dark, dangerous allure that called to her.

Get it together, woman. He's your training partner. Not your lover. No matter what kind of awesome fantasies and dreams she might have late at night. They were not involved romantically. Physically. Their relationship was just business. Gray was certainly not interested in anything more.

The man had literally called her the bane of his existence. Like that hadn't stung.

Her hand reached out. Flipped the lock. Yanked open the door.

And, typical Gray, he filled the doorway. Big, powerful. Too tall. Too muscled. Still wearing his white dress shirt, but he'd ditched his suit coat. His sleeves were rolled up, the collar of the dress shirt undone, and he was—

Barefoot?

When He Defends

She frowned at his feet. Was it weird to think that the man had oddly attractive feet?

"*Emerson.*"

Her gaze jumped back to his face. "You're not wearing shoes." Usually, Gray was perfectly attired. He liked fancy suits. He liked expensive clothes. He liked his gleaming dress shoes.

"They had the perp's blood on them."

She nodded. "Because you shoved your foot onto his shoulder and made him scream."

A muscle flexed along his clenched jaw. His chin tilted down slightly as he stared at her. His eyes—his eyes were a swirling mix that fell somewhere between gold and brown. In the light, they always appeared more golden, but as soon as shadows crept around, his gaze would go so very dark.

Sometimes, she could also almost swear his eye color seemed to change with Gray's emotions. When he was angry, his gaze went extremely dark.

It was dark right then.

"My shoes were taken as evidence. I have a backup pair, don't worry, but I didn't think it mattered what the hell I wore when I paid you this break-up visit."

Her shoulders stiffened. "We are not breaking up." First, they weren't a couple. Since they weren't a couple, they could not break up. She took a step closer to him. Even without his shoes, he still towered over her. An annoying trait. She'd always wanted to be taller. Since nature had not seen fit to help her out in that department, she wore her heels as often as she could.

"Oh, Emerson, we are, in fact, breaking up." He also took a step forward. Since they'd already been close, his step pretty much had their bodies brushing. Maybe an inch separated them. She could practically feel the heat from his body reaching out to wrap around her. His scent—rich, masculine, and, dammit, *sexy*—tempted her.

But, then again, everything about Gray tempted her.

Unfortunately.

She kept her chin up. Kept her spine ramrod straight. "You are not going to intimidate me."

"I'm not trying to intimidate you."

Emerson almost snorted at the denial. "Yes, you are. You're in my space. You're towering over me—"

"Everyone towers over you."

"They do *not*. I am an absolutely normal height for a woman." She would have just liked to be taller, but she was *normal*. "You're coming in here, with your shirt unbuttoned and looking all se—" Wow. *Stop*. Red light. Serious, red light. Flashing red. She had almost called him sexy. *Out loud. To his face.* Her eyes widened in quick shock before she whirled away from him.

Get it together.

One, two, three, four, five...she hurriedly took steps to put some distance between them. *Six, seven, eight*—

The connecting door clicked closed behind her. "Looking all...what? Don't think I caught that last descriptor," Gray said. "Please, do not leave a man in suspense."

She spun toward him. Glared.

"My shirt is unbuttoned—the top three buttons—because it's been one long-ass day." He rolled back his shoulders. "See, I was forced to take on this partner who had *zero* actual training."

Her hands clenched at her sides. She worked hard to keep her control in place. Truly, she did. She'd worked hard to get along with Gray. But the man was about to push her too far. "I have some training."

"You're not an FBI agent."

"I went to Quantico—"

"For some bullshit special program that your senator mom created just for you. She pulled strings, she shoved you down the Bureau's throat, and now you're the unavoidable pain in my ass."

Okay, that was the third time he'd called her a pain in the ass. Yes, she'd counted. Her teeth snapped together. "You're not exactly sunshine and champagne."

He blinked. A hint of a smile curved his lips. Only that smile—or what *could* have been a smile—immediately vanished. "You didn't follow orders at the garage."

The man loved orders. He issued them non-stop. "Were you a drill sergeant?"

He stared at her.

"I know you were a Marine. The way you love to bark orders makes me think you must have been a drill sergeant. You have that whole vibe about you."

He rubbed the bridge of his nose. "The term is drill instructor. When you're talking about Marines, they're called drill instructors." Flat. "Drill sergeants are in the Army."

"Oh." She had not known that.

"I was Marine, all the way. Semper Fi. A Marine, not a soldier. And, no, I was not a drill instructor. What I did is classified, and I don't share that information."

She blinked. "Not even with a partner?"

"I did not *ask* for a partner." His hand dropped back to his side. "Especially not one who nearly got herself killed this evening."

Now she couldn't help it, Emerson snorted.

He blinked. "What in the hell did you just do?"

Now she rolled her eyes. "I was in zero danger of dying. You had your gun on the perp the whole time."

He took a slow, stalking step toward her. "Jake Waller had a screwdriver shoved beneath your chin."

She didn't need the unnecessary recap. "Yes, I know. I still have the mark to prove it."

Something happened to him with those words. His gaze went flat. Hard. Brutally cold and even darker. "What?" he rasped.

Hadn't he known that the tool had left a mark? "Not a big deal. Barely more than a scratch. It was photographed, and an EMT treated me while you were talking on the phone." The brief treatment that had been completely unnecessary, by the way.

He advanced on her with a hard, angry stride. She held her ground, sucked in a breath, and waited to see what new insult he'd hurl her way.

Only, he didn't insult her. Gray stopped right in front of her. One big hand reached out, he caught her chin, bent toward her, and as he angled her chin up even more with a touch that was oddly gentle and incredibly careful, he growled, "Bastard. Why the hell didn't you let me put a bullet in his brain?" His fingers brushed lightly over the mark. Not a scratch really. The screwdriver hadn't broken the skin. A purplish bruise.

She'd always bruised easily.

His careful touch was doing strange things to her. But, full disclosure, she tended to have that reaction whenever they touched. Her heart raced. Her breath came faster. Tension pooled within her and...

I get turned on.

Definitely not the reaction she was supposed to have to her growly partner.

When He Defends

She hurriedly stepped back.

His hand lingered in the air for a moment before falling. Fisting at his side.

"We don't put bullets in the brains of our suspects." She thought her voice sounded suitably crisp. Points for her.

"Jake Waller killed three women that we know about, Emerson. You and I both suspected there were more. Based on all those trophies, we were right. Hopefully, we'll get him to reveal more about his vics. You saw the trophy case—uh, trophy toolbox. There was a whole lot of jewelry in that case. Lots of carefully preserved hair locks. More than would belong to just three vics."

Yes, he was right on that score. But *she* was also right. "You're not the bad guy. You don't get to pull the trigger unless it's necessary."

His brows rose. "Sounds to me like you're the one giving orders." A negative shake of his head. "That's not how our relationship works."

So, they had a relationship now, did they? Interesting. Maybe it was time to cut through the BS and get to the heart of the matter. "What is your problem with me?"

"Excuse me?"

Oh, she thought he'd heard her just fine. But she'd be clearer. Louder. "You've given me grief since the moment we met." He had. They'd met in person for the first time in a Mississippi jail. He'd been less than impressed with her then. And, apparently, he still was. "I'm good at profiling. I know killers. I found Waller's trophy box in about five seconds. You should be thanking me." She nodded. Her careful control might have started to crack. The tiniest bit. Her hands flew to her hips. "Instead, you're here, doing your big, bad wolf impression."

His dark brows flew up. "Say that again?"

"You're huffing and puffing and threatening to dissolve our partnership."

"You were supposed to stay in the car." His eyes glittered at her. "You are *not* an FBI agent. You're a freelancer who should not be in the field. When I give an order, it's not for shits and giggles. The orders are to keep you safe. To keep you alive. But if I can't count on you to follow even the simplest of directives, how am I supposed to trust you?"

She didn't need him to hold her hand every second of the day. Or to encase her in bubble wrap. She understood the risks of the job. "I've had self-defense classes."

His teeth snapped together.

"I know how to fire a gun. Though you haven't *given* me one to use in the course of our investigations yet."

"Because you are not an FBI agent," he repeated. "You got the gig because your senator mom pulled strings and shoved you down my throat. It was either accept you and start babysitting duty or get my ass demoted."

Now she blinked. She could feel heat stinging her cheeks. She hadn't known her mother had used her influence that intensely. She had not realized that Gray had been told if he didn't accept her as his temporary partner, he'd lose his job. "I'm sorry." Brittle. She whirled away. Hurried for her bag. Grabbed her phone. "I'll get this sorted out immediately." She dialed her mother. Pressed the phone to her ear and heard the rings. *One. Two. Three.* "You should never have been faced with the possibility of losing your job—*wait!*"

He'd just plucked the phone from her. Ended the call. Now he frowned at her. A faint line cut between his brows. "You didn't know about the demotion bit, huh? That was news to you?"

Miserable, embarrassed, she shook her head. The burn

in her cheeks was even stronger. *Not only did my mother twist arms at the Bureau in order to get me the position, she literally threatened Gray.* "No wonder you hate me."

"I don't hate you. Things would probably be one hell of a lot easier if I did. But then again, I've never been one for easy. Easy is boring."

The phone rang in his grip.

"That's my mother," she said, recognizing the ringtone.

"Figured as much."

"I'm going to tell her to reach out to her contact at the Bureau. To cancel any pressure she may have applied. Your job will be safe." An exhale. "And I will find someone else to work with at the FBI."

The phone kept ringing.

Gray's head angled to the right as he studied her and ignored the ringing phone. "You're not giving up this freelance gig, are you?"

No, she wasn't. Emerson shook her head. She wouldn't give up the gig, but she would give up the dream of working with him. *The man can never know I was a super fan. That I studied his case files long before we ever met.*

"Stubborn," he muttered, and then Gray answered her phone. "Hello, Senator Marlowe." His voice was curt. Annoyed. "Your daughter is busy right now. Can't chat."

Her eyes widened. No, he had not answered her phone at...her gaze darted toward the bedside clock. *12:43 a.m.*

"Who am I?" Gray laughed. A rough, oddly seductive sound. "I'm the man in her motel room, of course. Look, you get what you pay for. You wanted me to be with Emerson twenty-four seven, and I take that kind of work seriously."

No, no, no, no. She frantically waved at him. Tried to lunge for the phone.

He winked at her and effortlessly dodged her lunge.

Winked. The man did not know what he was doing.

"Oh, yes, this is Gray Stone. At your service, or Emerson's service, I should say. I'm here in her motel room—"

"What is wrong with you?" Emerson gasped. She snatched the phone from him on her second, desperate attempt and put it to her ear. "Mother, I want you to contact the FBI. I can't believe that you threatened to demote Grayson if he didn't—"

"Gray," he cut in to say.

"—if he didn't work with me."

There was silence on the line. Emerson's heartbeat raced in her chest.

"Hello, Emerson," her mother finally said in her perfect, polished tone. A tone that no longer held any hint of her Maine accent. She'd lost all traces of an accent years ago. Though, on the campaign trail, she would deliberately slip back to her roots, like dropping her "r" at the end of words. "I do believe I recently missed your call." A brief pause. "To what do I owe the pleasure of this late-night chat?"

Emerson held Gray's stare. She swallowed the lump in her throat and, even though she knew the answer, she asked, "Did you threaten to have Agent Stone demoted if he didn't agree to work with me?"

Another beat of silence. Then, "You wanted to work with Gray Stone very badly," her mother replied.

One of Gray's brows quirked up. Of course, he would have heard that line. *He still does not know I am a super fan.*

"I was simply trying to help you," her mother continued. "After some discussion, Agent Stone agreed to take you on in a mentoring capacity, so, really, there were no...threats. Let's not use that word, shall we? Let's not say—"

"You threatened him," Emerson cut in. "I didn't want you involved in this at all." She had never intended for her mother to use her political influence to get Emerson the job. She'd wanted to pave her own path. "I am telling you now— back off. Leave Agent Stone alone. Leave my work at the Bureau alone. I can handle myself." There. Done. "Good night, Mother."

Her mother hummed. "Sorry it was a failed experiment. I did tell you, though, numerous times, that the Bureau would never be the place for you. Far too rough and dangerous. You wouldn't be able to handle the pressure, isn't that what I warned you?"

Yes, over and over again, her mother had said Emerson couldn't handle the work. *You were wrong, Mother. You still are.*

"Good night, darling." Her mother seemed pleased. *Click.*

A failed experiment. Emerson made certain she didn't crush the phone in her too-tight grip. "There." She pasted a false smile on her face. "Situation handled. If I am really such a terrible inconvenience to you..." *A pain in your ass.* "Then consider the inconvenience over."

He studied her with zero expression on his face. Just standing there. All muscled and intense, and, damn him, sexy as he took her in. Assessed her. Judged her.

Then, slowly, he nodded. "If we weren't partners any longer, then I could do what I really wanted to do..."

What was he talking about? She tossed the phone toward the bed with a weary sigh. It had honestly been a soul-exhausting day. "What's that? Yell at me? Tell me how I'm the bane of your existence? Oh, wait, been there, done that. Super fun, just so you know. But, I can assure you, no need for a repeat performance."

He stepped toward her. His hand reached out. Curled beneath her chin. As before, his touch was incredibly careful.

And...sexual. This time, there was definitely a fierce, charged heat in his touch. And in his eyes. In fact, Gray stared at her as if he could—quite possibly—eat her alive.

There was no control in his stare. No anger. Just bright, burning lust.

"What is happening right now?" Emerson whispered.

"If we weren't partners and if you just said...*yes*..."

Her lips parted.

"I'd fuck you until you screamed with pleasure."

No, he had not just said that. Had he?

"You feel it, don't you, Emerson?" Gray growled. "The heat? The need? It's there when we touch. It builds up. Deepens. Burns right beneath the skin."

Yes, yes it did. And, yes, she felt it. She'd tried to pretend that she did not feel it, but, oh, yes, she did.

"If we weren't partners, I'd kiss you." His gaze had locked on her mouth. "I'd kiss you the way I've been dying to kiss you since the first moment I saw you—wearing those sexy as hell red heels of yours."

He remembered the color of the *heels* she'd worn at their first meeting? She had a ton of heels in a very wide variety of colors. She didn't even know what she'd worn the first time they'd met.

"You have this scent that drives me crazy. Summer nights. Jasmine. It's light and sweet, and I swear, it's like fucking innocence."

She stiffened.

Gray shook his head. "But there is no innocence in my world. Not in yours, either. And I don't want innocence from you."

She wet her lips. "What do you want from me?"

"Sin. The best, darkest kind of sin. I want to taste every single inch of you. I want my mouth all over you."

Her knees were getting weak, and her nipples were tight, hard peaks.

"I want you clawing at my back and coming harder for me than you ever have for anyone else in your life."

Oh, she could pretty much guarantee that.

"*If* you weren't my partner." His thumb brushed over her lips. The softest of caresses. "There are so many things I would do to you. With you."

Her lips parted. "You're making a lot of assumptions." Oh, no. Had she just—dammit. *Oh, yes. Yes.* She'd just licked the tip of his thumb. His surging pupils said he'd felt that sensual touch. Sue her. It had been deliberate. No accident. "I haven't said I want to fuck you." For the record.

"You also haven't said that you don't."

Because she *did* want to fuck him. Very, very badly.

"I don't fuck other FBI agents." Blunt. Hard. His eyes glittered at her.

Good thing I'm not an FBI agent. Not technically.

Gray's jaw hardened. And he—backed away. "But since we *are* partners, none of that will happen."

What? The man was a *tease*. The worst kind of *tease*. She was practically salivating and he'd just said—hold up. He'd just said, "We *are* partners." Big emphasis on the *are* part of the sentence. Her breath shuddered out. "You're not quitting on me any longer? You changed your mind?"

He took another step back. His nostrils flared, as if he was drinking in her scent. "When I give an order, it's not because I'm an asshole."

"Pretty sure that's debatable." The words just slipped

from her. Her eyes widened. Her hand flew up. Covered her mouth.

He stared at her.

She stared at him. Tension thickened. Seconds ticked past.

Her hand slowly lowered.

"Why the hell did you request me as your partner, Emerson? Why me?"

She swallowed. "Because I wanted the best. When it comes to hunting killers, you are the best." Undeniable.

"Even though I'm an asshole?"

One shoulder rolled. Her knees were still weak. *He thinks about kissing me? About fucking me?* She hadn't admitted that she thought about kissing him all the time. That she dreamed about fucking him.

"Orders are in place for a reason," Gray continued grimly. "Orders save lives. Either agree to do what I tell you, without hesitation, when we're in the field, or consider this partnership done."

Emerson could only shake her head. "I thought we were already done." Why else had he gone into the whole discussion about wanting her? Was the man just trying to torment her? If so, not cool.

"Yeah, I said that. Only those words came before you told the senator to fuck off. Before I realized you had nothing to do with threatening my job."

Okay. "And everything else?" She motioned between them. "That whole wanting to kiss me, wanting to fuck me bit? Was that just you trying to mess with my head?"

He laughed, and the rough, deep sound caught her completely off guard.

"No, Emerson." A smile lingered on Gray's lips. "That would be me, giving you the truth, because you've been messing with my head from day one." An exhale. "But I won't fuck another FBI agent."

Uh, as you keep pointing out, I'm not an FBI agent. I'm freelance.

"Fucking a partner will lead to increased danger and a boat load of trouble. You'll go falling in love with me, and I'll just break your heart."

Well, wasn't he just full of himself? Her jaw nearly hit the floor. "How do you know that you won't fall in love with me?" Was that so beyond the realm of possibility for him?

He stared back at her. "The choice is yours."

"What choice?"

"I can be your partner, or I can be your lover. You pick." He turned on his heel and strode for the connecting door.

This could not be happening. "You are making an awful lot of assumptions!" Emerson rushed after him.

He spun. They nearly collided. His hands flew out and curled around her shoulders. She jolted at the contact. Hissed out a breath as sensual energy seemed to pour through her blood.

"That's what I'm talking about," he said, as if satisfied. "You think I don't see it? You're good at controlling your expressions, I'll give you that, but every now and then, your eyes will give you away. And when I touch you...*I feel it.*"

She wanted his mouth on her. Right then. Right there. Her body practically vibrated with need.

"Call me a liar," he dared. "Tell me that I'm wrong. Tell me that you don't want my mouth on yours more than you want your next breath right now."

Her breath had frozen in her lungs.

"I'm good at reading people. At knowing what they want most. At understanding the darkness they keep chained inside." His head tilted. "I've got so much darkness. If we're not careful, it could wreck us both."

She thought about just grabbing him by his shirtfront and yanking him toward her. Slamming her mouth onto his. "We might kiss and feel nothing." A possibility.

The intensity in his eyes only deepened. "Or we might kiss and fuck right where we stand."

Why do that? There was a perfectly good bed just a few feet away. Had to be far more comfortable than fucking where they stood.

"Partner or lover," he said. "You pick. You decide."

Her gaze searched his. Desire twisted inside of her. She did want him, damn the man. More than she'd probably ever wanted anyone in her life. But she also wanted to keep working with him. Because Gray *was* the best when it came to getting into the minds of killers. He was better than she was, probably because he'd had so much valuable field experience. Because he'd been up close and personal with too many monsters over the years.

And they'd left their mark on him.

"Sleep on it," he murmured. "You can give me your answer in the morning."

He was going to walk away. She knew it. She also knew...

"Fuck it," Emerson snapped. She grabbed his white shirtfront, and she hauled him toward her.

Their mouths collided.

Chapter Three

"I don't have delusions. I won't ever be like him."
– Emerson Marlowe

WORST MISTAKE EVER. GRAY KNEW IT. ACCEPTED THE fact deep in his soul. Kissing Emerson was a mistake.

So why did it feel so good? Why did *she* feel so good? Emerson had grabbed his shirtfront. She'd yanked him toward her. Gray could have stopped the forward momentum. A simple enough task to do.

Only he hadn't stopped it. He hadn't pulled away. He'd leaned toward her.

Because he'd been dying to know how she would taste. Because his control was weak. Because he'd watched a savage bastard hold her in a brutal grip and shove a screwdriver beneath her chin, and Gray had thought about squeezing the trigger of his gun and taking another monster out of this world.

He kissed her because he was riding a wave of

adrenaline. A wave of lust and dark need. He should have walked away from her. Should never have given her the option to be his partner or his lover...He should have kept the words to himself.

What the hell was I thinking?

But, the instant his lips touched hers, the instant he touched that soft, satiny mouth...

All rational thought fled. As if he'd ever been particularly rational where Emerson was concerned. Her lips parted for him. His tongue snaked inside her mouth, and he was just utterly *done*.

Lust exploded, even more powerfully than he'd anticipated. Primal and basic. A consuming need that swallowed him up because her taste was even better than he'd imagined. His hands locked around her hips, and he hauled her ever closer toward him. Her breasts pressed against his chest. Her tight nipples were pebbled, and he wanted to rip away every barrier between them. Strip her. Taste her. Fuck her.

Her body was flush against his, but that wasn't good enough. He lifted her up with his grip on her waist, and her legs wrapped around him. Her mouth opened even wider. Their tongues met. She kissed him with a raw, wild abandon.

Warned her. Told her that I'd want to fuck her right here, right now.

And he did. She had to feel the hard, swollen cock shoving against her.

A moan rose in her throat, and he greedily swallowed the sound. His heart raced in his chest, and he turned with her, took two steps...

A bed is close by. Don't have to fuck her against the wall. Can take her in the bed.

When He Defends

The lust he felt was too strong. Part of him knew that. Adrenaline and danger were a dangerous brew that could rip apart anyone's self-control. He needed to let her go. To step back.

Instead, they hit the bed. He tumbled down on top of her, making sure that he didn't crush her much smaller body with his. He kept kissing her. Her hands curled around his shoulders as she held him in a fierce grip. She was as greedy as he was. As desperate. Her hips arched toward him even as her legs remained locked around his hips. His mouth tore from hers so that he could kiss a path down her neck. Did he press too hard? Was he marking her? Was he—

"Open the fucking door!"

Gray froze. His breath sawed in and out.

The shouted command was followed by a fierce pounding. *At Emerson's motel room door.* Oh, the hell, no. He shoved up on his hands and stared down at her.

Lust still blazed in her eyes. So did confusion, though. She blinked those intense, unforgettable eyes of hers up at him even as a furrow crept between her brows.

"Guessing you're not expecting company," he said.

"Open the door, bitch!" Another shout.

She shook her head.

Jaw locking, he reached for her legs. Slowly pulled them off his hips. Whoever the hell that was at the door—the jerk would pay. Both for interrupting at the wrong time and for calling Emerson a bitch. Gray eased from the bed.

She scrambled to her knees.

"Do not even *think* of answering the door," he told her.

She blinked at him again. Licked her lips. "Gray?"

Finally, she'd called him by the shortened version of his name. But then again, he'd been dry humping the woman in bed, so calling him Gray damn well seemed appropriate.

He double-timed it to his room and grabbed his weapon. In seconds, he was back in her room, and she was—thankfully—still in the bed. She'd listened to him. Followed an order. Impressive. Or maybe he'd just been really fast, and Emerson hadn't gotten the opportunity to move, but, either way, he'd take it as a win.

Gray headed for the exterior door. He checked through the peephole in the too-thin door. The bastard on the other side was drawing back his fist to pound again.

Gray yanked the door open. "Can I fucking help you?" he snarled.

The man gaped at him, and then, in the next instant, raw rage filled his face. "You're fucking the bitch? You're fucking *my* girl?" He lunged toward Gray.

Gray brought up his gun. "I'm a federal agent, asshole. You need to calm the hell down. Right now."

At the sight of the gun, the jerk scrambled back as his jaw dropped open.

"The only person staying in this room is *my* partner, and you damn well don't call her a bitch." Gray filled the doorway. This prick was not getting past him. He could smell the alcohol pouring off the guy. "You need to go somewhere and sleep off the booze. That's a pro tip for you. Otherwise, your ass is about to be in serious trouble."

The man—young, probably early twenties but with a hairline already receding and a chin that had gone weak—blinked blearily. "Room two?"

"This is room twelve, dumbass. Twelve." He felt the change in the air behind him. A light shift. Emerson hadn't made any sound to alert him, but he knew she was right behind him. Her scent teased him.

The prick at the door twisted his head as he eyed her. "You're not Misty."

When He Defends

"No," Emerson's flat voice. "I am not Misty."

The drunk creep yanked a hand over his face. "Got to find Misty. Bitch won't leave me." He turned away. Almost fell. Managed to catch himself at the last moment as he staggered off...probably for room two.

Gray narrowed his eyes on the target.

"Gray?" Emerson touched his shoulder.

As always, her touch burned through him, but his focus was on the drunk man. A man who peered at the numbers above each door at the small motel. The weaving drunk was counting down, getting closer and closer to his target.

"He's going to find Misty," Emerson said, as if reading Gray's mind. "I don't think we should let that happen."

Damn straight, he wasn't going to let that happen. This whole scene...Gray surveyed the fading exterior of the motel. The pothole-filled lot. The flickering light near the VACANCY sign. An old ice maker humming nearby.

A place right out of my nightmares.

The drunk guy approached room two. Anger twisted his features.

Gray advanced.

"Gray?" Emerson's soft voice.

He kept marching after the prick who'd called Emerson a bitch.

The bastard lifted his hand. Pounded on the door for room two. *"Open the fucking door!"*

Ah, familiar words. Clearly, he liked to announce himself the same way each time he tried to break into a room.

Whoever was in room three immediately turned off their lights.

Room four did the same. The bright light in the window went dark in a blink.

The drunk guy pounded his fist into the wooden door. "Misty!" He lifted his foot and kicked at the doorknob. "Bitch, open up!"

"Did you miss the part where I told you that I was a federal agent?" Gray asked, voice curious.

Emerson had followed him. Of course, she had. He made sure that he moved his body and stood in front of her.

"What?" Drunk and Obnoxious spun toward him.

"FBI Agent Gray Stone." Gray nodded. Then he reached back, caught Emerson's hand, and shoved his gun into her palm.

"Do I look like I fucking care?" The drunk bobbed. Lifted his foot to plow it into the door again. And—

Gray caught him by the shoulder. "You're destroying private property. You're not allowed to do that."

"Get your damn hand off me!"

Gray removed his hand. "You're destroying private property."

"I'm getting my girl! Misty, open the fucking door! Open the door now or you will pay, I swear, you will, and so will that brat-ass kid of yours!"

The door to room number two flew open. A woman stood there. Was she even twenty-one? Big, dark eyes. The left one was lined by a purplish bruise that was clear to see even in the weak light from her room.

A black eye. And what looked like fingerprint bruises on her throat.

"Go away, Trevor," Misty told him. "We're done."

Yep, they were.

Tears trailed down Misty's cheeks.

And, behind her, a small boy—maybe two years old? Three?—held tightly to her leg. His eyes were an exact mirror of his mom's as he stared up at Trevor with terror on his face.

Trevor surged for the young woman. But Gray jumped into his path. He faced off with the bastard. "The lady says you're done. That means you need to stay the hell away from her."

Trevor swung at him.

Emerson screamed.

Gray took the hit. The jerk drove his fist into Gray's stomach. Not even a particularly impressive hit. Gray had taken way worse. Hell, when his buddy Kane threw a punch, it was like getting hit by a bus. This punch? More like having a basketball bounce off your stomach.

Mostly just annoying but...

Gray leapt into action. He grabbed the guy's wrist, yanked it behind Trevor's scrawny back, and had the jackass on his knees and howling in about three seconds. "Gonna need my handcuffs," he announced to Emerson. An Emerson who had lunged forward and now had the gun aimed—a rock-steady aim, by the way—at Trevor. "They are in my motel room. Will you get them for me, please?"

She lingered.

He glanced her way as Trevor snarled and twisted.

"You're not going to do anything...reckless while I'm gone?" Suspicion laced Emerson's voice.

Her lips were swollen. From his kiss. Her hair a bit disheveled. She held the gun and glared at the perp, and, damn, she was sexy.

I crossed a line with her. I should have held back. But he hadn't. His control had broken. Because Emerson was a weakness for him.

"I'm hardly the reckless type," he assured her. He

tightened his grip when Trevor heaved hard. "The handcuffs, Emerson. I could use them about now."

She darted away.

I'm only reckless when it comes to you.

He watched her rush away. And then...

He hauled Trevor to his feet. Flipped him around and faced him. Even let go of the creep. For the moment. "You the reason that Misty has a black eye?"

"Fuck off—"

"Dumbass, you just assaulted a federal agent." He'd deliberately told the guy he was a Fed so there would be no confusion. Gray had known the prick would take a swing, sooner or later. "That means you're getting a swift ticket to jail tonight."

Trevor tried to hit him again. Gray let him. A punch that rolled off Gray's shoulder because the idiot couldn't hit for shit and was drunk as hell.

"That's twice." Gray nodded. "You don't get another hit. I'll swing next time. You'll go down. You'll wake up in jail." He positioned his body in front of Misty and the kid. *Too much like a nightmare from my past.* He kept his eyes on a glaring Trevor even as he asked Misty, "He the reason for your black eye?"

No response.

"And the fingerprint marks on your throat? Did he leave those, too?" Gray pushed. Because he'd seen them, too.

The kid didn't make a sound. No crying. No screams. Nothing.

"Misty, don't say a word!" Spittle flew from Trevor's mouth. "I'll make you so damn sorry if you do!"

Gray's hands fisted at his sides. "No, you won't." Absolute certainty. "You won't do a single thing to her." He would see to it.

When He Defends

"I've helped you, Misty!" More rage. More spittle. "You and that dumb bastard kid of yours!"

A hard gasp from Misty.

"I let him in my house, I gave him food—*I am the reason you're both alive!*"

Gray rolled his eyes. "No, you're not, you sonofabitch. You're the reason she's got bruises. And the reason the kid is too scared to speak."

"He *can't* speak!" Trevor bellowed. "Good for nothing kid can't—"

Gray prepared to take the bastard *down*. A snarl broke from his throat because this attack was about to be brutal.

"I'm leaving." Misty's paper-thin voice cut into the night before Gray could destroy the jerk. "I don't love you, and I'm not letting you hurt me anymore. I'm done!"

Hell, the fuck, yes. "Great choice, Misty," Gray applauded. "Top-notch. You deserve one hell of a lot better. So does the kid. Trust me on this one. *You deserve more.* From where I am standing, basically *anyone* will be better than this loser."

A choked yell broke from Trevor. He barreled forward. This time, Gray was the one to deliver a punch to the jerk's stomach. All of the air left Trevor's lungs in a whoosh as he doubled-over in pain.

"Look at that," Gray bent toward him, "you just walked into my fist. So clumsy. Bet you've told plenty of stories about Misty being clumsy, haven't you? Stories to hide the BS that you did to her." He positioned his head near Trevor's ear. "You will never get near Misty or her kid again. You will never put your hands on her again. *Not on either of them.* Because if you do..."

Heels clicked as Emerson rushed back. "I have the handcuffs!"

Trevor lifted his head. His blood-shot eyes locked on Gray's face. He blinked. Twice.

Gray smiled at him. A warm smile. Friendly. Because they did have an audience now. "I will make your life a living hell," he told Trevor softly, voice lethal. Then, louder, he added, "You're under arrest for assaulting a federal officer...and, hey, Misty, you want to press some charges, too?"

* * *

THE BLUE LIGHTS swirled in the motel's parking lot. Trevor glared as he was shoved into the back of the patrol car.

Gray sent him a friendly wave. "Enjoy prison, asshole! See if you like being on the receiving end of punches! An exciting new life awaits you. So many new friends. So many new ways for you to become the bitch."

"Gray," Emerson chided. "I get that I'm still learning the ropes, but I don't think you're supposed to taunt the perps."

He shrugged. Considering that he wanted to be ripping the jerk apart, he figured that taunting was certainly the lesser of two evils. He could see Trevor's mouth moving frantically, and Gray was certain the camera in the car was picking up all sorts of interesting things—statements that Trevor would certainly regret making later. "Not my fault if he gets mad and makes threats...or confessions."

Gray shifted his position slightly, bracing his legs apart. He'd grabbed some shoes, not like he wanted to be standing in the parking lot barefoot. He'd answered the questions for the responding officers, gave them a full report, and, hell, yes, he was gleefully watching as Trevor was taken away.

One less perp on the street. One less bastard who gets off on hurting those who are weaker.

The couple in room three had come out. Backed up Gray's statements. Apparently, they'd been watching through their blinds. Watching, not intervening.

But when the cops had come swarming with their sirens blaring, the couple had run out.

Trevor would not be hurting anyone else for a while.

"Thank you." Soft. Hesitant.

Misty.

She'd lingered near him. Had hunched her shoulders at a few of Trevor's eruptions but had stood firm. Emerson had remained at her side the whole time. Not pushing. Not asking a ton of questions. Just being there. Emerson was a steady, reassuring presence. He'd noticed that about her on a few occasions with other vics. She soothed and comforted, and he swore, she almost seemed to do it just by breathing.

She doesn't soothe me, though. Just the opposite. When he was around Emerson, he felt amped up. Far too out of control.

"I appreciate you coming to my aid, Agent Stone," Misty said.

He glanced at Misty. Her tears were gone. The hunching in her shoulders had eased. The little boy with her still curled one arm around her right leg. *Timothy.* That was his name. Gray had learned that Timothy was four years old, and he was deaf.

The kid peered up at Gray. Gray winked at him.

The kid's eyes just got bigger.

"Guess it was my lucky night, huh?" Misty asked. She sent Gray a weak smile. One that he caught in the swirl of the lights. "Having you here. Had no idea a Fed was staying at the same motel."

He studied her. Hated those marks on her. She was twenty-one. Her birthday had been last week. Talk about a shit-poor birthday present—*being stalked by your ex*. But Gray would make sure that things changed for Misty and Timothy. There were strings that he could pull. He'd pull them. Hard. "The more distance you have between you and Trevor, the luckier you are."

Her lower lip trembled. She looked down at her hands. Twisted them. Then let one hand fall so she could stroke her son's hair. "You probably think I'm weak, don't you? Pretty pathetic. Being with someone like him. Someone who hurt me so—"

"Misty."

She looked up at him.

He kept his voice gentle, something that was hard because he truly did not have a great deal of gentleness in him. "It takes a whole lot of strength to walk away." More than most people would ever realize. He wasn't most people. And he understood her far more than Misty would ever know. "Just because he might have told you that you were weak, don't you ever believe him, understand?"

Her lip trembled again, but her chin lifted.

Damn. As he stared at her and her son, it was like staring back at another time. Another place. Another freaking rundown motel in the middle of nowhere. He looked down, dropping his gaze behind her, almost expecting to see—

No, no, it's not my life. Not my past. I see Timothy.

"You are incredibly strong, Misty," Emerson told her. "Gray is right. Never doubt that. The weak person is the one who hurt you."

Damn straight. Gray dropped to his knees before Misty, putting him much closer to Timothy's height. His hands

When He Defends

formed fists with his thumbs on the outside, and then he made an X, bringing those fists over his chest, with his right hand over the left. Then he swung his hands out. He pointed at the kid. *Safe.* Gray made the motions again. *Safe. You. You are safe.*

Misty inhaled sharply. "You...you know sign language?"

Yeah, he did. Gray pointed at the kid. *You.* Gray's hands moved toward his shoulders, claw shaped. As his hands pulled away from his shoulders, they curled into fists. *Brave.* He did the sign one more time. *You are brave.*

Timothy smiled at him.

"H-he's been working on his signs," Misty said. "I had him in a preschool for kids who are deaf, and he's so smart, and he's been learning so fast. He's *so, so* smart. Timothy just needs a fair chance in life, you know? I was leaving Trevor because of him. Because Timothy deserved more. Because—"

"You both deserve more," Gray told her flatly. He pointed at Timothy. *You.* Gray's hand raised. His fingers were slightly parted. His middle finger moved toward his head. He touched his temple. Flicked the hand outward. *Smart.*

You are smart.

Timothy let go of his mom and tossed his little body at Gray. At first, Gray stiffened, then he slowly patted the little boy's shoulders. *Oh, hell, yes, I'm gonna make sure that you and your mom have that fair chance.* They would never be cowering in fear again. Done.

The boy slowly let him go. He smiled at Gray. Went back to his mom.

"Thank you," Misty whispered.

He slowly rose to his feet. Gray's breath eased out. "You did the right thing tonight."

"You have my card, Misty," Emerson said. "You contact me anytime."

"I'm...I'm gonna go home to my mom in Georgia. I already called her. The cops, um, they said I have to fill out some paperwork. Then Timothy and I can go." Her feet shuffled nervously. "Could you, um, would you—one of you—um, go with us? To the station, I mean? I'm just—I'm scared."

"Yes," Gray answered. He'd go. He'd take steps to make sure she had every resource she needed in Georgia, too.

"Yes," Emerson replied at the same time.

His gaze collided with Emerson's.

"We'll be with you," Emerson promised Misty. "Every step of the way."

He could not look away from Emerson. And he should. He absolutely should. Because Gray was very afraid at that moment...

Emerson is seeing too much of me. Seeing into him. And discovering the secrets that he tried too hard to hide.

* * *

THE SUN WAS STARTING to rise when they got back to the motel room. Weariness pulled at Emerson. All she wanted to do was fall into a puddle. A puddle that—hopefully—landed in her bed.

Gray had made arrangements for Misty and her son Timothy to be transported to Misty's mother's home. He'd also made a few, secretive phone calls. Calls that her instincts said were all geared around Misty and her protection.

As soon as he parked their rental at the motel, a weary sigh slid from her. "You're really a good guy, aren't you,

Gray?" Gray. The shortened version of his name slid easily from her now.

Because I almost had sex with the man.

Something that they would have to discuss soon.

Gray exited the vehicle. She started to push open her door, but he beat her. Opening it for her. With his face expressionless, he told her, "I'm good to some people."

Yes, he'd certainly been good to Misty and to Timothy that night. She rose from the vehicle. Her heels tapped on the cement as she edged closer to him.

He slammed the car door. "But to most people, I'm a real nightmare."

Chapter Four

"Did I grow up intending to be an FBI agent? Uh, no. No, the plan was much different. What was it? Trust me on this. You don't want to know."
– Gray Stone

She stared up at his face. The strong angles. The stubble that covered his square jaw. Shadows lined his eyes, and the golden brown of his irises seemed to shift and swirl as he gazed down at her. She thought of how gentle he'd been with Misty. How he had knelt to be on a closer level with Timothy as he signed to the boy. Emerson slowly shook her head. "I don't believe you're a nightmare." Quite the opposite.

"That's just because you don't know me that well." He turned away. "I'm sure you're ready to crash."

Beyond ready. But she had things she wanted to say to Gray. Questions she needed to ask.

"We'll have to pay a visit to Jake Waller later. Tie up

When He Defends

loose ends. Then we'll be getting the hell out of Briar." He glanced down at his wrist, at the gleaming watch there. "But we can spare at least five hours of rest. I'll talk to the clerk at the motel's front desk and arrange a late checkout for us."

She touched his wrist. Right near that gleaming watch.

He tensed. "You don't want to do that."

"I think we need to talk, Gray."

His head turned toward her. "Not right now, we don't." A low warning filled his words. "You need to rest. I need to rest. We'll regroup. Talk later." He swallowed. "You don't want to be touching me right now. Trust me on this."

"Why would you think that you're a nightmare?"

He pulled away. Backed away. "Don't try to profile me, Emerson. It's a bad idea."

She held her ground. She would not be intimidated by him. "You know a victim, don't you? Someone close to you. Very close."

He marched for the motel's small office. "Don't know what you're talking about."

Oh, but he did know.

So she waited. Right outside of the small office. He went in, talked with the female clerk, got them the late checkout, and when he came out of that door, Emerson made sure she was standing in his path.

He growled. A sound that should not have been sexy, but, oddly, it was. Deep and dark and it pulled at something equally deep and dark inside of her. Something she'd worked extremely hard to keep hidden. "It was the way you reacted to Misty and her son. There was a crack in your mask. I saw it. For just a moment, she was personal to you. She reminded you of something—someone—from your own past."

"Misty wasn't personal. I'd never met the woman in my

life, not until our fun-filled stay here at the Motel from Hell. Late checkout is one p.m., by the way." He advanced.

Again, she did not retreat.

"Who was it?" Emerson asked him. "A friend? A lover?"

His eyes flashed. "Are you asking me if I *hurt* someone, Emerson?"

"No." Immediate. Then, "Yes."

His teeth snapped together. "You think I would—"

"Not the victim. No, I don't think you'd ever hurt a victim."

Some of the tension eased from his shoulders.

"But I think you'd hurt the perpetrator."

He smiled, and the smile did not reach his eyes. "I'm not the judge and jury. Punishment isn't my department." That was a shark's smile. Terrifying in its beauty.

And sharpness.

She exhaled. "We should take this conversation inside." Not that anyone was out there to hear them, but—

He took her hand.

The move surprised her so much that she jerked. Jumped.

He quirked one brow. "Emerson, are you afraid of little old me?"

No, she wasn't. In fact, he was one of the few people she didn't think she would ever fear. "You wouldn't hurt me. I'm not a predator."

His fingers twined with hers. His touch scorched her, but she didn't say a word as he led her back to her room. Room twelve. He stopped at the door. "Get some sleep."

He let go of her hand.

"Was it your mother?" Emerson pushed.

Hit. She saw it on his face. The flash of pure savagery. His mother *had* been a victim in the past.

When He Defends

But he shook his head. "Don't go down this road with me, Emerson."

"You're a protector, straight to your core." She understood so much now. "Some protectors are born. Some are made. The instinct to help the victims—that's what drives you. I wondered how you were such a good profiler. Now I get it. You're so good because you're working extra hard to understand the victims and to help them."

"No." He leaned toward her. Put one hand on the frame of the door near her head. "I don't understand the victims. I understand the perps. I know how they think. I know what they want. I know what they need. I understand them completely, and that's how I become their nightmares."

She almost forgot to breathe. "Gray?" A squeak.

"You are right about one thing, though. I know a victim." His lips thinned. "My mother left the sonofabitch who hurt her when I was five years old. He tracked us to a motel much like this one." A shake of his head. "When he came banging at the door, everyone looked away. The lights went out in the nearby rooms, just like they did tonight. People pretended not to hear his yells. Not to see him breaking down the door. Everyone needed it to be someone else's problem. It was *my* problem."

She wanted to grab onto him. Hold him tightly. "Come in so we can talk."

"No." Another flat denial. "You don't..." His hand fell as Gray backed up a step. "I'm too raw. I can't be near you right now. You don't want me close the way I am."

She did want him close. "What happened when he broke down the door?" *He...*Gray's father?

"That's a story I don't share." His gaze cut around the area, then came back to her.

47

"You know sign language." It was how he'd communicated with Timothy.

"I know sign language." A roll of one shoulder.

She stared at him.

A sigh slid from his lips. "Not a big deal, Emerson. My aunt was deaf. My mom made sure I could communicate with her. I also speak French, some Russian, and a little bit of Chinese. Anything else you want to know?"

Just a million things.

"How about you save the rest of your questions for another time?" He edged toward the nearby door. Room thirteen. "Get some sleep, partner. I'll see you soon."

"Gray!"

He stood in front of the door to his room. Didn't open it. Not yet.

Partner. She blinked. "Am I still your partner?" Emerson turned her body toward his.

The tension between them seemed to thicken. She could practically see what they'd done before flash between them. The kiss. The lust. The tumble onto the bed.

Is that why he won't come into the room with me? Because he doesn't want us to pick up where we left off?

"You're my partner." His stilted reply. "That's what you'll continue to be."

Ouch. Okay, that hurt. But then again, she'd been the one just picking hard at his painful past. She got that he didn't like to be vulnerable. She more than understood. And it wasn't fair to parade his past out for her to see. At least, it wasn't fair unless she intended to reveal her own pain. "My father was schizophrenic." The words just came from her. Flat. Unemotional. "Delusions drove him to take his own life when I was seven years old."

"*Emerson.*"

"For years, I was terrified that the same fate would happen to me. Schizophrenia is supposed to have a strong hereditary component." She'd pretty much made the study of schizophrenia her life's focus. In order to be a psychiatrist, she'd had to get her MD. So many years of study. Of research. *Of fear.* "I grew up with a ticking time bomb inside of me. Always afraid, just waiting for warning signs to appear. Disorganized thinking and speech. I feared when my mind would become scattered and the words I wanted to say wouldn't emerge." Should she confess that a ticking, time bomb terror sometimes still came to her in the dark...and in the light? "I worried about hallucinations." *I still worry.* "Most people don't fear that they'll see things that aren't there. I spent years trying to make sure that everything I saw *was* real." And living in fear that one day, it wouldn't be real. That she wouldn't even realize when she was hallucinating. But her fear didn't stop there. "And then there is the trifecta. The delusions. My father suffered from so many delusions at the end. Delusions that he was being hunted...that he was being tracked and persecuted by those closest to him. Those delusions led my father to run blindly and leap straight off the cliff near my mother's home in Maine."

Sympathy burned in his eyes. And, oh, horror of horrors, was that pity, too? Gray was looking at her with pity now when he'd stared at her with fierce desire hours before? Pity was the absolute last thing that she wanted from him or from anyone. *"Don't."* A sharp snap as Emerson realized that she'd just made a serious miscalculation in her relationship with him.

I shouldn't have told him. Why, oh, why did I tell him? I don't tell anyone. Her father's condition was a closely guarded family secret. Or it had been, until she'd blurted out the truth because she was going on twenty-four hours of no sleep, shaking with adrenaline, and fueled by too much fear.

She didn't normally make mistakes like this one. But it was too late to pull the words back.

Gray was stepping toward her. Reaching for her.

She had to minimize the disaster, immediately. "You were right." Brisk. "We need to sleep. We'll regroup later and talk about our partnership after we've rested." When she was less likely to spill more deep, dark secrets.

"Emerson—" His hand almost touched her.

She fumbled and pressed the keycard against the lock. The little bar flashed to green, and Emerson shoved open the door. Darkness greeted her. She didn't remember turning off the light, but she must have done it before they'd gone to the police station with Misty and Timothy. Emerson kicked the door shut. She didn't immediately turn on the lights. Instead, she stood with her back pressed against the door, with her heart racing far too fast in her chest, and she let the darkness surround her. Comfort her.

It was so easy to hide in the dark.

"Emerson..." She heard Gray's voice quite clearly. After all, the door was paper-thin.

But she didn't respond to him.

Was he going to knock? Demand that they talk? Was he going to tell her how sorry he was about her father? Was Gray going to look at her with more pity when she needed him to stare at her with that wild desire? A desire that had made her feel so incredibly alive and *wanted*?

He didn't knock.

Didn't do anything but walk away. When she strained, Emerson could pick up the soft pad of his steps. He was leaving her. Check. That was exactly what she'd asked for.

When He Defends

They needed space. She needed it. Emerson waited until she heard the creak of his door opening, and then her hand reached out, and she hit the light switch. Illumination immediately flooded overhead, shining down on her and the room.

Chaos.

Emerson's eyes widened.

Furniture had been overturned. Her suitcase had been ripped open and the contents scattered across the room. Her clothes appeared to have been torn—or slashed—into pieces.

And, big, dripping red letters hung over the bed, letters that formed—

You'll die.

Letters that promised her death.

Emerson stopped breathing. Her eyes snapped closed.

Don't be a delusion. Don't be. I can't—I can't be like him. Her greatest fear, right there, surrounding her, but maybe, maybe when she opened her eyes, things would be normal again.

Her eyes flew open. Her breath expelled.

You'll die.

The chaos and destruction remained.

* * *

HE COULD HAVE HANDLED the scene differently. Could have done a thousand different things instead of just gazing at Emerson like the cold-blooded bastard that he was. The woman had poured out her heart to him, and, in turn, he'd reacted by gaping at her. Had he really buried his emotions down so deep that he didn't know how to respond fucking *sympathetically* to someone? To her?

But by the time Gray had realized that he'd frozen, it had been too late. He'd tried to reach out to her, but Emerson had pulled back. Shut down. No, shut him out.

And letting her go had seemed the kindest choice.

Especially since he'd already screwed up colossally with her earlier. *Should never have gone into her room. Should never have kissed her. Should never have gotten so close to fucking her.* Why the hell had he told her how he really felt? He should have kept his need to himself. So what if he'd seen the same lust in her eyes, if he'd caught her watching him with her hungry stare as she nibbled on her plump, lower lip?

Yes, he'd understood that she was attracted to him. But he could have kept his own damn mouth shut. Ignored the attraction.

He had not.

The last twenty-four hours had been a real cluster of a situation for him. If Trevor the Jerkoff hadn't interrupted Gray and Emerson...

I would have taken her, and there would have been no going back. Not for either of them.

He pressed his keycard to the lock. The light flashed green. With his jaw clenched, he pushed open the door, flipped on the lights and—

What. The. Hell?

Battle-ready tension poured through Gray because his room had been completely trashed. The mattress had been dumped on the floor. The sheets ripped away. His suitcases had been emptied, his suit bags opened and...

"Oh, the fuck, no," he breathed as he shot forward. But, the fuck, yes, some punk with a death wish had *slashed* his five-hundred-dollar suits. A punk who would pay.

Gray yanked out his gun as he spun and surveyed the

scene. Anger pumped in his blood. Red letters had been spray-painted on the wall. Letters that dripped and distorted but were still clear enough to understand.

Leave. One word. Just that. *Leave.*

The welcome wagon had clearly come to greet him in Briar, Tennessee. He would have preferred a gift basket and not slashed suits and a destroyed room but—

Emerson.

He was already running toward the connecting door. Gray doubted he'd been the only one to get an unwelcome visitor. The perp wasn't in his room any longer, and Gray had a sudden, stark fear that Emerson had walked into her motel room just to find some bastard waiting on her.

"Emerson!" Gray shouted her name. He grabbed for the connecting door on his side. Opened it. But *her* door was still locked. Screw that. He didn't hesitate. Just lifted his foot and kicked in the door that barred her room. It flew forward even as he burst into Emerson's motel room. "Emerson!"

A fast glance took in everything.

The trashed bed.

The clothes that had been ripped and thrown around the room.

The painted threat on the wall over her bed. *You'll die.*

And...Emerson. Frozen near the motel's front door, with her back pressed to the wood. But her gaze whipped toward him. Her breath shuddered out. "Gray?"

"Did you search the room?" He was already doing it even as he asked the question. Peering into the closet. Looking under the bed. Checking the tiny bathroom. "The bastard is gone." Fury bled in every word. "The fuck you'll die. Can't believe some angry prick left that message for you." He bounded toward her.

She seemed rooted to the spot.

Worry rose to twine with his rage. "Emerson?" His right hand retained its grip on the gun, but his left reached for her. Touched her shoulder.

She flinched. "I-I don't have delusions."

What? He glanced over his shoulder. "No, baby." His stare returned to her. "This isn't a delusion. Some creep broke into your room *and* mine. They are both trashed."

She shook her head and seemed to snap to attention. "Right. *Both.*" Another shake of her head. Her gaze sharpened. Darted to his gun. Then back to his face. "You're okay?"

"No, I'm not *okay.*" He nearly roared with his fury. "The prick slashed my suits."

Her eyes widened. "Oh, no. Not the suits."

She could not be mocking him. Not then. "Emerson..."

"Did you call me...baby...earlier?"

Damn. He might have. "No idea." Yes, he had. Definitely. "We need to make sure we weren't robbed. My laptop was in the room's safe. Didn't even check to see if it was still there." Because he'd hauled ass to her. "Search to see if anything of yours was taken." He whirled away from her. Glared at the wreckage. "Do you *know* how many fingerprints are in motel rooms? No way will a crime scene team find anything useful." And there sure as hell hadn't been any cameras outside their rooms. The only camera he'd seen had been in the small check-in office.

That office that would be his next stop.

He hurried back to his room. Opened the safe. *Good.* The laptop was still there. Not that seeing it did anything to lessen his fury.

"Nothing was taken."

His head jerked toward the connecting doorway.

Emerson stood there. Beautiful, fragile Emerson in her high heels and with her dark hair falling softly around her face and smudges of exhaustion beneath her gorgeous, sapphire eyes.

She hadn't slept all night. Neither had he. And this piss-poor motel was not providing any security. He should have done better with her. He'd just—hell, he'd thought they'd be in and out of Briar, Tennessee. Not like he'd planned for a long haul.

I should have taken better care of my partner. This won't happen again.

Because that was what Emerson was. *Partner.* Not a lover. He could not, *would not* cross that line. It was too dangerous. Not because of her. Because of him. Because as he'd learned when he finally tasted her, his control did not hold when he had Emerson in his arms.

"Gray?"

"You're not fucking dying," he snarled.

"Good to know." Her gaze dipped to his bed. Over it. To the message painted there. "Guessing someone isn't keen to have us in town, huh?"

"Probably one of Trevor's buddies. Word must have spread about his arrest." And Gray had left *Emerson's* room when Trevor came knocking. So he'd shined a bright signal on their location. But, still... "I'm talking to the desk clerk."

"I'm coming with you."

Sure, she was. Damn straight. He didn't want to let her out of his sight.

In moments, he and Emerson were entering the small check-in office. The bell overhead jingled when they entered, and he couldn't help but tense.

Fucking bells jingling make me nervous now. Because of another case. The first he'd worked with Emerson.

"You again?" The young clerk grimaced at him. "Thought you were all settled with a late checkout." She blew a big bubble. Popped it. Sucked it back in her mouth.

A game show played from the TV on the wall. One of those twenty-four-hour game show channels.

He ignored the TV. He *had* tucked his gun into the back waistband of his pants. No sense terrifying the woman working the desk. "Our rooms are trashed."

She grimaced. Raised her dark brows even as she twirled a lock of very blond hair. "Yeah, that's pretty much the status for all the rooms here. Sorry. Not like it's the Ritz. You get what you pay for, you know?"

"They aren't trash. They are *trashed*," he emphasized. "They are—"

"Someone broke into our rooms," Emerson cut in to say. "Destroyed our belongings. Spray-painted our walls."

The clerk stopped chewing her gum. Her eyes widened. "Are you serious?"

"No, I joke about stuff like this for shits and giggles," Gray snapped.

"Gray," Emerson tried to soothe.

He put his hands down on the counter because he was not in the mood to be soothed. He was in the mood to kick ass. *My suits are destroyed.* Worse, someone had been in Emerson's room. Someone had threatened her. With his eyes locked on the clerk, he questioned, "Did you see *anyone* near our rooms while we were gone to the police station?"

The clerk—her name tag identified her as Sherry—shook her head. "But I wasn't exactly watching your doors, you know?"

She seemed to say "you know" a great deal.

"Supposed to stay in here," Sherry added. "Answer the phone and stuff."

"You have any other cameras around here that might have caught sight of an intruder?" Gray pushed.

Again, Sherry shook her head. But she asked, seemingly curious, "What was painted on your walls?"

"Oh, the usual. 'You'll die,'" Gray quoted. "'Leave.' Typical, fun greetings from a small town."

Sherry resumed her gum chewing. Slower now. "Does this mean you don't want that late checkout?"

He growled.

Emerson's fingers skated up his arm. "Who is in room four?"

What? Gray's head swung toward her. He found her staring straight at Sherry.

"When Trevor was out there screaming for Misty," Emerson explained, as if she could hear the question he hadn't voiced, "I saw the lights turn off in room four. They went off in room three, too."

Gray nodded. "People trying to hide from trouble. Acting like they're asleep or not there so they don't have to get involved."

Emerson's head dipped in agreement. "Only the people in room three came out when the cops arrived. They gave statements. No one ever answered the door in room four. I noticed that the lights were still off when we passed the room moments ago."

"Well, it is late," Sherry mused. "Or, you know, early, depending on how you look at it."

Behind them, someone solved the big puzzle on the game show. There was thunderous applause from the TV.

Gray ignored the applause because Emerson had just made him very, very curious. "Who is in room four?"

Sherry tapped on her computer. "I'm not just supposed to tell you guest names...but, seeing as you're a Fed..."

A Fed without a warrant, but sure, whatever.

Sherry's dark brows snapped together. "No one." She looked up. "No one is checked into room four." Her lips pursed. "You must have made a mistake. Lights were probably always off."

No, they had not been. He'd seen the lights. So had Emerson. "If no one is in the room," he said, keeping all emotion from his voice even as rage still twisted within him. *Someone broke into Emerson's motel room. Someone trashed her room. Mine.* "If no one is inside, then there is no reason you can't unlock the door to room four and let us in."

"Well..." A pop of a bubble. "Sure, why not?"

Why not, indeed?

She led them to the room. Unlocked the door and swung it open. "You can see for yourselves," Sherry declared as she poked her hand inside and flipped on the lights. "No one has been—" But her words stopped.

Because someone had been inside. A can of red spray paint sat in the middle of the bed. Something that had been deliberately left behind. As if...

As if you wanted us to know that you were here.

Gray pulled his gaze off the spray can and glanced at Emerson. She stood behind him, but was peering into the room, and he knew she'd seen the spray paint, too.

Leave. His message.

And, for her...

You'll die.

The hell she would.

"That's weird," Sherry noted, voice catching a little bit. "The spray paint isn't supposed to be here, you know?"

"I know," he returned grimly.

Chapter Five

"To figure out the way to break killers, you just have to understand their weakness. Everyone has a weakness, after all. The best profilers—and agents—know how to exploit weaknesses." – Gray Stone, from an undated lecture to FBI recruits at Quantico

ONE WEEK SINCE BRIAR...

"AIM AND SHOOT."

Emerson raised her brows at Gray. "Thank you," she said barely containing an eye roll. "I had no idea what I should do here at the shooting gallery."

"Smartass, why don't you just focus on hitting the targets?"

She could feel eyes on them. Far too many eyes. "I know how to shoot."

"Great. You'll prove that to me right now."

They'd been back in Atlanta for two days. They'd stayed in Briar—at a *new* motel—for a time in order to make certain the case against Jake Waller was air tight.

Gray had sprung this practice routine on her with zero warning when she'd walked into the FBI office that morning. She'd already checked the weapon. The target waited. But she didn't put on her ear protection and get into firing position. Not yet. "What's the purpose of this little exercise?"

"To make sure that you can shoot."

"Smartass," she returned without missing a beat.

From nearby, Emerson was pretty sure she heard a snort from another agent.

Gray put his hands on his hips. "Fine. The purpose is to make sure that when we enter dangerous situations, I know that I can trust you to cover me."

"You think I can't handle myself?" Now that was insulting.

"I think you skipped out on a whole lot of training, *freelance consultant*."

Someone was certainly in a mood. But, actually, Gray had been in a *mood* since the motel break-in at Briar. Cold, distant, fully activated asshole mode. Uh, *mood*. Or maybe mode, too. Whatever.

"Before we go into the field again," his take-no-shit voice told her, "I want to make certain all the basics are covered with you."

Oh, he did? "If I prove that I'm a stellar shot, does that mean I get to start carrying my own weapon in the field? Because, otherwise, this whole exercise is pointless." She wanted a gun. Either he gave her one or she'd just bring her own gun that she normally kept locked securely at home.

"Put six bullets in the heart and two in the head, and you can carry your own weapon in the field."

The agent nearby wasn't laughing any longer. He sidled a bit closer even as he cleared his throat. "Uh, jeez, maybe make it easier, boss."

"Maybe mind your own business, Rylan. *Now.*"

"Minding my own business, sir, yes, sir." Rylan Tate rushed back.

Emerson tested the weight of the weapon in her hand. "You don't have to bite off anyone's head."

"I wasn't biting—"

"If you're angry with me about something, just say it." She was *dying* for the man to say something. An icy wall had been built between them. Was it because of what had *almost* happened in her motel room between them? Or because of her oversharing about her dad? A cold lump formed in her gut because she feared that he didn't think she was capable of handling the job. Not anymore. *A ticking time bomb.* "You're wrong if you think I can't handle myself."

"Six in the heart. Two in the head."

She put down the gun. Grabbed her ear protection. She already had on protective glasses. Standard equipment at the shooting range. "How about give me a little space?"

He backed away. Put on ear protection.

She didn't bother glancing at the agents who'd all gathered to watch. Emerson knew she was the show they'd come to see. The consultant, having to prove she could handle the job.

Her breath expelled slowly. She'd been at this shooting range before. When she'd *first* gotten the position as consultant. She'd been out there with various supervisors, and she'd demonstrated that she certainly knew how to handle a weapon.

But, um, there had not been a requirement for six in the heart. Two in the head. Not when she'd fired at the target before.

She picked up her weapon. Shifted her stance. Gray didn't understand her at all. Or her mother. Because Emerson's mother had been in politics for a very long time. But Maxine Marlowe had also come from an extremely wealthy family, one that kept guards close at all times. Emerson's mother had made sure that her daughter was always surrounded by protection when she'd been growing up.

And perhaps Emerson had convinced some of those guards to give her shooting lessons. A lot of lessons.

She stared at her target.

Six to the heart. Two to the head. Sure, she could do this. Hopefully.

She fired.

And when she pulled off her ear protection a few moments later, the applause had already started.

"Nailed it!" Rylan called out even as he pushed the button to bring her target forward for all to see. As that target surged toward her, almost seeming to fly, Emerson could see that she had, indeed, hit her marks. Sure, one hole on the heart was a little close to the left side, but it had still fallen within the designated area. She'd *done* it.

Six to the heart. Two to the head.

"Happy now?" Emerson demanded as she whirled toward Gray.

"That's not the right word." His expression was inscrutable. Typical Gray.

Other agents called out their congratulations. He, however, did not.

"I think you're gonna have to marry me," Rylan announced.

Emerson jerked in surprise. Her body swung toward him.

Rylan—handsome, with close-cropped, blond hair and warm brown eyes that always seemed amused—grinned at her. "With shooting like that, you need to marry—"

"No," Gray broke through his words. "She does not need to marry you. Not in any universe. And don't you have some actual work you need to do?"

Rylan shrugged. Mischief danced in his eyes. "You think that you can do better on the target, Agent Stone? I mean, Emerson here just proved herself. You think you still got what it takes to nail a target like she just did?"

At least six agents inched closer.

Emerson could not help herself. She put the gun down. Motioned toward Gray. "Six in the heart. Two in the head." A deliberate challenge.

Without another word, Gray took up a firing position. Not in the lane she'd just used, but to the right. "Set it up!" he shouted.

And the lane was set up. He checked his gun. Nodded.

He fired until the weapon was empty.

More than eight shots.

Rylan pushed the button for the target to advance toward them.

There was no applause. There was just dead silence. Sort of a stunned silence.

All of the holes were tight and close—basically on top of each other—right on the heart. And in the head. Tight. Close. Accurate. Deadly.

"Want to marry me, too?" Gray asked blandly.

"Uh, no, thanks," Rylan returned as he backed away and put his hands up. "I'm good."

* * *

ONE WEEK *and two days since Briar...*

"WE'RE SPARRING?" Emerson crept forward in her sneakers. She'd made sure to change into running shorts and a t-shirt after getting the text from Gray saying they were meeting to workout. At five a.m. "I thought we were going for a run."

His gaze swept over her body. "That explains the shorts." His stare lifted. Pinned her. "Self-defense practice. That's why I asked you to meet me in the training room."

"Five o'clock in the morning." She nodded. "For self-defense. Sure, why not?" Emerson squared her shoulders even as she edged closer to the mat that waited for her.

Gray stood in the middle of that blue mat. "Didn't want us to be disturbed by any of the other agents. As it is, Rylan follows you around like a lost puppy."

Uh, he did not. "Be careful, you sound jealous."

"Is that what you want me to be?"

She stilled. Totally stopped her creeping-forward movement. Because this was as close to a personal conversation as they'd come since Briar.

"I'm not jealous." He rolled his neck. "Not my business at all who you fuck."

Emerson blinked. "Then why are we having this fun pep talk?"

When He Defends

He growled.

Don't find the sound sexy. Do not. "Unless you've changed your mind." Now she advanced fully onto the mat. Stopped about a foot from him. Maybe she should have taken off her sneakers. He'd taken off his. Oh, well. Too late. Too late to ditch the shoes and too late to call back the words she'd already spoken. "Did you decide you want us to be more than partners?"

His nostrils flared. "How much self-defense do you know?"

A lot. Instead of answering, she shrugged. Yes, she was feeling *difficult*.

A muscle flexed along his jaw. "I want you to get out of some basic holds. Don't worry about hurting me. You can't."

"Never thought I could, not for a second." She sent him a hard smile. "You've been avoiding me."

"The hell I have. I've been with you in every briefing session and every case update."

"Fine, you have been avoiding having private talks with me and you have—"

He had her ass on the mat. He'd taken her down, and he covered her. "You saw me coming, yet you did nothing to stop my attack."

She stared up at him. One of his legs was between hers. That rich scent of his teased her nose. Gray wore black sweats. A tight black t-shirt. He looked so freaking sexy. She had seen him coming, obviously, but she hadn't, uh, responded. Probably because she'd been trying to ignore how sexy he was in the black t-shirt. "You usually wear suits," she blurted.

"Not to sparring sessions."

Of course. Obviously.

"If I were a real attacker, you'd be dead, Emerson."

If you were a real attacker, I wouldn't be lusting after you. "Are you afraid of me?" she asked, bluntly.

He blinked, jerked back, and, using that moment of surprise, she shoved up with her arms, twisted, and flipped Gray over so that when their bodies stopped heaving about, she was on top of him. On top as in, she straddled him.

It took exactly two seconds for her to realize that position was a serious mistake. She flew off him. Took a couple of quick steps *away* from Gray.

"Why would I be afraid?" He rose slowly to his feet. "I let you go, by the way."

"Fair enough. I let you tackle me, by the way." Another smile. More brittle this time. "I think you're afraid because one minute you're trying to fuck me, then you learn my deep dark secrets, and you act like I have the plague. I don't, FYI."

Now he surged toward her. "You think I'm keeping a distance because of what you told me about your father?"

Her chin notched up. Her hand also rose, and she jabbed him in the chest. "I think you kissed me like your life depended on it and then—*Gray!*"

He'd caught her wrist. Using his hold, he spun her around and looped his arm over her. She found herself with her back flush against his chest and stomach, while his arm in front of her was a seemingly unbreakable bar.

"I am the last person who would ever judge you because of your father." His breath whispered against her ear. "People in glass houses and all of that."

Surprise rushed through her, even as Emerson drove her left elbow back against him as hard as she could. He grunted but didn't release her. Instead of trying to rush forward to get out of his grip, she stepped back, looped her foot behind his ankle, and then she slammed her whole body back, making them both fall. But as he toppled, she rolled free and bounded back to her feet. "Why is your house made of glass, Gray?"

He smiled up at her.

Oh, damn. Gray's smile was absolutely, one hundred percent lethal.

She backed away.

He rose, slowly. "Come now, Emerson. You already know. You profiled me, remember?"

His mother had fled an abusive relationship. I think he is a protector now because he saw his mother abused when he was a child. He wants to protect those who are weak. "I spoke with Misty yesterday."

"Did you." Not a question.

"She's at home in Georgia."

"Um."

"With her mom. With Timothy. Really crazy thing—she said that a bank account had been set up for her." Emerson paused. "She started crying when she told me how much money was in the account."

There was zero change to Gray's expression.

"You know anything about the account?" Emerson pushed.

"Maybe it's one of those crowd sourcing things." He shrugged. "Or an anonymous donation. Those are really hard to track down. Especially if the donor doesn't ever want to be found."

She was staring at the donor. "She also got contacted by the teacher at a hearing-impaired school in her mother's town. A doctor reached out about Timothy, too. All sorts of contacts are appearing."

"Emerson, are we going to talk all day or should I just tackle you again?"

Tackle me. I dare you. "You made sure Misty and Timothy would be secure. You're helping them. Because you're a protector."

"Pretty sure that her ex would call me something else." A cold smile came and went on his face. "So would Jake Waller."

Jake Waller was being held without bail. And currently being charged with eight counts of murder and kidnapping. *Eight.* The toolbox had helped them to discover the other victims.

Gray was clearly not going to admit that he'd gone the extra mile to help Misty, so she'd try another tactic. "Where is your father, Gray?" she asked.

He began to circle her.

Dammit. She started to circle him, too. *Circling each other.* Tension slithered beneath her skin.

"In the grave, rotting." A roll of one shoulder. "Or maybe in hell, burning. Either way, win for me." His gaze didn't leave her. "My father was an abusive bastard. Sadistic. Narcissistic. No empathy. No remorse. But the guy was utterly fantastic when it came to manipulation and deceit. And really, really good at the old superficial charm tricks. Good when he wanted to be, anyway."

Goosebumps rose onto her skin.

"Classic psychopathic personality disorder. And, of course, seeing as how you're a doctor, a psychiatrist, then you know that some say there is plenty of evidence to suggest that can be inherited, too. Nature or nurture. But sometimes, they both fuck you over." Gray flexed his wrist. "You know, it still hurts from where you broke it."

Horrified, her gaze jumped to his wrist. She *had* broken

his wrist, a while back, on their first case. But only because she'd been trying to save his life, and she'd slammed her body into his in order to protect him from a hail of bullets. But if the injury still pained him... "We shouldn't be fighting! I don't want you to hurt it again and—"

He'd gotten too close. His leg swept behind hers. She was falling down, again, dammit. But she grabbed him and twisted on the way down. If she was going down, then Emerson intended to take Gray with her.

He landed first. She fell on top of him.

"I lied," he told her. Gray's hands locked around her hips. "It doesn't hurt at all. See, I'm good at manipulation, too."

Emerson blew a lock of hair out of her eyes. "Tell me something that I don't already know."

"I'm not staying out of your bed because I'm worried you might be like your father. I can assure you, I don't think about your father at all when I look at you."

Her lips parted.

"I'm staying out of your bed because I lose control too easily with you. I don't believe I would be a safe lover for you to have." His hold tightened on her wrist. "And I think you crave safety. Despite the fact that you spend your days and nights trying to understand killers, I think—at your core—that safety is what you want most. Maybe that's the whole reason you do try to understand the monsters out there. You want to stop them, don't you? To save the world."

"The victims," Emerson whispered. Her legs had slid between his. She levered up, pushing her hands against his chest. "I want to save them."

"Sometimes, we're too late for that, and all we can do is stop the predators."

Her gaze fell to his mouth. No more sexy smile. No

taunting grin. She could remember, all too easily, what it felt like to have his mouth on hers.

"Don't," Gray warned.

She inhaled and forced her stare to rise and hold his. "Am I supposed to act like I don't feel the giant cock shoving against me?"

He cursed.

"Because I do feel it. Super hard to miss it, in fact." *Because it is super hard.*

His hands immediately let her go.

She rose, slowly. Maybe she deliberately slid her body against his.

He hissed out a breath. "Mistake."

Was it? "I was supposed to give you my decision, remember? Partner or lover? Wasn't that the big question that you posed in Briar?"

"Forget that." He was on his feet, too. His body seemed extra tense. "Partner. I am your *partner.*"

"I don't like either-or situations. Why does it have to be one or the other?" She didn't circle him. Just held her ground. "I'm sure there is some HR paperwork somewhere I can sign that says things between us are one hundred percent consensual."

He stiffened. "Emerson."

Yes, so she'd just made it abundantly clear—at least, Emerson certainly thought she had—that she wanted to be his lover. She held her breath. Waited for his response.

"Not a good idea for partners to sleep together. Emotional involvements can be dangerous." Rough. Rumbling.

Heat burned her cheeks at the rejection. Her breath expelled. "I don't think you're dangerous to me." *Let it go,*

When He Defends

Emerson. The man just said no. He's not interested. Gray changed his mind. Whatever. Let. It. Go.

He closed the distance between them. She tensed because, sure, he was probably planning another sneaky attack, and she truly didn't want to hit that mat again. But he didn't attack. Just stopped right before her. Towered over her.

Her head tipped back. Sometimes, she forgot just how big he was. Only now, his size was especially evident, particularly since she wasn't wearing her trademark heels.

"I am more dangerous than you realize." Deep and dark.

She swallowed. "If you changed your mind about us, that's fine. I get it. Heat of the moment and all of that." Under normal circumstances, she never, ever rambled. Silence was her friend. She liked to listen. Observe. Evaluate. This was not a normal circumstance, though, and she was rambling like mad. "You don't need to give me an explanation. You don't have to say—"

"I want to fuck you here and now."

Oh. Well. Okay.

But he didn't touch her. Just said those deep and hungry words. Just watched her with his intense, ever-so-dark eyes. Not gold. *The darkness has spread.*

"This had better not be another distraction technique," she muttered. "I'd appreciate it if you'd say exactly what you mean to me. No games, for once."

"I want to fuck you here and now," he repeated.

There was rough longing in his voice. Savage desire.

She found herself leaning toward him. *I want the same thing.* Emerson opened her mouth to say those words.

"But that's not going to happen." Gray held his position.

"Why not?"

"Because me without control? That's not something you want to see."

Uh, yes, yes it was. She was more than eager to see—

The workout room door flew open.

"Are you two sparring?" Rylan's voice rang out. "Holy shit—uh, sorry, Agent Stone. I just, uh, didn't think you ever sparred with anyone these days. Not unless it was your military buddies when they come in for some of those joint task force operations." He bounded forward.

Emerson forced her gaze toward him. Rylan wore gray sweats. A blue t-shirt with FBI emblazoned across the chest.

"They are former Marines," Gray said, his voice very careful and very flat. "And they give me a challenge, so I like sparring with them."

"Is Emerson a challenge, too?" Rylan asked.

She didn't like the mocking smile that he flashed her way. *Careful. I will put you on your ass, Rylan.*

"Yes, she is," Gray responded. No mockery. Truth.

Her stare whipped back toward him.

"A definite challenge." His gaze scorched her right before Gray turned away. "Get changed, Emerson. We've got profiles to work." He started to pass by Rylan.

"Hey, how about a quick sparring session, Agent Stone?" Rylan wanted to know. "Let's see if you live up to the hype." He reached for Gray's arm.

Two seconds later, Rylan hit the mat with a hard groan.

Gray stared down at him.

Emerson knew her gaze had to be huge. Gray had taken Rylan down with brutal efficiency and with a heck of a lot more force than he'd used with her.

Rylan gasped, "Definitely living up to the hype."

Gray stalked for the exit. Emerson scrambled to catch him. She grabbed his arm. He spun toward her, and she half expected to find herself hurtling through the air the way Rylan had just done.

Only that didn't happen. Gray just stared at her. "Something you need, Dr. Marlowe?"

When in the world had she become *Dr. Marlowe* again? He'd just said he wanted to fuck her on the mat, and now he was pulling this *Dr. Marlowe* bull on her? "Someone is running hot and cold."

His eyes *blazed*. "Just hot. So watch yourself."

No, she was done with that. "You went easy on me."

He didn't blink.

"On the mat," Emerson clarified. "You weren't using your full skill set or strength against me. You were holding back." Angry, she shook her head. "Don't ever do that again."

"Fuck that. I'll always hold back my strength with you. You don't hurt delicate things in my world."

"I'm not delicate. Don't hold back with me. I can handle anything that you throw my way."

His lips began to curl. His eyes to gleam.

Rylan groaned again. "Hey, Emerson, help a guy up, would you?"

"Help your own self up," Gray snapped at him. He leaned toward her. "You sure about that? You really think you can take all of me?"

"Try me and find out." Wait, did that sound sexual? Maybe. Definitely. Whatever. *His* words had seemed sexual, too. "Don't hold back with me. I *can* handle you."

"We'll just see about that."

Then he walked away. And her heart kept racing.

* * *

ONE WEEK and four days since Briar...

"WHAT's it like working up close and personal with the Man of Stone?" FBI Agent Agnes Quinn asked the question as she raised a chilled beer bottle to her mouth. Her dark red hair had been twisted into a braid that trailed over her right shoulder. Soft tendrils escaped to frame her oval face.

Man of Stone. Right. Emerson had learned that was the secret nickname for Gray shortly after she'd started working as a consultant at the FBI. A play on his last name, of course, but also on the fact that the other agents thought nothing ever touched him. That he could see the most chilling cases and remain totally unmoved.

But after watching him with Misty and Timothy at that rundown motel, after hearing about his past...

The nickname is a lie. Emerson didn't touch the beer bottle that had been placed in front of her. "I'm learning a great deal from him." That seemed like a diplomatic response. Also one that was true.

"He *sparred* her," Rylan announced to their group. He wiggled his dark brows dramatically.

There were stunned gasps from the agents at the table. They'd gathered at the bar—apparently, meeting at O'Sullivan's was a weekly tradition when the group was in town—and when they'd extended an invitation to Emerson to join, she'd agreed. Why not? Not like she had anything else happening on a Friday night. Her social life was non-existent. Hard to have a social life—or a dating life—when her thoughts were consumed by one man.

The Man of Stone.

"He sparred me, too," Rylan admitted as he took a long

pull on the beer. Rylan cleared his throat and confessed, "Man had my ass down on the mat before I could blink."

More laughter. Some clinking of beer bottles.

Covertly, Emerson studied the group. All FBI Agents. Rylan Tate. Agnes Quinn. Malik Jones. Trinity Coleman.

Trinity didn't drink her beer, either, just ran nervous fingers around the mouth of the bottle. "Is it weird that he scares me?" The faintest hint of a Texas accent came and went in her voice. "Because he does. I mean, don't get me wrong. I want to know about killers, too. But—there's knowing and then *knowing*, get me? Like, if you're in their heads that deeply, maybe something is off about you." Then, seeming to realize what she'd just said, her dark eyes widened. She yanked the beer toward her lips and took a couple of quick swallows. "Forget I said that," she burst out as she clinked the bottle back down on the table. "Forget it. And if anyone *dares* to pass that along to Agent Stone, I will bury you."

"No worries," Rylan assured her as he sprawled in the booth. His arm brushed against Emerson's. "If you're not scared of Stone, then something is probably off with you." An incline of his head toward Trinity. "I mean, did you hear about the time he was taken prisoner? Tortured for days?"

Beneath the table, Emerson's fingers pressed to the tops of her thighs. "What?"

"Oh, yeah." Rylan glanced around the busy bar. They'd picked a spot in the back, away from the small band that played on the stage. The lighting was dim. The music slow. His gaze darted back to the group. "I'd just started working with his team at the time. Get this. One minute, he'd been all secretive and shit with some joint-task-force case. Him and his military buddies."

"Marines." This came from Malik. Agent Malik Jones

was definitely the quiet type. Quiet. Still. Watchful. No accent in his voice.

"Right. Right. His Marine buddies. One minute, Stone is dealing with them, and the next, the guy just goes totally dark. I have no idea what's happening. Supervisors won't tell the team shit."

"Maybe you shouldn't be telling us this," Trinity murmured, biting her lower lip.

But Rylan waved that away. "Not like it's classified. I mean, the man vanished for days. Then had to stay in the hospital because he was beaten to hell and back." A low whistle. "When he finally arrived in the office again, Stone looked like the walking dead. Can you imagine how much pain it would take to put him down?"

Emerson's hands curled into fists. Her nails bit into her palms.

"And about that case he was working...the task force case...the one that got him snatched and tortured..." Rylan hunched forward.

Everyone at the little table leaned inward, too.

"It was all about some seriously high-profile witness." His voice was low. Barely above a whisper.

Everyone leaned a bit closer.

"He made the witness disappear. Poof. As in, gone from the face of the planet. He does that stuff. Works task force stuff with that US Marshal buddy of his, Tyler Barrett."

She'd met Tyler before.

"Agent Stone made the witness vanish while he was running some covert investigation. Only he knew where the person had gone—because his Marshal buddy had gone dark with the witness. The investigation apparently turned into a major clusterfuck, with even some powerful folks at the Bureau getting involved. Some of those individuals were reportedly dirty as hell." He swallowed. "The bad guys needed the witness eliminated. So, Agent Stone was taken. Gone." He snapped his fingers. "Like that."

"Bet he fought like hell." From Malik. His intense stare didn't waver as he studied Rylan.

"You know it." Agnes saluted Malik with her beer bottle.

"And I bet he didn't spill a single secret." Malik nodded. "He's one of those types that would die first before giving up an innocent." Admiration filled his tone.

"He almost did die," Rylan informed him. "The dude was seriously the walking dead, had to be carried out when he—"

"If you're going to tell my story, get the details straight."

Holy hell. Emerson jumped. So did everyone else at the table. They'd been positioned close to the back of O'Sullivan's. They should have seen anyone approaching, but Gray had just snuck up on them all.

"Dammit!" Beer dripped down Rylan's shirtfront as he leapt to his feet and grabbed napkins to mop up the liquid. "How did you sneak up on us?"

"How, indeed." Gray stood behind Rylan. "There's a back door, genius. And you always come to this bar on Friday nights when you're in town. The group's behavior is very predictable." His gaze swept the group. Lingered on Emerson. "Most of the group. Someone is a new member." He did not look away from her. "Collecting more data for your profile on me?"

"I'm just having a drink." She motioned to the beer bottle.

"You don't drink, Dr. Marlowe."

"Emerson," she whispered.

Their gazes held.

*Now I'm the one asking him to call me by—*Wait. "How do you know that I don't drink?"

His lips curled into a half-smile. "Because I have a thorough profile on you." His gaze left her. Took in every person at the table once more. Finally landed on Rylan. "I have a profile on every single one of you. I know your strengths and your weaknesses."

The group had gone dead silent.

After a moment, Rylan cleared his throat. He stepped to the side and motioned toward the round table. "Would you, uh, like to join us?"

"No."

Her brows shot up. *Way to be rude, Gray.*

"Gossiping about an FBI superior, huh, Rylan?" A nod from Gray. "Expected."

"Ouch," Agnes murmured.

"That wasn't the first time I've been tortured by someone who wanted me to give up a witness." Gray's voice was so mild he could have been talking about the weather forecast, and not a torture session. "I've learned to deal with pain. Guess that's necessary for the Man of Stone."

"Oh, shit." Agnes slumped in her seat. "He knows the nickname. We're all in serious trouble, aren't we?" Her fingers fiddled with the end of her braid.

"For telling stories? Nah." A shrug of one shoulder. Gray seemed so utterly unconcerned. "But try and get the details correct, would you?"

Rylan coughed. "What, um, what did I get wrong?"

"I didn't nearly die. Big detail that was incorrect. Total hyperbole. I still had plenty of fight left in me."

Trinity wet her lips. "But you *were* taken prisoner? Tortured? And someone in the FBI was involved?"

"I was taken prisoner." A nod. "And, yes, actually, I was

betrayed by someone who should have been working to protect us all."

Jaws dropped.

"What?" Malik exclaimed.

"My torturer enjoyed using a knife. Some of the cuts were a bit too deep. I bled out more than I should." Spoken casually. "So all the blood loss made it look like a bigger deal than it was." Another shrug. "No worries. I lived to fight another day."

Everyone stared at him. Just stared.

Finally, Malik asked, "What happened to the people who took you?"

Gray's smile was brutal. "What do you think happened?"

A shiver slid over Emerson.

Gray shrugged out of his suit coat and passed it toward her. "Should have worn a dress with sleeves, Dr. Marlowe. The temperature is supposed to drop tonight."

She reached for the coat. Their fingers brushed. Heat singed her. "I-I don't need—"

"Take it." Flat. Then he stepped back. Nodded curtly. "Enjoy the night, everyone." He turned and strode away.

She had his coat in her hand. It was warm from his body. It carried his crisp scent. And he was walking away from her without a backward glance.

"Tell me that was weird," Rylan mumbled. "Come on, I'm not the only one who feels like he was stalking us, right? I'm not the only one who thinks something is seriously up."

"Good night." Emerson was already on her feet. "I can't take his coat. Got to give it back." She grabbed her purse. Dipped her head toward everyone. "See you all soon."

Then she was bobbing and ducking through the crowd. "Gray!" Emerson called out his name and she was—

Running straight into Gray. Because he'd stopped in the middle of the bar. Turned back toward her. His hands flew out and clamped around her shoulders. "Did I forget something?"

"Yes," she said, very definitely. "Me." Then she stood on her tiptoes, yanked him toward her, and kissed him.

Chapter Six

"I will protect my partner. Always." – Gray Stone

HE WAS A STALKER.

Gray knew it. Understood it. Should probably change his actions and be *less* of a stalker, but that shit just wasn't going to happen. Ever since that night in Briar, Tennessee, when a killer had put his hands on Emerson, Gray had turned into a full-fledged stalker where his partner was concerned.

His protective tendencies had only amplified after the painted message had been left in Emerson's motel room. Gray was worried. Every instinct he had screamed an alarm.

You'll die. Those words in Emerson's room haunted him. They also pissed him off. No one would hurt her. Not on his watch. Screw that shit. So...

He'd begun to stalk her. To make certain she was safely

home at night. To make certain no predators were hanging around her place. To make certain...

There are no threats.

And, yes, he'd been testing her. He'd needed to make sure the woman could shoot to protect herself. Sure, he'd seen her files. Knew that she'd passed the shooting drills before, but he'd wanted to see her skills up close and personally.

He'd been impressed when he'd watched her fire at the target. It took a lot to impress him.

Then, there had been the morning when he'd had the total jackass idea of sparring with her. Just to make sure that she'd be able to hold her own against a bigger opponent. But the instant he'd seen her in those short shorts—*hello, torture*—his dick had saluted, his mind had gone dead silent, and he'd had to fight the urge to pull her into his arms.

So, he'd taken her down on the mat. She'd escaped his hold. Again, impressing him. Then she'd taken *him* down.

Turned him on even more.

When they'd regained their footing, she'd stood before him, beautiful, determined, and she'd just boldly announced that she wanted him. He'd tried to warn her away. Done his damn best. But...

She hadn't backed down.

Rylan had interrupted before things went too far. Rylan who always watched her a bit too much. *Like I'm one to judge.* Rylan who always lingered around her a bit too much. *Again, who the hell am I to judge?*

But...

He didn't want Rylan around her. Truth be told, Gray didn't want any other guy putting his hands anywhere near her.

So, yes, his stalker skills had been activated. He'd

followed the group to the bar when he realized Emerson was accompanying them. He could have lied to himself and said he followed to make certain that she was safe. But this particular stalking adventure wasn't about safety. It was about jealousy.

She'd gone to the bar with Rylan.

Watchful, fun, and ready-to-entertain-her-at-any-moment Rylan.

Getting the drop on the group had been too easy. Seriously, too easy. They were Feds—fine, Feds and one consultant. They should have been aware of their surroundings at all times. But, instead, they'd been gossiping about his past, and they hadn't been aware when he'd snuck in the back door literally feet away from them.

Amateur mistake.

And...now...

She's chasing after me. He'd turned when he heard Emerson call his name. She'd darted through the crowd. He couldn't even see the table of Feds behind her. They were blocked by a line going to the bar. But Emerson—

She barreled toward him. His coat was tucked under her arm. She'd shivered, so he'd given her the damn coat to wear, not to carry around. His hands reached out and curled around her shoulders. "Did I forget something?"

"Yes." Very definite.

Oh, he had? What had he forgotten?

"Me." Her hands fisted in his shirtfront even as she shot onto her toes, and she kissed him. Holy hell, she kissed him. In the crowded bar. A bar with FBI agents.

She. Kissed. Him. Open mouth. Teasing tongue.

He stiffened. Even as lust and longing poured through every cell in his body, his muscles tightened. Her mouth was soft and sweet, and he wanted to savage it with his raw need and lust. Wanted to damn the consequences and any watchers and kiss her the way he wanted. *I want to kiss her. Fuck her. Claim her.*

Emerson whipped back, as if just realizing what she'd done. "You...aren't kissing me. Not, uh, back, I mean, and I'm—I'm sorry! I—I shouldn't have chased you. I shouldn't have kissed you!"

Screw it. He took the coat from her.

Emerson blinked.

He moved behind her. Put the coat on her shoulders.

"What is happening right now?" she whispered.

"You're coming with me." Gritted. Speech was nearly impossible. He put his arm around her shoulders. Pulled her against him. Took her out of that bar. His expression must have been helluva fierce because everyone got out of his way, immediately, and then he was outside. *They* were outside. The busy Atlanta street seemed to hum with energy. He turned to the left, his arm still around her shoulders. Gray guided Emerson away from the bar's busy entrance. To the side of the building on a much quieter street. He turned. Pinned her between the building and his body. His hands flew up to cage her.

"I...probably should not have done that."

There wasn't much light on the side of the building. The darkness surrounded them. Pulled at him. "Yeah, you definitely shouldn't have. Too late now, though." He leaned closer. "Do it again."

"Wh-what?"

"Do it...again." He should not. Hell, no, he should not but... "Kiss me again." Kissing her was not the way to stay platonic partners. He'd intended to keep his hands off her that night. Actually, his hands weren't on her. They were flat against the brick wall behind her. It was his mouth that was about to be on her.

Jealousy seethed inside of him. Because when he'd gotten to that bar, Rylan had been sitting right beside her. Rylan's arm had been brushing against hers. Rylan had been leaning into her, practically kissing her cheek.

Sonofabitch. I'm jealous of a green agent. And it sucked. It freaking sucked. He wanted Emerson, and he didn't want to share her with anyone. Ever.

Her hands rose and pressed to Gray's cheeks. A silken touch. He leaned toward her. She rose up. She. Kissed. Him.

They were alone. No prying eyes. No Feds at a nearby table. Just him. Just her. Just the darkness.

His mouth opened. Her lips parted. His tongue sank into the sweetness that waited for him, and every cell in his body seemed to become electrified. His dick was already saluting her. Need burned beneath his skin. A hungry desire to take and take and take.

To take until the desperate lust eased.

Until he stopped dreaming about her. Waking up at night, her name on his lips, the sheets tangled around his legs and his dick hard and aching for her.

You can't go back from this.

Did he want to go back? Or did he want to grab tightly to her and never let go?

Danger. Serious fucking danger.

He hauled his mouth away. She cried out in protest. He wanted to put his mouth right back on hers and drink up every single sound she might make but... "Why the hell did you kiss me, in there?"

"Because it seemed like a really good idea at the time." Husky. Sexy.

His back teeth clenched. "You know that we could have been seen," Gray gritted out.

Soft laughter trickled from her. He was pretty sure that he might have stopped breathing.

I love the sound of her laughter.

"Being seen was the whole point," Emerson confessed.

His hands pressed harder against the wall as he fought the impulse to touch her. To drag her close.

"Though the crowd did get thicker than I anticipated. Can't be certain that we *were* seen," she mused. "I did try, though. Maybe an A for effort, am I right?"

She might drive him insane. And he might enjoy the ride. "Why did you want to be seen kissing me?"

"Because I wanted everyone to understand that *I* was the one pursuing you. You weren't applying pressure, using your big, bad clout at the FBI to get impressionable me into bed."

He snorted. Impressionable, his ass.

"You weren't getting me to do anything I didn't want. By kissing you there, in front of everyone, I was making it clear that you were the man I was choosing." An exhale. "Even if you weren't choosing me back. You rejecting me right in the middle of the bar was a major possibility. And, FYI, you kinda did reject me. So if any of the team saw us, they probably have no idea if we're making out or if you're currently kicking me out of the Bureau. Not like you kissed me with mad passion in the bar."

It had taken all of his willpower not to literally gobble her up. "You shouldn't play dangerous games with me."

"Why not? They're the only kind of games that you like to play."

He wanted to kiss her again. No, he wanted to do one hell of a lot more than that. He wanted to completely devour her. He wanted her mouth. He wanted her naked. He wanted his hands on every inch of her body. He wanted his mouth on every inch of her. He wanted to lap her up and have her shudder and buck against him as she came.

"Giving you the green light," Emerson said. "In case there was any confusion."

Fuck me.

"I made my choice. Partner or lover? That was the question you posed to me. Well, I choose both. I've never been an either-or kind of girl. I take what I want. I want both options with you. And I think we can have them."

He should unclench his jaw. Move away from her.

"This is the part where you respond," she prompted. Her voice trembled a little bit. "The part where you have to say or do something."

Usually, he *was* the chatty one, at least chatty by comparison to his very small group of real friends. His Marine buddies, all lethal bastards who would gladly bleed for each other in a heartbeat. But, right then, with Emerson, he wasn't sure what to do.

Or what to say.

I want her. I want to take and take.

But...

Could they be both? Hell, no. This was going to explode in his face. He knew it with utter certainty. When the flames came, he'd have no one to blame but himself. But that didn't mean he couldn't enjoy the fire for a time.

"Gray?" Emerson prompted. Her hands had lowered to press to his chest.

In the distance, he heard the rumble of motorcycle engines. Quite a few of them.

"Are you going to say anything or just leave me hanging?" Emerson asked him.

Oh, darling, I would never leave you hanging. "Your timing is interesting."

"What?"

Gray nodded. "I appreciate you helping me lay the groundwork for our new case."

"I have no idea what you're talking about." A pause. "Are you drunk?" Suspicious.

He laughed. Couldn't help it. Even as the growl of those engines got louder. Closer. "The scene in the bar—if we were spotted—just plays in our favor."

"Uh...good?"

"Because we'll need that for our cover."

"Cover? What cover? Gray, make sense, would you? Make sense."

He kissed her. Just put his lips back on hers, plunged his tongue into her mouth, and tasted her. *So incredibly sweet.*

Time was running out. He had just a few moments to take what he wanted. And he wanted *her*.

* * *

THEY'D COME out of the bar together. He hadn't seen the FBI bastard go in the nearby bar, so he hadn't expected Emerson to come out with the jerk's arm around her shoulders and seemingly wearing the man's suit coat.

But he'd been waiting. Watching. Some days, it seemed as if he'd always been watching Emerson. Did she know? Could she feel him?

She should know. She *should* feel him.

So when she came out with the agent, he wondered if it might just be a taunt. A way to piss him off. Tricky, tricky Emerson. Such a naughty tease.

Only then the man steered her into the shadows. He

pushed her up against the wall. Then FBI Special Agent Gray Stone put his mouth on Emerson. He kissed her. She kissed him back. There, in the shadows. In the darkness.

He watched. He didn't attack. Even though rage twisted and coiled inside of him.

Emerson, what are you doing?

He'd been angry before, back in Briar, when he'd seen the FBI agent rush out of her motel room. For a moment, his temper had taken control. He'd wrecked her room. Wrecked the Fed's room. Left a warning for them both.

But then they'd stayed apart. He'd thought—maybe they'd taken his warning to heart. Or...or maybe he'd even been wrong. Maybe they had been talking about a case, and that was why Gray Stone had been in her motel room so late. Not because they were fucking. Emerson wouldn't fall for someone like him, anyway. Stone would be too boring for her. He didn't have enough darkness to call to the real Emerson.

But she was kissing him. Right then. Right there. Stone was kissing her.

He slowly pulled out the knife that he always carried. Started to advance.

And the howl and growl of motorcycles erupted into the night. He stepped back, darting into the shadows once more even as his head whipped toward the growls. He saw the lights from the approaching bikes. Shining—glaring—through the darkness. Oh, no. Had he been seen in the lights? He scurried back more. *Even more.* More hurried steps away from Emerson and the Fed, fast steps until he was almost running, but he figured the growl of those motorcycle engines would hide his retreat. Wouldn't they?

Can't be seen. Can't be caught.

Rage blasted inside of him even as...

A glance over his shoulder showed him that the motorcycles were heading straight for the darkness that held Emerson and her Agent Stone.

Don't disappoint me, Emerson. If you do, I'll kill him first...and send pieces of him for you to find.

* * *

THE GROWLING AND snarling of motorcycle engines yanked Emerson back to reality. She shuddered against Gray. It sounded as if a whole stampede of bikes was heading their way.

"Don't be afraid," Gray told her. "I've got this."

This? What was this?

He turned away from her. Put his body in front of hers, and those growls just got even louder. Even rougher as the small side street they were on suddenly filled with at least a dozen big, black motorcycles.

What is happening here?

She grabbed Gray's shoulders and shoved up on the balls of her feet. The riders all wore dark helmets, with their masks pulled down to cover their faces. The first bike had stopped about five feet from Gray. The driver of that bike still gripped the handlebars as the motorcycle idled.

"You're loud as hell," Gray called out. "How about you try making a less dramatic entrance next time?"

The lead motorcycle revved again.

Oh, no. Emerson's stomach seemed to drop. She knew that Gray had a ton of enemies in this world. She *hadn't* known about his abduction and torture time. How had she missed all that? The powers at the FBI had buried that truth, but the gossip mill had kept some of the details going.

And now...

When He Defends

This.

The leader raised his hand. Made a circling motion with his gloved fingers. All of the other riders immediately turned and drove away. More snarling engines. More growls. Rather deafening in the small street.

But the leader remained. He turned off his Harley. Climbed off the motorcycle. He wore a black jacket. Battered. His hand rose to grab his helmet. He dropped it on the seat and then began to close in on Gray.

Slow steps.

Emerson remained on her tiptoes so that she could try to see him better. Dark hair. Thick. Hard jaw.

Would it kill them all to take this scene into better lighting?

"You taking the case?" the man asked.

What case? Emerson tried to dart around Gray.

He moved to the side, effortlessly blocking her dart. "Working on it right now."

"Uh, huh. Looked to me like you were working on something different." Mocking.

She realized that the flash of headlights had probably illuminated her and Gray quite well.

"It's called laying groundwork," Gray returned. "Setting the scene."

Her hands fisted. She'd thought what they were doing was called kissing.

"She's my partner, Dr. Emerson Marlowe."

Partner.

"Oh, I know exactly who she is." The stranger seemed pleased. "Glad she's the one you picked for the job." A brief pause. "You'll take him out?"

"I'll...apprehend the suspect." Careful words.

Enough of this nonsense. She elbowed Gray out of her

way. He rumbled a warning to her, but she ignored that warning and faced off with the stranger. Gray's height. Gray's build. If only she could see his features clearly. "Who are you?"

"Sweetheart, names aren't entering this game."

"I'm *not* your sweetheart," she returned instantly.

"She sure as hell isn't." A lethal warning from Gray. "Watch yourself."

Soft laughter. "Is that you getting into character, too? The jealous lover? Bet you've never played that role in your life. A real bitch, isn't it?"

Her gaze raked the stranger, going from the top of his head—thick, dark hair—and traveling down. Old t-shirt. Jeans. Black boots. His voice was deep, held no accent, but seemed...*something is familiar about him.* "Do I know you?" Emerson asked.

"Better if you don't," he said. "Ask Gray. He'll tell you it's always better to pretend you have no clue who I am."

Okay. Now she was even more curious. Her head turned toward Gray. "Are we meeting with a motorcycle gang leader in a dark alley? Because that's sure what this seems like. Is he some sort of source for you?"

The stranger laughed. A deep, rumbling sound. Again... *familiar.*

Gray sighed. "Emerson, first, it's a narrow street, not an alley. And, second, calling someone a gang leader isn't polite. Third..." Gray pointed at the biker. "You're the one who likes to pretend. Not me."

There were a whole lot of undercurrents flowing in that narrow street.

"Fuck politeness," the biker said. "By the way, I saved you both from a mugger tonight. So when this case is over and you're tallying up how much I owe you for putting this fucker in the ground, add that to my list, would you?" He turned away.

"*We're not putting anyone in the ground,*" Gray snapped.

"Sure." The biker waved his hand toward them. He'd almost reached his bike. "You find him, pull him out of the dark, and I'll bury him. Done. You know how I love to handle the dirty work."

Footsteps rushed toward them.

Emerson wasn't overly surprised to see the rest of the FBI team advancing. The arrival of the motorcycle gang had been *loud*. Rylan was even reaching for his weapon as he eyed the leader.

"Stand down," Gray snapped.

Rylan froze.

The biker climbed on the Harley.

Emerson found herself rushing toward the stranger. "What mugger?" Her heart drummed. Unease slithered through her.

A faint beam of light fell on his face. High cheekbones. Strong blade of a nose. "Some creep was sneaking up on you and Gray. Had a knife in his hand. Went scurrying into the dark when my crew arrived." He started the bike. The engine growled. "You're welcome."

Someone had been sneaking up on her and Gray?

The biker's gloved hands rose. His index fingers pointed upward. The rest of his fingers curled down. His fisted hands quickly pressed together. The index fingers did *not* touch. A fast motion that she almost missed. One index finger dropped and slid against his chest.

Her eyes narrowed.

"Loverboy," the biker called out. "Do a better job of watching your six. I can't always handle the task." The engine revved. "Might want to jump back," he advised Emerson.

She didn't have to jump. Gray wrapped an arm around her waist and hauled her back. The biker drove away even as his motorcycle growled and shuddered beneath him.

Emerson's hands lowered to press against Gray's hold. "You can let me go."

"Yeah..." His breath blew against her ear. "I don't think so."

The rest of the team scrambled toward them. Rylan was no longer reaching for his gun. "What in the hell is happening?" he demanded. "Do you *know* who that guy was? Shit, shit, I can't believe he was right *here*."

Emerson did not, in fact, know who he was.

"I know," Gray said. His tone came off as bored. Sure, why not? Normal night for him, huh? *Nothing to see here.* A make-out session in the dark, bikers, a would-be mugger...

He was sneaking up on you with a knife. Her breath heaved out as she shoved at Gray's hold. "Let me go. *Now*."

He let her go.

Trinity bounded forward. "Pretty sure that was Cassius Striker. He's the leader of one of the most notorious motorcycle clubs in the US, and he was just *here*. Just, what, talking with you both?" Her voice rose. "While the rest of us were drinking inside?"

"Yeah, it was Cass." Again, Gray seemed *bored*. "It's called talking with a source, something I am sure you can all understand."

"Cassius Striker is your source?" Malik rocked back on his heels. "Sorry, Agent Stone, but I have to call BS. No way that man trades intel on his MC."

"He trades intel when he wants to find the killer who

recently took out one of his members." Gray glanced at Emerson. "You dropped the coat."

Crap. She had. She rushed to grab it.

He beat her. Picked it up. Put it back around her shoulders. His touch didn't linger.

She wanted it to linger.

"Be in the office at 0600 tomorrow," Gray directed the group. "I'll brief you on the case, but Dr. Marlowe and I will be the primaries. We'll be working undercover."

"Undercover?" Rylan edged closer. "Undercover as what? You gonna pretend to be a member of Cassius's MC?"

"No, I'm going to pretend to be Dr. Marlowe's husband. Pretend to be hopelessly and completely in love with her."

She wasn't the only one to have her jaw hit the ground. The whole group was stunned.

"Any other questions?" Gray drawled.

Everyone shouted at once.

"Too fucking bad," Gray returned. "See you at 0600." His fingers curled around Emerson's elbow. "Now I have to go brief my wife."

Chapter Seven

"Pretending isn't hard. Hell, I pretend every single day of my life. Pretend to be normal. Pretend to fit in. Pretend to care. Not like this is my first undercover assignment. I can pretend in my sleep." – Gray Stone

"I'M SORRY ABOUT YOUR COAT." EMERSON STOOD inside of her rental. An upscale condo in Atlanta's Art District. Moments ago, she'd disarmed her alarm. She shrugged out of the suit coat and extended it toward Gray. She grimaced as she noticed the dark stains on the back of the coat. "You know what?" Emerson snatched the coat back before he could take it from her. "I'll get it dry cleaned."

"Forget it." He tugged the coat from her fingers. "I can handle some dirt, Emerson."

"Oh, so I'm Emerson again, huh? Thought I was Dr. Marlowe. Seemed odd, I have to say, considering all of the times you chided me for calling you *Grayson*."

"Grayson was my father's fucking name. I don't particularly like it."

She blinked.

"So, what's happening here? Do I stand in the doorway all night or are you going to invite me inside?"

He'd followed her home. Trailed her up the stairs to her second-floor condo. Seen her to the door. And now he wanted inside. Emerson cocked her head to the right. "If you come in, will you give me truth or lies?"

"Emerson, Emerson, Emerson. Did you just call me a liar?"

"No, I asked if you would give me truth or lies. It's a straightforward question. One you didn't answer." She held her ground. "If you come in, do you intend to kiss me again?" A second question that deserved an answer.

Gray rocked forward, then caught himself. He shoved the coat under one arm. "You know what? It's probably a better idea for me to head out. I'll brief you at 0600 with the others." He turned away.

"Gray?"

"Yeah, Emerson?" Gray glanced over his shoulder.

She would not admit that she loved the way he said her name. The deep rumble and roll. The slightly rough edge. Fine, she would admit to *herself* that she loved the way he said her name. She would not admit that fact to anyone else. "Get your ass inside."

He flashed his smile.

Lethal.

She backed up. "Do you use that smile to your advantage often? Flashing it when you want to be charming or extra sexy in order to get what you want?"

He quirked a brow even as he entered her place and shut the door behind him. He tossed the coat onto her entrance table. "I think you just said I was both charming and sexy. Thank you. That should work well for our cover." His gaze darted around her place. "Huh. Not what I expected."

She wasn't going to be distracted. "The cover thing was for real? We have a new case? One where we'll be working undercover?" *As lovers?*

"You requested to work with me because you wanted more field experience, yes?"

She'd requested to work with him because Gray understood killers extremely well. The man was a legend. Also a hard ass. And a sexy distraction. Plus, a million other things that she had not fully expected. "Yes." A cautious response.

"Then consider your wish granted. You're about to get a crash course in field work."

Um, good?

He studied her critically. "You are great at profiling."

"Thanks for noticing," she muttered.

"I figure you'd like to have a shot at profiling on the spot, seeing potential suspects up close, and zeroing in on a target in real time."

Okay, he was dead serious. Excitement pulsed in their veins. "So there *is* a real cover."

"Real. And dangerous."

She thought about exactly what he'd said before regarding the case. "*Why* are we going to pretend to be a couple?"

"Because there is a killer targeting couples. They are his prey of choice. Three couples are dead so far. Two honeymooners. One couple celebrating their tenth anniversary. Guess someone just doesn't like love." His mouth tightened. "We're going to find that someone. We're going to be his next victims. And we're going to turn the tables and stop him. There. Done. Easy."

There seemed to be nothing easy about the plan from where she was standing. "When did you find out about this case?"

"Yesterday. Cassius brought it to my attention."

The gang leader had brought the murders to his attention?

"That couple that was celebrating their tenth anniversary? They happened to be friends of his. Cassius has taken a special interest in the case. If we bring down the killer..." His gaze held hers. "He's promised that he will greatly *owe* the Feds. I'm sure you understand how having Cassius in my debt could be a very beneficial proposition."

Her arms wrapped around her stomach. "Cassius wants to kill the guy."

"Yes, true."

"He *intends* to kill the perp."

Gray didn't argue.

She felt like a recap was in order. "You're going to find the killer. But you're *not* going to turn him over to Cassius, are you?"

"The plan," a smooth response from Gray, "is to stop the perp. To lock him up. The same way we locked up Jake Waller." He began to pace around the condo. "I get that the place is a rental. But there are zero personal touches in the space. You left everything as is, huh? Whatever the decorator put in, you kept."

She turned to watch him peruse her space. "It came fully furnished. No sense in changing things. You keep having me zip off to different parts of the country so it's not like I'm here for long periods of time." Where would they be heading for this latest case?

"That's a convenient excuse, Emerson. But why don't you try telling me the real reason there is nothing of you in this place?"

Emerson sucked in a sharp breath, completely caught off guard by his response. "Excuse me?"

"Oh, you heard me." But Gray turned his head toward her. "Want my theory? You don't have personal effects because you're not putting down roots here. Just like you haven't put down roots at the last three places you've lived. You rarely stay anywhere longer than a year."

"My work keeps me busy. You, of all people, can surely understand that." Her voice was steady.

"I understand a great deal. Far more than you realize." He waved toward the bookshelves. Shelves that were carefully decorated with things that weren't books. Vases. Small statues. Art pieces. "You're an avid reader, Emerson. But no books?"

"I tend to read on an e-reader." How did he know she was an avid reader? She hadn't read around him.

"No doubt, plenty of people do that—*I* do it often. Makes it easier to travel with books. But, come on, I'm sure you've bought plenty of physical copies over the years."

"Having books like *The Mind of a Killer* on your shelf hardly make guests feel comfortable."

"That's cute."

Now her brows shot up. "It's cute that I want to make people feel comfortable?"

"No, it's cute that you act like you have guests. You don't."

"You're here now. Hate to point it out to you, but that makes you a guest."

"Hmm. I'm here because I forced my way in. You didn't give me a spontaneous invitation."

No, she had not.

He strolled toward her. Casual. Graceful. That was something she'd noticed about him early on. Despite his big size, the man was extremely soft on his feet. Sneakily soft. Predatorily soft. Gray stopped directly before her. "You didn't invite any of your new FBI friends over. No dinner with Trinity. No night cap with Rylan."

"Your point being...?"

"You don't make friends easily, do you, Emerson?"

"No." And she envied him that ability because she knew that he did have a close circle of friends. His former Marine buddies—the ones who'd bled and fought together. They had a bond that she found to be quite amazing.

"You don't take lovers often, either, do you?"

Well, he'd just gotten very, very personal. In a blink. Tricky. Her chin notched up. "How often do you take lovers, Gray? All the time? Every other week?" A sharp snap entered her voice. Jealousy.

Great. Jealousy and envy, all in one two-minute period.

"I'm not a monk, but I don't have one-night stands all the time, either." A pause. "Two months ago."

Her brows shot up. "Excuse me?"

"I was with my last lover two months ago."

She did calculations in her head. Wait...

"Yeah, right before I met you. Funny thing, that. I met your infuriating and gorgeous self, and I couldn't get you out of my head." He turned away. "So playing your lover on this case won't be hard for me. But it will be a struggle for you."

"*What is happening here?* And why on earth would it be a struggle for me?" He was making her head spin. Deliberately, she was sure. Emerson suspected that Gray was trying to keep her off-balance.

"You're not used to being with a man. Having him touch you. Call you endearments. Make public displays of affection." He ran his hand over the back of her sofa. "Been two years, hasn't it? Since that prick colleague of yours took your work and tried to pass it off as his own? Don't know why you ever got involved with that loser. If you ask me, he was never worth your time."

"*Gray!*"

He turned his head toward her once again.

She swallowed. "How do you know about Nathaniel?"

He snorted. "Dr. Nathaniel Hadaway? Oh, easy. He came to see me today."

He could not have shocked her more. Her ex had gone to see Gray? *That very day?* "You are kidding me." If he was kidding, the joke was not funny. Not even remotely.

"Nope. Dead serious. Your Nathaniel—"

"He's not mine, and I am certainly not his." Nathaniel *had* tried to steal her careful research. He'd put his name on her paper and submitted it to journals. Total jerk. But how had Gray learned what the other man had done? "Why did he come to see you?"

"He'd learned that you were working with the FBI. He wanted to let me know that I was making a mistake in taking you on as a partner. That you would, ah, I believe the words he used were 'fracture in a field setting' and that I should terminate whatever arrangement I had with you."

The drumming of her heartbeat filled her ears. "That sonofabitch."

"Such language." He tut-tutted. "Dirty mouth." His eyes gleamed, more gold than brown in that instant. As if he enjoyed her dirty mouth.

Knowing Gray, he probably does.

"Don't act like you don't enjoy it." The words just fired from her.

He laughed. "See? That's why you were just *wasted* on him. Such a prick." A sigh. "Told him to get his ass out of my office, by the way. In response, he told me that he'd be back. Wanted me to consider the offer he made to me. Said he'd see me later."

"What offer?"

He rubbed the bridge of his nose. "The offer to replace you. Nathaniel felt that he could understand violent criminals far better than you could. Seeing as how you are so emotionally fragile and all that."

"I am *not* emotionally fragile."

"He did make a point of letting me know that you'd only had one serious relationship—a relationship with him —but that he'd had to terminate the relationship because he could not handle all of your emotional barriers."

This was not happening. Emerson didn't know if she should be furious or hurt or embarrassed or— "That sonofabitch," she said again. "He's trying to steal you from me!"

Gray blinked. "I can assure you, I have zero interest in Nathaniel Hadaway."

She rushed toward him. Grabbed his arms. "He's trying to take my job. Probably thinks he can do a ton of papers on the criminal mind based on your cases. He's trying to use you!"

"Isn't that what *you* think, Emerson? Aren't you using me, too?"

"I think—I think that I want you!"

He looked down at her hands as they gripped his arms. "Do you." Not a question.

"I want to work with you. You know that. I want to

learn from you. And yes, I just *want* you." There. Done. Said. "I think I've made that pretty clear. *You're* the one putting roadblocks in the way of what could be one very good time." Bold words but inside, she was twisting apart. Emerson could not believe Nathaniel had gone to see Gray. That her ex had just savaged her that way with all of this emotional fragility BS. The jerk would not get out of her life even though she'd told him to stay the hell away multiple times. "I'm not emotionally fragile."

Gray's head tilted. His eyes met hers.

"I can handle an undercover case." Fine, granted, it would be her first *ever* undercover case, but she could do it. She *would* do it. "After all, I have the best trainer in the world, don't I? I have you." She should let him go. Definitely. Only she didn't. "Teach me. Show me." *Kiss me.* Nope, she held that back because she'd already stripped her pride bare for him.

"Is this going to be one of those situations where you promise to follow orders…only to then go out and do whatever the hell you want?" His head lowered toward her.

If she'd been doing whatever the hell she wanted, then Emerson would be doing *him* right then and there.

"Nathaniel is a fucking ass, by the way," Gray informed her. "Insufferable. Arrogant. And his voice is nasally as hell."

"Agreed," she whispered back. His mouth was inches from hers. Inches.

"What did you ever see in him?"

"I thought he could understand me."

"Yeah, he can't. Knew it as soon as he said that emotionally fragile bullshit."

She blinked.

"Your body is delicate. Your mind and your heart aren't."

Her heart drummed.

"And even with a build one hell of a lot smaller than my own, you still do a damn good job of tossing me onto my ass so maybe I need to take it back and say your body isn't even that delicate. Hell, you're steel. Through and through. Better?"

She smiled at him.

He growled.

She'd never found growls sexy. Until Gray. Every time he growled, she sort of quivered.

The faint lines near his mouth deepened. "If we're gonna play lovers, you have to get used to my touch."

That would prove difficult. "Pretty sure I'll never get quite used to it. Every time you touch me, fire races beneath my skin."

His eyes widened. "Emerson."

"How does it feel when I touch you?" She was truly curious.

"Like I'm coming to life."

That had—that had almost been poetic—

"Fuck it."

Okay, not so poetic.

But she didn't care because his mouth was taking hers. He'd hauled her closer against him, and his lips took hers, and this was what she'd wanted. *He* was what she wanted. He was kissing her hotly. His mouth wildly passionate against her own.

Could they fake being lovers? Could she handle the undercover assignment? Absolutely. Because kissing him and touching him...easy.

Her mouth opened wider. His hands curled around her

hips. The need flared brighter and harder inside of her. She wanted to yank open that perfectly pressed shirt of his. To run her hands over his chest. She wanted to let herself go and not care about the consequences.

Nathaniel—no, he'd never really understood her.

But she had the feeling that Gray did.

"Gray..." She pulled her mouth from his. "Gray, I—"

Her doorbell rang.

Emerson blinked.

His gaze swirled. Gold and brown. Darkness swallowing the light. The ringing doorbell seemed to echo around them. Neither of them moved.

The doorbell rang again.

Gray slowly pulled away. "You expecting someone?"

No, not at all, she was not. Hadn't they already established that she didn't have visitors? Gray had been dead-on target with that analysis. She never invited friends over. Mostly because she didn't have a great deal of friends.

"This late?" Gray asked. An edge entered his voice. "Got a...friend you need to tell me about?"

She turned away from him. Grabbed her phone from the bag she'd tossed aside after entering her condo. "If that's your way of asking if I'm dating someone, the answer is no. You're the only man I'm interested in fucking." Her fingers swiped over the phone's screen. "For the record."

"Good." He peered over her shoulder as she used her app to see who was ringing her doorbell. And when they saw—

"Bastard," Gray snapped.

Yes, indeed. Her visitor was a bastard.

Before she could even put her phone down, Gray was stomping for the door.

"Uh, Gray!" Emerson called after him.

"It's almost eleven o'clock at night," he tossed over his shoulder. "He doesn't get to be at *your* place, at this hour. Dipshit."

Dipshit?

The doorbell rang again. Gray hauled open the door.

The man who'd been ringing the bell—three times—blinked owlishly. Emerson caught a quick glimpse of him and his stunned face because, apparently, he had not been expecting Gray to answer her door.

"Uh, ah, Agent Stone," Nathaniel Hadaway began. "What are you—"

"What in the hell are you doing at my partner's door at eleven o'clock at night?" Gray barreled over Nathaniel's words.

"I-I—"

Nathaniel wasn't usually the type to stutter or flounder at all. Normally, he was overly pompous and in full know-it-all mode. But Gray's voice had a lethal edge, and she could practically see the fury pouring off him. That fury seemed to have terrified Nathaniel.

"Emerson is *not* for you," Gray blasted. "Your dumbass lost that chance long ago. I told you before, stay the hell away from her and get out of my town."

"But—" Nathaniel rose onto his toes. Even on his toes, he was still inches shorter than Gray. Nathaniel strained to see her. "Emerson, I just want to talk! For old times' sake, just give me a moment. Tell your—your partner here to let me in!"

Um, how about no? Emerson tapped on Gray's very broad shoulder. He turned his head to look at her.

"Please," Gray said, voice softening just a fraction as he stared at down her, "let me kick his ass out of the building.

It would bring me such joy, and don't you want me to be happy?"

"Emerson!" Nathaniel's near shout. A nasally shout.

She peered over at him. Then back at Gray. The two men could not have been more different. Nathaniel with his polo and khakis, his slightly rounded chin and slicked back hair. Slender, at least four inches shorter than Gray even when Nathaniel was on his toes.

Weak.

And Gray...practically vibrating with energy. Rage? Handsome face tense, body strong. Muscles ready to attack. Dressed in his expensive pants and shirt but poised to strike at any moment. Because while he might dress the part of the gentleman, the truth was that Gray held a savagery barely in check, and it was a savagery that had called to her from the first moment they'd met.

No, it was Gray himself who called to her.

"Dammit, Emerson! This isn't personal," Nathaniel suddenly snapped. "It's a matter of life or death. So cut the dramatics, get your new partner under control, *and let me in.*"

Chapter Eight

"What do I think of Emerson's ex? I think the guy is a freaking idiot. With a very punchable face. Some people have those, you know. Genetic quirk."
– Gray Stone

His hands had fisted at his sides. It would be so easy to deliver a quick and brutal upper cut to Nathaniel Hadaway's weak jaw. Super simple. One punch, and bam, done. He would get so much joy out of the act.

This prick fucked my Emerson? Gray's fist lifted.

Emerson grabbed tightly to his arm. "He said life or death."

Gray locked his jaw. *Pretty sure the jerk will say anything to get in your pants again, baby.* Only, that shit was not happening. The moron would be getting nowhere near Emerson. Or her pants.

"Let's hear him out. It will take like, two minutes, tops." Her head turned toward Nathaniel. "Did you hear that?

Two minutes." Icy words. "That's all you're getting from me. Because that's pretty much all you ever gave to me."

Whoa. Whoa...

Had that been Emerson making a sexual dig?

Nathaniel flushed, and Gray could not help but snort. Two minutes? That's what this idiot had given Emerson? Oh, Gray would totally rock her world.

I'll make sure she comes so hard that she forgets this dumbass creep. He would make her come *in* two minutes. But that would be the start. The start of one seriously long, hot night.

"We don't need to get personal, Emerson." Nathaniel sniffed. "It's not my fault that you have emotional barriers that leave you unable to respond to a lover."

First, Gray laughed. Hard. Because he was pretty sure he'd never been with anyone as responsive as Emerson, and he hadn't even *had* her yet. Just kissed her. Touched her. But he'd felt the hunger in her body. She'd kissed him with a frantic passion. Her moans had made him crazy. Her nails had bitten into his shirt, and her body had twisted and pressed eagerly against his, promising him the hottest paradise of his life.

So, to say she couldn't respond...*bullshit.*

Except, he realized Emerson had stiffened. He immediately turned fully toward her. She'd paled. Her gaze had dropped down. Her chin dipped low and—*nope. Not happening.*

Did she think he'd been laughing at her?

Never.

His fingers curled under her chin. He lifted it up, slowly, deliberately, and when her incredible blue eyes were on his—eyes that held the hint of tears—he smiled at her. "He's completely clueless, isn't he?"

Her lips parted.

He almost kissed her again.

"I can have you coming in two minutes." He considered the matter. "Actually, probably in one. Shall we find out? Want to make a bet with me on it?"

Color came rushing back to her cheeks. She blinked quickly, and the tears vanished.

"You're fucking each other?" Nathaniel's nasally voice was getting on Gray's last nerve. "Well, that makes sense, I suppose. There is no other way that Emerson would have gotten the job. I mean, even with her mother's clout, you would not have agreed to work with her unless you were getting something from the deal. I'd heard that you told the senator to go to hell at her first overture, but then you changed your mind and now this makes more sense to me. So much more sense. *Fucking someone to advance up the ladder, eh, Emerson? I would have thought that was beneath you."*

"Usually I'm beneath her," Gray drawled. "Or she's beneath me."

"Gray!" Emerson shook her head. Hard.

Fine. He'd play nicely. No, wait, he wouldn't. The bastard at the door was her *ex*. And he'd just insulted her. "You were wasted on him," he told her, very definitely, then he reached out, fisted his hand in Nathaniel's pale green polo, and yanked the idiot inside. "Two minutes. Talk fast, then get the hell out. Emerson and I have better things to do than just piss away time with you."

Emerson hurried back a few steps, as if she didn't want to be too close to Nathaniel. Gray noted the move. Wondered a bit about it. He shut the door and watched his prey.

Nathaniel smoothed back his hair. His fingers trembled a bit as he glanced toward Gray.

"Agent Stone and I are not f-fucking," Emerson began.

Oh, fine, so she was going to give the guy the truth, was she?

"Yet," Emerson added. Then she nodded.

Gray blinked.

"But if we do, that's none of your concern. And if we fuck, it has nothing to do with me advancing up any ladder."

"Yeah," Gray agreed. He cut a disgusted glance at Nathaniel. "It just has to do with us wanting to rip each other's clothes off in a haze of passion. That happens to some people." He had to force his jaw to unclench. "Insult her again, and I can guarantee, it will be the worst mistake you ever make." He'd given the guy fair warning. What happened next would be on Nathaniel. Gray's gaze slid back to Emerson.

Her arms crossed over her chest. "What is the big life-or-death issue? Why are you here?"

Nathaniel's stare shot around her condo. Then his eyes darted to Gray. "I need to speak with Emerson alone."

Was the guy serious?

Precious seconds ticked past as Nathaniel just looked at Gray.

Finally, Gray laughed again. He couldn't help it. Nathaniel was being a bit unintentionally hilarious to him. "Dude, your two minutes are ticking past." He stepped forward.

Nathaniel backed up.

"You don't get to insult Emerson one moment and then ask to talk to her alone in the next instant. No way I'm leaving you on your own with her. Not happening."

And if you insult her again, my fist is flying. I did warn you.

"She started it," Nathaniel was quick to point out as he sounded like an absolute two-year-old instead of a licensed psychiatrist.

"Nathaniel." Brisk. Emerson did not move from her spot. "If you have something important to say, do it."

"Fine." He whirled toward her. Advanced fast in her direction.

Gray tensed.

"You need me," Nathaniel passionately told Emerson.

Uh, the hell she did.

"Bring me on as an associate in your field work exercise at the FBI," Nathaniel urged her. "You know that I understand criminals better than you do. *I've* worked in numerous prisons, I've interviewed serial killers, I've published *two* books on their psychopathy, and I have the option to write a third on the process of actually tracking down an active killer."

Oh. Gray got it. He nodded. "You have a book deal on the table. Only you need a plot for said book. That's why you were at my door earlier, trying to get me to ditch Emerson and replace her with you. That effort didn't work out like you'd hoped, so you came here to beg and get her to bring you onto the team."

Nathaniel's spine stiffened. "I do not beg."

"Whatever. It's not working. Emerson doesn't have the authority to bring you on. Only I do. So fuck off. It's not happening. Pretty sure I told you that earlier." He looked at his watch. "Longest two minutes of my life," he muttered. "Even longer than the time when a serial killer jabbed an ice pick into my arm and started twisting it."

Emerson gasped.

Nathaniel actually took a quick, almost eager step toward him. "That happened?" Interest lit his pale green gaze. The color of his eyes almost matched the sickly color of his shirt. "Can you tell me about it? How did it feel? What were your thoughts when the ice pick first went into your arm?"

Was the creep serious? It sure looked like he was. "Can I tell you about it? Just did. How did it feel? Like an ice pick was being shoved in my arm. What were my thoughts?" Gray tilted his head to the side. "That the killer would have to work one hell of a lot harder because I was not easy prey, and the second I was free, he would be a dead man. And I would be sure to make his death *hurt*."

Silence.

Nathaniel swallowed. "Fascinating." But he looked a little squeamish. One hand fanned toward his face.

Gray rolled his eyes. "Not really fascinating. Just facts. But story time is over. The door is waiting. Next time, don't lie to get your way back in Emerson's life." *You actually won't be getting back in her life at all.* He advanced and clamped a hand around Nathaniel's shoulder. "Do I need to walk you the seven steps back to the door?"

"But I can help! I'm better than Emerson when it comes to killers! I can figure them out!" He locked his legs. "Tell me about the new case you're working."

Unease slid through Gray. "Who said I had a new case?"

"I—" Nathaniel backed away. "I have my sources. And I know that something big is happening for your team."

Gray smiled at him. "You can't help on this particular case. I'm afraid that Emerson is irreplaceable to me."

"I can do anything she can!"

"Doubtful. Don't think people are really gonna buy you as my blushing bride."

Nathaniel's eyes got very big. Then very small. "What?"

"Oh, didn't I tell you the good news? Sorry, probably didn't have time with you busting in and being all life-or-death dramatic. Emerson is going to be my wife. And it's time for you to get the hell out."

* * *

"SHE'S NOT REALLY your wife. It's a cover." Nathaniel talked fast.

"No shit, Sherlock." Gray followed on the guy's heels. He'd decided the prick needed a personal escort out of the building. He'd also wanted a word alone with Emerson's ex. *Who the fuck told you about the new case?* He'd just ordered the team in for the 0600 briefing not even forty minutes ago.

"Emerson has never done undercover work."

They were heading down the stairwell. Their steps seemed to echo around them.

"I'm aware." The top of Nathaniel's head showed his thinning hair. That would explain why he kept his hair slicked back.

"She will crumble under pressure," Nathaniel warned ominously.

"She will not." *But you will crumble beneath my fist.*

They reached the landing.

"Emerson should be in the halls of academia." Nathaniel reached for the door handle. "She won't be able to maintain a false persona for long. She's no chameleon. Social situations have always been awkward for her. That's why she has few lasting relationships. Only surface friendships. It's why she watches instead of speaks first." He hurried outside.

Gray followed, his steps slower.

And Nathaniel kept right on talking. "She's constantly trying to understand criminals because she thinks there is something wrong with her, deep down, and if she can unravel their deviant behavior, then Emerson believes she can understand herself."

Enough. "Hey, asshole."

Nathaniel spun around.

"I don't need you to tell me anything about Emerson. I understand her perfectly. And, honestly, dude, say less. Because you know jack shit."

Nathaniel glowered. A nearby light fell clearly on his angry features. "I think I know her intimately."

"Two minutes? Nah. Not really. You don't. You barely know her at all after two minutes."

Nathaniel sucked in a breath. "It's not my fault that she's frigid."

Gray's hands fisted at his sides. "Weird. To be frigid, she sure burns me alive every time I touch her."

Nathaniel lunged forward but seemed to catch himself at the last moment. Maybe because he realized Gray could —and would—lay him out in an instant.

"Are we going to have a problem, Agent Stone?" Nathaniel asked. "Because I thought we could both be professional."

"Fuck professional. And, yeah, we are going to have a problem. We *do* have one, actually." Then, because he was pretty sure he knew just where Nathaniel had gotten his inside information, Gray fired, "Senator Marlowe."

Nathaniel's Adam's apple bobbed. "What about her?"

When He Defends

"She likes controlling Emerson's life. She's also a major donor at the university where you work."

"It's...her alma mater."

"She picked you out for Emerson, didn't she? Probably thought you would fit her. Only you didn't. You just disappointed Emerson."

"How dare—"

"Ease up, stud. Not talking about sexually, though, clearly, you disappointed her that way, too."

Nathaniel huffed out a breath.

"You stole her work." He remembered Emerson's anger. "Broke her trust. You can't do that with her. She's not big on forgiveness." Was that why he had been so careful to put all of his cards on the table with Emerson? Because he'd realized that about her from the beginning? *Trust is important. And too damn fragile.*

Gray decided to share a few details, just to see what reaction he could get from Nathaniel. "The senator wanted me to be a puppet on her string. Reporting every action Emerson took at the FBI." Gray shrugged. "I told her to fuck off. Doesn't mean others at the Bureau aren't still reporting to the woman, though. And I can't help but connect the dots right here, right now. Yesterday, I tell my superiors that I'm taking a new case..." A case that hadn't been on the FBI's radar at all, something personal because of Cassius. "And then you walk in my door *today*. Spouting about how you should be working with me, and it shouldn't be Emerson. So I'm guessing something changed in the senator's world. She wants Emerson out of the FBI. She thinks playtime is over. The senator sent you to take Emerson's place."

Nathaniel didn't deny the charge.

"I wasn't wild about Emerson being my partner, not on

day one." Truth. "But *no one* will take her place. She wants to run this mission, then she'll run the fucking mission."

"I can *help*."

"No, you can get in my way." He considered the matter. "You can also piss me off. Piss off Emerson, too. We don't have time to waste on that BS. So get in your Benz and get the hell out of here. Your services are not needed."

But Nathaniel lingered. "You don't understand. *You can't count on Emerson*. Her mother—look, the senator is *worried*. It's Emerson's life on the line, all right? The senator is worried that Emerson is—"

He broke off.

Gray stared him down. "Don't leave me in suspense. Just what is it that the senator fears? Because one day, she's demanding that I work with Emerson, and then I turn around and have you shoved in my face. A man can get whiplash for that type of exchange."

"I'm not here to watch you. I'm here...here to watch over Emerson." Nathaniel smoothed back his hair. "The senator is worried that Emerson may be...fracturing. There is a family history that you do not know about."

Actually, he did.

"And the senator is concerned that Emerson may be following in her father's footsteps. Starting to suffer from paranoia. Having delusions. The senator is worried that Emerson is slipping into the darkness." Sympathy deepened his voice. "Someone has to help Emerson. Someone has to watch over her. With my qualifications, I'm the perfect man to assist her." His hand fell back to his side.

So Gray stared him dead in the eyes—dead in the prick's lying eyes—and called, "Bullshit."

Nathaniel's mouth opened, then closed. "Excuse me?"

"Bullshit." He thought that was pretty clear, but just in

When He Defends

case, "Bullshit." The third time he said it, he did it just for fun. "Emerson isn't slipping into any darkness. You're also the last man who can handle anything about her. And here's a pro tip for you."

"What? I-I'm telling you the truth!"

"No, you're not. And about that pro tip..." He pointed toward the guy's hair. "When you lie, you smooth your hair. Dead giveaway."

"I—" Nathaniel's hand began to rise, but he caught himself.

"It's been fun. Nope, it hasn't been. It's just been annoying. Don't let me see your ass again." Gray turned away. He'd gotten too many lies from that conversation, but he was pretty sure that he *had* discovered one truth.

The senator was screwing around with FBI business. That would be stopping.

And the only person who would be *handling* Emerson?

It's gonna be me.

Two minutes, his ass.

Chapter Nine

"Do I think some people are born evil? Hell, yes."
– Gray Stone

EMERSON'S BREATH SAWED IN AND OUT. SHE COULDN'T believe that Nathaniel had come to see Gray and then showed up on her doorstep. The bastard was trying to discredit her with Gray.

But Gray isn't falling for Nathaniel's tricks.

Nathaniel. Smart. Deviously so. Driven. Driven to steal other people's work. Manipulative. He'd sure tricked her into thinking that he might actually care about her, only for her to find out that he'd been using her all along.

Her mother had been furious when Emerson had broken things off with Nathaniel. Emerson, on the other hand, had just been relieved.

Only now he's showing up at my door. Nathaniel could just stop that crap. They were not working together. She hurried through the condo. Darted in her bedroom and rushed straight through to her attached bathroom. She wanted to splash some water on her face and get her control back before Gray arrived back at her place.

He's giving me the chance to work undercover with him. I will not screw this up. I will not—

Her heart seemed to stop. Emerson had just looked into her bathroom mirror. A mirror that reflected her fractured image back to her. Fractured and distorted because the mirror had been smashed. Cracks ran across its surface like hundreds of tiny spiderwebs. Her hand lifted, as if she'd touch one of the cracks. But she stopped before making contact. Fisted her hand.

Then she was running out of her bathroom and back into her bedroom. Rushing toward her dresser and the mirror connected to it. She hadn't even glanced at the dresser before. Or its mirror. But now her focus was on it completely.

Fractured. Smashed. A dozen broken images of me.

Her head shook. One mirror being smashed...okay... maybe some random accident had happened.

Uh, exactly how did a random accident happen, Emerson? When you weren't even here? So the accident theory was weak, granted, and when you added the fact that it wasn't just one mirror that had been shattered, but *two*...

She backed away from the dresser and its mirror. Her steps were much, much slower now. Her heart thudded in her chest. This had...happened before.

Her hand rose to her neck. Slid around to the lower right side. A small scar. Barely an inch. Usually hidden by her hair. An old scar.

I got away.

She backed up more, then she turned and lunged. *One more mirror in my place.* In the small, half bath off her den.

Her heels tapped over the flooring as she raced for that bathroom. She threw the door open.

Broken. Twisted. Spiderwebs across the surface. Except a big chunk of the mirror was missing. Right in the center. A big chunk, maybe six inches long and two inches wide, was missing. And she thought of another time. Another place.

When a chunk of a broken mirror had been used like a knife.

She retreated from the bathroom. The drumming of her heartbeat was far too loud, and her right hand touched the scar on her throat.

That long ago night, the broken piece of mirror had been placed against her throat. It had cut into her, deep enough to make her bleed. To leave a scar.

A hand touched her shoulder. "Emerson—"

She screamed and grabbed for that hand. She twisted and heaved, and her foot went beneath her attacker's ankle. She was going to take him down and get out. He wasn't going to hurt her again. She would not let him hurt her.

But her attacker remained upright. He shifted his position, dodged her attack, and suddenly, Emerson was up against the wall. He'd moved lightning-fast, and he had her hands pinned on either side of her head.

"Emerson," Gray snapped.

She blinked. Her breath heaved.

Worry had a faint line slanting between Gray's brows. "No way did you just get the sudden, random urge to spar me."

Her heart was about to shoot out of her chest.

"What's happening?" he demanded.

"L-look at the mirrors."

"What?"

"The mirrors." Her wrists twisted in his hold. He didn't

let go. "They're all broken." Or at least, she thought they had been smashed.

No, no, don't second guess yourself. The breaks are real. Someone smashed the mirrors. But in order to do that, someone would have needed to break into her home.

What if he's still here? She hadn't searched the rooms thoroughly. When she'd arrived, Nathaniel had come pounding at the front door right after she and Gray had entered the condo. There had been no time for a search of the premises.

And that was why she'd freaked and attacked Gray when he touched her. Because she was so afraid the attacker was still in her home.

"Your mirrors are broken?" The line between his brows deepened. "And that made you try to toss my ass on the floor?"

"Go look." Her voice was too husky.

Slowly, he let her hands go. Frowned at her. "I don't like it when you're scared."

Yes, well, she wasn't particularly fond of the feeling, either. Her hands dropped.

Only for him to immediately manacle one wrist again. "Where I go, you go."

That sounded like an excellent plan. He led the way to the half bathroom. She edged in behind him. Saw the shattered mirror and their twisted reflections.

"I'm guessing you didn't break the mirror?" His voice had gone grim.

Emerson shook her head and told him, "The bedroom."

"Right. Stay behind me, would you?" He bent, and his right hand pulled out his gun from the holster on his ankle. His left maintained that unbreakable, manacle grip on her wrist.

He crept toward her bedroom, moving soundlessly, and she stepped out of her heels so that she, too, would make no sound. He glanced back at her, and his frown seemed to deepen as he noticed that she suddenly was smaller.

Then he was in her bedroom. She'd left the door wide open. He eased toward her dresser. His jaw hardened even more as he took in the broken mirror above the dresser. Emerson pointed toward the attached bathroom.

He sees it, too. The broken mirrors are real. Someone came in my home. Broke them all.

Not just someone.

"What in the fuck is going on?" he rasped. Then in the next instant, "I'm searching the condo."

Yes, good, brilliant. They should search the condo. They headed out of the bathroom. He let go of her wrist, but she quickly grabbed his arm. "A chunk of glass was missing from the half bath. Be careful. He used the glass like a knife before."

Silence.

Then, utterly lethal and rumbling with rage, *"Before?"* Gray repeated.

She let go of him. Her fingers rose to her neck. Slid over the faint scar. Emerson nodded. "Before. Y-years ago..."

"He's a fucking dead man."

* * *

"You didn't have to bring me to your place." Emerson stood right beside the couch in Gray's den, with her overnight bag near her feet. "We both checked my home. The intruder was gone." Her gaze tracked around the room. Lingered for just a moment on the wide bookshelves to the right. Her eyes seemed to take in each book. For just a moment, he could have sworn that her lips even moved as she began to count the volumes there.

One, two, three...

Gray's teeth snapped together. *Emerson counts when she's stressed or scared.* A habit he'd picked up on early in their partnership. And he knew with certainty that she was terrified right then. How could she not be? Some sick sonofabitch had broken into her home. Shattered her mirrors.

He was furious that she'd been terrorized. Add the fact that this shit had happened to her before? *Oh, the hell, no.* Every protective instinct that he possessed was in overdrive. Then again, his protective instincts were always on high alert where Emerson was concerned.

He'd insisted on calling the cops. Filing a B&E report with the local cops, though they'd been pretty useless on scene. There had been no sign of a forced entry at Emerson's place, and the cops hadn't exactly bought that someone had just come inside in order to break some mirrors.

Gray bought the story. The mirrors had been a message. A taunt. A threat. All of the freaking above. *Those broken mirrors terrified Emerson.* Exactly what the perp had wanted.

"Let me be very clear." He knew his voice was too rough, but there wasn't a damn thing he could do about that situation. He felt rough. He'd tossed his dirty coat after entering his home. Taken off his ankle holster and secured his weapon, too. Now Gray jerked at the buttons on the ends of his sleeves. With quick, angry motions, he proceeded to roll up both sleeves. "There is every need for you to stay with me. Someone broke into your house tonight."

"Yes."

Just that. Her eyes—solemn, scared, sad—held his.

"He was good enough not to leave any marks at the doors, and he didn't set off your alarm." He'd watched her disarm the alarm right after their arrival at her condo. "That means you're not dealing with an amateur."

She shook her head, sending her hair sliding over her shoulder. Her hand rose to her neck. Then dropped almost instantly as if she'd just caught herself.

Screw that. He marched toward her. A hard, angry stride. His hand lifted toward her.

Emerson flinched.

Her flinch cut straight through him. "I'm not going to hurt you. I would never do that." One vow he'd made long ago...

You never, ever hurt someone weaker than you.

Her long lashes flickered.

"I want to see what happened to you." *I want to utterly destroy the bastard who hurt you.* The person who'd smashed the mirrors had been long gone by the time Gray searched the place but...

Sure seems suspicious as hell that Nathaniel Hadaway was at the scene of the crime. He'd told the cops about Nathaniel. They'd agreed to question the guy, mostly just because Gray was FBI—an FBI agent with a lot of power in that town—and they'd been intimidated as hell by him.

Gray fully intended to follow up their investigation with a questioning session of his own with Nathaniel.

"It's hardly anything now, really. The scar is very old."

Hardly anything. Bull. In all the time he'd known her, she hadn't ever touched the scar. But now, with the events of this night, her fingers kept fluttering toward it. He understood. She'd deliberately trained herself not to touch it, not to draw attention to the scar because she'd wanted to bury that night and the fear it had caused in her. If she'd touched the scar too much, people would have noticed. People like him. And questions would have been asked.

His secretive Emerson didn't like it when she was the one asked questions. *Too bad, sweetheart. I have a boat load of questions I'm going to ask, and you will tell me everything.* Because he had to know every detail about her. If someone was threatening her—and he was certain that someone was, in fact, after Emerson—then knowledge was what he needed so he could stop the creep dead in his tracks.

"I want to see what happened to you," Gray repeated. His hand carefully brushed back her hair. The chandelier overhead provided plenty of light as they stood in his den. A place filled with one hell of a lot of personal mementos.

Emerson's home had been empty, but his place...it was his refuge. Filled with items that he'd carefully selected over the years. Nothing random. Everything special. If a book made it onto his shelves, it was because that book was a keeper. Something he'd read and reread over and over again. The things he kept always had great value to him.

But, like Emerson, he hardly ever invited people inside his home. Only a select few crossed the threshold. His Marine brothers. His family.

Emerson.

Her head tilted to the side. "You probably can't see the scar. It's been years..."

He could see it. About an inch long. A little white line on her golden skin. His index finger brushed lightly over the scar. He found himself leaning toward her. "What happened?"

"A slice from a broken piece of mirror."

His back teeth snapped together. That was exactly what he *thought* had happened. "Who did it?"

Her hands rose. Pressed to his chest. Not to push him away. Not to pull him closer, either. Just to touch him.

He felt her touch rock through his entire body. Her scent wrapped around him. Sensual. Jasmine. And still somehow—innocence.

"I-I never saw his face. I was seventeen."

Seventeen? What the actual hell?

"I was at my mother's home."

Her mother's home? Shouldn't that have been *her* home? What an odd way of phrasing things. Gray filed that telling descriptor away, for the moment.

"I'd come home for the weekend. I usually stayed at a boarding school, but we had a three-day weekend. I didn't think anyone else was there. Just me. I walked into my bedroom, and I realized the mirror on my wall was broken. Cracked and missing chunks, and I backed away, and as I did...he came up behind me." She swallowed. "He put the piece of broken mirror against my throat."

His muscles locked.

"I was terrified. I could feel him behind me. He was so much bigger. And he..." An exhale. "I fought him." Flat. "I'd been trained by my mother's security staff. When he tried to push me forward, toward the door, I fought him. I kicked and twisted and used my elbows, and I got away." Her gaze rose to lock with Gray's. "I felt the mirror cut me. I didn't care. Blood dripped down my throat when I ran. I got out of the bedroom. I rushed down the stairs. I didn't look back, not once. I was too afraid he'd be right there. On my heels, slicing at me with that broken mirror. I got to the front door, and I ripped it open, and—my mother was there. My mother and her head of security, Owen Porter."

His fingers slid over the small scar once more.

She shivered.

"They didn't catch the bastard," he said.

"They didn't catch the bastard." Her lips pressed together, as if she was trying to hold words back.

He didn't want her holding anything back. "Emerson?"

Her hands curled and fisted against his shirtfront. "I can do the undercover job. Don't let this change anything. I *can* do it."

"I have zero doubt that you can do any job, and I don't see why it would change a single thing." But it *had* changed things. He was lying to her. It had changed things because...

I don't want to let you out of my sight. I want to protect you. I want to destroy the bastard who scared you. Correction, I will destroy him.

Her lashes flickered. "Do you mean that?"

"Why would it change anything?"

"My mother and Owen didn't find an intruder that night. There was no sign of a forced entry, and my mother's home had a top-of-the-line security system."

Just like tonight. No sign of an intruder, and he didn't set off the security system. "Just means the guy is good." Which was *bad*.

"They thought it meant...I did it."

His jaw nearly hit the floor. "What?"

She dropped her hands. Took a step back. Another. One more. "I didn't. I didn't smash the mirror in my bedroom that long ago night. I didn't injure myself because I wanted attention or because I wanted to be a victim."

What the fuck? Her mother had thought that crap?

"I'm not delusional."

He sucked in a breath because he understood exactly where this was going.

"I'm not," she repeated with harder intensity. "My attacker that night was real, even if I'm the only one who saw him. And he was real tonight. *I* didn't smash those mirrors."

A curt nod. "Never thought for even a second that you had."

"My mother made sure that incident never got out when I was seventeen. She was so sure I'd made it all up." An exhale. "I never told anyone other than my mother and Owen what happened. Not until now. Not until you."

"You're seriously saying that an assault on a seventeen-year-old was swept under the rug by your senator mother? The bastard could have raped you, could have killed you, and she did *nothing?*"

Emerson flinched.

Gray knew he needed to calm the hell down. He also knew that his rage wasn't going to be cooling anytime soon. *This is Emerson.*

Her gaze had fallen to the floor. "She was afraid I was like him."

"Eyes on me, Emerson."

Her stare whipped up.

Calm the fuck down, Gray. Yes, he knew that he should get a grip. He also knew that wasn't happening. His control was as cracked as those mirrors. "You aren't your father."

"I don't have delusions," Emerson whispered.

"No, baby, you don't."

She wet her lower lip. "You just called me baby."

Yeah, he had.

"Are you getting into your—our—cover story? That why you're suddenly using an endearment?"

He could lie, say yes. "Is that what you think I'm doing?"

"I don't know." Her gaze started to fall away.

"On me, Emerson. Eyes on me."

Her stare collided with his.

"You've got a stalker," he told her.

Slowly, she nodded.

"You've known he's been in your life for a while, haven't you?" Rage slithered within him.

"Since I was seventeen. He's been in and out of my life since then. Doing small things."

Trying to make you think that you were slipping into the same delusions that claimed your father? He locked his jaw. "How often does he leave you messages saying that you're going to die?"

Her breath shuddered out. "That was new."

"Was it." Not a question. *You should have told me what was happening.* But he was figuring things out. Fast. *The prick followed her all the way to Briar.* Like that wasn't hugely problematic. As problematic as say, threatening to *kill* Emerson. Damn red spray paint on the motel room wall...

The paint had been a warning for him to get away from her. *Leave.* Why? Because her stalker thought Emerson belonged to him?

The hell she does.

And when Gray had stayed close, the guy had gotten mad, stepped up his sick game, and smashed her mirrors?

"He's trashed my room before. Broken valuables."

And it made sense. Shit. He'd read her wrong. Gray reevaluated. *"That's* why you don't have anything personal at your place. Because he just destroys what matters to you."

Her chin lifted.

"You didn't go to the police?" *Keep the rage back, Gray. Hold it in check.* "I get your mother wanted to cover up the first attack, but when the prick stayed around, you never told the authorities?"

"I did. When I was in college. Then med school. In college, the campus police told me it was just a prank. Probably some frat guys having fun."

He growled.

"In med school, I, um, hired a PI. My mother wouldn't hear of me making a public charge, so I went on my own to the PI. He didn't find anything. Never figured out who'd come into my room and destroyed everything." A soft sigh. "I've contacted other local cops over the years. See, something always happens, wherever I go. Sooner or later. He's been a ghost, always dodging me, leaving no trace, and it's not like you can get a restraining order against a ghost."

He needed to breathe. Hard when he just wanted to fight. "Name."

"Excuse me?"

"What was the PI's name?"

"Daniel Stewart. He was in Boston."

Gray filed the info away. He would be reaching out to the PI. "How many times has this shit happened in your life?"

"Hard to say...because sometimes, he doesn't destroy things. Sometimes, I'm pretty sure he just slips inside, and he takes things."

"Fucking fuck, Emerson!" The rage just exploded.

She nodded. "Yes, exactly. Fucking fuck. I'm sick of it. Of him. I'm sick of getting security systems that don't keep him out. I'm sick of calling cops or getting a PI to investigate and having them turn up nothing over and over again."

He remembered how shut down she'd been when the cops arrived. Her stilted responses. *No damn wonder. She'd been through this routine too many times.*

"He's played with my life for years. All I want is to find him. To stop him."

"Done and done," Gray vowed.

Those incredible eyes of hers widened. "What?"

"You think I'm going to let some jackass get away with tormenting my partner? Hell, no, sweetheart. Hell, no. We're finding him. We're stopping him. We're becoming his absolute worst nightmare."

Hope flashed across her face. "You're truly going to help me? You believe me?"

"Yes." He eliminated the distance between them. Cupped her chin. "*Yes.*" He wanted to rage at the fools who hadn't helped her before.

"But we have a case. The perp who is killing the couples. It has to be the priority. Not me. I can wait."

The hell she could. "I can multi-task." In his sleep. "You're a priority. Know it. Understand it." Absolutely, she was. His top priority. "Besides, it works."

"Uh, say again? What works?"

The extra-close proximity she was about to have with him. The way he'd be her freaking shadow from here on out. "You're not staying on your own until I have the jackass stalking you locked away. He made a death threat in Briar." Sure as shit, Gray believed the bastard had been the one leaving the spray painted messages in Briar. "He was in your place tonight. That's *two* encounters in a very close span of time." Talk about acceleration. And he knew that acceleration equaled dangerous trouble. "You'll be staying with me from now on."

Her lips parted.

"Until we catch him," Gray hurriedly amended. *Don't come off so strong. Tread with caution where Emerson is concerned.* "Us staying together will fit the cover for our case, and it will also allow me to make certain my partner is safe. Two birds, one stone and all that."

"He's never left evidence behind. Not even a fingerprint. I, uh, insisted on a full scene check a time or two."

He was sure she had. "Just means the jackass wore gloves. I'll find him. It's what I do. Find monsters. Lock them away."

"I had cameras up in my places, too. He'd just disable them. No video footage of him was ever taken."

"I'll get him, Emerson. Believe me." A pause. Then, rougher, *"Trust me."*

She stared into his eyes. Her lips began to curl. A smile. Slow, big, real, the smile spread across her full lips. Her expression warmed, as if a weight had been lifted from her delicate shoulders. "Thank you." Emerson threw her arms around him and held on tight.

She was warm and soft and...*fuck me, she is precious.*

His arms closed around her. He was enraged that she'd been dealing with a stalker since she was seventeen years old. And had she let the stalker intimidate her? Change her? No. His Emerson had hauled her ass into prisons and psych wards as she faced off against monsters and tried to figure them out...

All while she'd been battling her own monster.

"Thank you, Gray," she whispered.

His fingers dropped to her waist. Tightened. "I don't want your gratitude." She didn't need to thank him for a damn thing. This was what he did. His job was to stop the predators.

Emerson eased back.

His fingers lingered on her waist.

"What do you want?" Emerson asked, voice breathless.

Oh, she was not ready for what he wanted. And he *could* be a gentleman—or pretend to be one—and not just act like a lustful bastard where she was concerned. His gaze cut away from her.

"Gray..."

"You can sleep in my bed. I'll take the couch."

"Gray."

He should stop touching her.

"Eyes on me, Gray."

Surprised that she'd just tossed his own words back at him, his gaze whipped toward her. Emerson stared directly at him. No fear. Eyes so blue it almost hurt to look into them.

"What do you want?" Emerson repeated.

You. No way did he say that. He would not. Because he was not gonna make it seem like the price for his protection was sex. It wasn't. He could want Emerson physically and want to protect her at the same time. He could multi-task. Hadn't he just told her as much?

"Not gonna say?" she murmured. "Fine. Then I'll tell you what I want."

The den felt hot. Nah, he was hot.

Emerson did not look away from him. He could not look away from her as she confessed, "I want you."

Fuck. Then...*yes!*

"I want you to finish what you started at my place. Kiss me, Gray."

Chapter Ten

"I will not be afraid of the monster in the dark. I will not be afraid of the monster in the dark. I will not be—know what? Maybe I am the monster in the dark."
– Emerson Marlowe, a very, very long time ago

THE DRUMMING OF HER HEARTBEAT FILLED Emerson's ears as she stared into Gray's gleaming eyes. He believed her. He'd stood by her when the cops were at her house. He'd insisted on taking her to his place when they left.

He believes me. He wants me.

I'm desperate for him.

"Partners," Gray rumbled.

She flinched. Yes, yes, that was what they were, but Emerson wanted so much more.

"Lovers," he said.

She nodded. They'd be both. For the undercover mission. But in reality, too. "Doesn't change anything." She needed him to understand this. "I'm not asking for some undying commitment from you."

"No?"

"No." She would go into this with her eyes wide open. "I get that you're not into forever."

"And how do you get that, sweet Emerson?"

Simple. "Because I've profiled you."

"And you think you know so much about me." His lips hitched into a mocking half-smile. "Don't be so sure of yourself."

Emerson did not think she knew everything, certainly, but she did know enough. "You don't want forever. That's fine. That's not what I'm looking for, either." Truth be told, the possibility of forever terrified her. *What if I did become like my father, and Gray had to watch me break apart before his eyes?* "Not forever." Harder.

"What is it that you're looking for, besides, of course, two unforgettable minutes?"

*Two unforgettable...*Oh, crap. She felt heat sting her cheeks. "I shouldn't have said that about Nathaniel." Even though it had been true.

"He's a fucking idiot. Say anything you want about him. *He* had no business saying you were frigid."

The heat left her cheeks in a rush. Suddenly, her face just felt cold. "I..." Emerson didn't know what to say. Because the truth was... "I didn't, ah, climax with Nathaniel. I'm not the most responsive..." Her words trailed off. How humiliating was this? But if she was asking him to be her lover, he needed to understand everything. "I'm too guarded. I can't let myself go. Being in the moment is too hard for me, and I—" An exhale. "I think things can be different with you." She hoped they would be different. Wasn't that one of the reasons she wanted this so badly?

Wanted him so badly? "I touch you, and I need. I want. I've never felt so much desire for someone."

His mocking smile vanished. "Are you this honest with everyone in your life?"

"No, but I like being honest with you."

A muscle flexed along his jaw. "What in the hell am I supposed to do with you?"

Well, if he was going to ask, she'd answer. "Fucking me would be a great start."

His lips thinned. But his eyes gleamed even more. Then, "You do need to have practice for when we pose as lovers."

Um, sure, practice. They could call it that.

"But more than that..." His head lowered toward hers. "You need to understand that I can make you come in less than two minutes."

Admirable goal, but, no, he couldn't. Nice try, but—

"Emerson?" His mouth was right over hers. Maybe an inch away.

"Yes, Gray?"

"Stop thinking. Just feel." His mouth took hers. Open. Warm. Passionate. His tongue dipped into her mouth. Teased and tempted.

Her hands curled around his shoulders as she held on tight. *Happening. This is happening.* Gray was happening. He was kissing her, his hands were snaking down her body, and he was—wait, lifting her?

Her hold tightened on him as Gray lifted her with seemingly effortless strength. He carried her though the house. She lost her high heels along the way as he moved perfectly through the darkened rooms and soon she was in his bedroom. *Not* so dark in there. The overhead light poured down on them. He lowered her to stand right next to a massive bed with dark covers. His hands slid over her body. Her clothes seemed to melt away as he stripped her, falling in a pool at her feet until she stood before him, completely naked. Utterly exposed beneath the light.

While he was still totally dressed.

That was wrong, wasn't it? Shouldn't Gray be naked, too? It would certainly speed along the process and make her feel a whole lot less vulnerable.

"On the bed, Emerson."

She backed up. Her knees hit the bed. Her hands rose to cover her breasts as a wave of uncertainty filled her. "I'm not coming in two minutes." That was not a fair expectation to set.

He smiled at her. "Wanna bet?"

Then Gray was on her. Kissing her. Only, this kiss was different. Not as tempting. Not as controlled. Hotter. Deeper. Wilder. As she stood there with her legs hitting the back of the bed, his strong hands swept over her body. Pulled her hands away from her breasts so that *he* could touch her. Skimming those big fingers over her breasts. Teasing her nipples.

She gasped into his mouth.

One of Gray's hands dipped lower. Slid down her body even as the other plucked her nipple.

Her legs parted for him.

That seeking hand dove between her thighs. Pushed at her core. His fingers slid over her clit.

"Baby, you are gonna be so wet for me."

She was certainly getting there already.

Gray slid one finger inside of her.

Emerson rose onto her toes with a gasp, even as her fingers flew up to clamp around his upper arms.

"So tight."

Well, yes, it had been two years so...

"Emerson, baby, you're still thinking."

She was. Her mind seemed to be spinning at a hundred miles an hour. He was still dressed. She had to get him naked. She had to make sure he enjoyed what was happening. She had to—

"Time to feel," Gray rasped His hands moved in a blink to cup her waist and he pushed her onto the bed. He came down on top of her. No, not fully on top of her. He leaned over her. His hands dropped and spread her thighs. Wide. He stared down at her exposed core, and her hands dove to cover her sex as another wave of vulnerability surged through her.

Only for Gray to catch her hands. To push them to her sides. "No more hiding." His body shifted. He eased down beside the edge of the bed, crouching. Her legs dangled off the bed. He was between her dangling, spread legs.

His head lowered.

His breath rasped over her clit. Emerson's breath choked out on a wave of longing. "Gray?"

He put his mouth on her. Her hips jerked. No, jolted. He clamped his fingers around her waist and pinned her to the bed as he suddenly just *feasted* on her. Lips, tongue. Tasting and taking and plunging that wicked, wicked tongue into her body. He went from zero to *consuming* in a blink.

Her hands grabbed the bedding. Fisted it. Her hips surged up against his mouth.

He licked her again and again. Growled and savored her and seemed to get hungrier, more frenzied with each swipe of his tongue.

She looked down at him. Thanks to the light, she could

clearly see Gray. *Right between my legs. Grayson Stone is going down on me.*

One strong hand let go of her waist. His fingers slid between her thighs to join his mouth. He was stroking and teasing and licking and nothing had ever felt so good in her entire life.

His other hand rose to tease her nipple. To squeeze and pluck.

Sensation took over. A flood of pleasure as her whole body tightened in anticipation. She was on a tightrope of desire. At any moment, that rope was going to snap. She'd fall, but oh, that fall was going to be *good*.

His tongue lashed against her clit. Over and over and over and the rope snapped. Emerson was falling. Surging down hard, and she choked out his name as she came. The orgasm blasted through her entire body. Not some brief flash of pleasure, but a hard, surging wave that battered at her as the pleasure seemed to completely envelop her. Emerson could hear her own gasps and moans as she thrashed against the bedding and against Gray, and he kept right on lashing her with that wicked, ever-so-wonderful tongue of his.

And then...

The drumming of her heartbeat slowly eased. Her lashes lifted. She was pretty sure she'd squeezed her eyes shut when she came. Now she looked down at Gray. He slowly raised his head even as he remained crouched between her spread legs as they hung off the side of his bed.

"Sweetheart." He licked his lips, as if savoring her. "I am a man of my word."

She should form some kind of response. Have some actual speech.

"Less than two minutes."

Holy crap, it had been.

"You were utterly wasted on Nathaniel Hadaway." His hands curled around her thighs as his face darkened. "You'd be wasted on anyone but me. That's why I am going to fuck you until you can't think of anyone but—"

The ringing of a doorbell cut through his words.

His teeth snapped together. He lifted his left hand. Glared at the stainless-steel watch around his wrist as he—what? Looked at the time? "Fuck," he breathed.

Someone was at his door? Then? "Why..." Emerson stopped. Wet her lips. Her voice was way husky. Probably from all the gasping and moaning and, potentially, screaming. She was a little hazy on the details. Had she screamed? Maybe. Possibly. Probably.

I wasn't thinking. Just feeling.

Something that she didn't usually do. Gray was certainly correct on that score. Usually, she couldn't shut off her thoughts. But with Gray, she'd let go. She'd trusted him enough to let go.

She swallowed and tried speaking again. "Why is someone always interrupting us?"

His gaze had been on the juncture of her legs. Slowly, that burning stare rose. Lifted. "Fate doesn't want me taking what I want." His fingers curled possessively around her. Pushed against her clit. One finger even dipped into her.

Her breath heaved.

"But I'll have you." His hand pulled back. He rose. Grabbed the cover from the foot of the bed and yanked it up and over her. "Do not leave this room."

"What? Gray, wait!"

He'd already turned to leave her. "I'll have him gone in a blink. You stay here."

The bedding covered her from shoulder to ankle.

When He Defends

While Gray stood there, dressed in his fancy shirt and his expensive pants, and barely had a hair out of place. He looked cool and confident, slightly pissed.

"We will finish what we started." With that, Gray stalked out of the bedroom. He pulled the door shut behind him. *Click.*

Her heart still raced. Her body still trembled. In her core, she could feel aftershocks of pleasure still reverberating through her body. All from his mouth. That wonderful, sexy mouth.

That had been incredible. She'd like more, please. So much more.

She'd also definitely, one hundred percent, been missing out over the years.

Emerson stared up at the ceiling. At the light on the ceiling. Goosebumps rose onto her skin, and she felt pretty wild and decadent sprawled in his bed, completely naked beneath the comforter.

Gray is going to come back. We are going to wreck this bed. She'd never wrecked a bed in her entire life, but Emerson was super looking forward to the task.

And then she heard, very distinctly, from Gray...

His angry voice snarled, *"I'm going to kill you."*

She clamped the comforter to her chest and leapt out of the bed.

Chapter Eleven

"Why do I hunt killers? Someone has to do it. I'm good at the job. And maybe...maybe I like hunting them. Guess that makes me just as much of a predator, huh?"
– Gray Stone

GRAY SHUT THE FRONT DOOR AND GLARED AT THE MAN who'd just entered his home. "I'm going to kill you," he told him, the words coming out as an angry snarl.

Cassius Striker quirked a brow. "Is that any way to talk to family?"

Gray grabbed him. Shoved him against the nearest wall. "Watch it."

Cassius—Cass—blinked. Then his brown eyes narrowed. That sharp stare swept over Gray's features. Then he smiled. "Sneaky SOB, am I interrupting you, again?" Laughter hummed beneath the words. "Are you busy with that hot new partner of yours?"

Gray heard the faint click of a door opening. His

bedroom door. Hell. His eyes closed for just a moment. "She can't follow orders for shit." He didn't let go of Cass just yet. "Watch what you say with her."

"Why? Don't think the sexy partner can handle some painful truths?"

Gray shoved him harder against the wall. "First, she can handle anything. Second, you don't get to notice that she's sexy."

"When she comes down the hallway naked, I sure as hell do."

Naked? No, no, no, no. Gray let him go and whipped around because he had, indeed, left Emerson naked in the bedroom. If she was walking toward him naked, if Cass was seeing every beautiful inch of her—

Cass burst into laughter.

And Emerson crept forward. Fully dressed once again, minus her high heels, but sexily disheveled as she stared at Gray and gripped—holy hell, Emerson had his back-up weapon in her hand. The weapon he'd left in his top nightstand drawer.

"Heard you threatening to kill someone," Emerson announced as she sent a frown toward the laughing Cass. "Thought you might need backup."

Cass's laughter stopped. Probably because he'd just spotted the gun that she held. "Uh, Gray?" He cleared his throat. "How about tell her that I'm not here as a threat? Get the pretty lady to put down the big gun."

Gray pursed his lips. Maybe he should let Cass sweat it out a bit.

"I forgot that the two of you had plans to meet tonight." Emerson's brisk voice. "What with everything else that happened, I let that slip my mind. I should have realized when your doorbell rang that he was coming to follow up on that chat in the alley."

"You *told* her I was coming?" Cass's surprise was clear.

"No, I damn well didn't." Gray advanced on Emerson. "What do you mean, you forgot? I didn't tell you anything about our meeting."

She lowered the gun. Carefully placed it on a nearby table. Her hair wasn't in its normal smooth style. Instead, it was tousled. Her cheeks held a hint of color. Her lips were still swollen from his mouth. *Dead sexy.* He wanted to punch Cass for even staring at her.

But her words had distracted him, for the moment.

"You know sign language," Emerson said. She put her hands behind her back. Rocked forward. Didn't add anything else.

He waited.

There was still nothing else added. "And...?" Gray prompted.

She shrugged. "And I've been watching your hands extra closely since I realized that important fact. Sign language is a great way for you to communicate with others if you want to send a message but make certain you don't leave a verbal trail. But while you can't *overhear* sign language, you can see it, if you're paying close enough attention."

"I didn't sign anything with Cass." He was certain of that fact.

"No." Her gaze slid past him, to a Cass who was still standing near the front wall. "But he did. Didn't know what the movement meant at first. Had to look it up on my phone." Then she mimicked the quick sign that Cass had made near O'Sullivan's, bringing her hands up with her index fingers extended. "'Meet,' right? 'Meet me,' perhaps?

You didn't have the sign for 'later' included, but I figured that part was understood. You told Gray that you intended to meet up with him later. And it's later."

Cass gave a low whistle.

"He looks like you," Emerson mused as she cocked her head slightly to the right. "Same jawline. Hair has the same texture, even if the color is a bit different. Eyes are different, too, but the cheekbones are the same. The resemblance is probably why he felt so familiar to me. Guessing he's a relative? Not a motorcycle gang leader, after all?"

It took a lot to surprise Gray in this world. But Emerson just ticking off her facts when he'd kept this particular secret for ages? *Shit. Am I just sloppy where she is concerned?* Was he not on his guard enough?

But it had been *Cass's* mistake. Hadn't it?

Hell.

Cass ambled toward her while Gray remained rooted to the spot. Cass stopped about a foot away from Emerson. Took her measure. "Sweetness..."

She stiffened. "Trust me, I am not your sweetness."

No, she fucking belongs to me.

Whoa. Whoa. Whoa. Where in the hell had that savagely possessive thought just come from? Because she was his partner?

Uh, nah. Gray's chin lifted even as Cass cut him a quick glance. *It came from the fact that I just had her coming against my mouth.* "Not yours," Gray repeated flatly.

"Someone sounds possessive. Which is new. And vaguely concerning." Cass's brows climbed. "Gray, come on, man. It's me. You and I both know that you are not about to bare all with her. I mean, sure, you'll fuck her. So I guess you'll be baring all that way. But you won't take her into your confidence. Partner or not." He motioned dismissively toward Emerson. "So how about you direct your *partner* back to the bedroom and then we can get down to confidential business?"

Gray focused on Emerson. Her face had gone doll blank. All emotion gone, but he knew Cass's words had hurt her.

Cass could be an asshole.

It was a family trait.

He elbowed Cass out of the way. Cass, who was Gray's size. Who had his same build and temperament but had gone down a different path in life.

"By the way, new partner," Cass rasped, "I can be both family *and* a gang leader. Haven't you ever heard of a family's black sheep?"

Her eyes weren't on Cass. They were on Gray. He could see that she'd shielded herself. As if she expected him to take Cass's side. To tell her that this was not her affair, even after he'd had her coming beneath him moments before.

"I came out to protect you," she told Gray with careful dignity.

His chest ached. "I appreciate that." His head inclined toward her. "Thank you, Emerson."

"You think I don't ever follow orders."

Could she be more adorable? "I know you don't."

"Tell me to walk away. I will."

"Yeah," Cass muttered. "I need to get down to business. Don't have all night. Time's ticking. My bike is stashed around the corner, and I had to sneak around to make sure no nosy neighbors spotted me."

Gray caught Emerson's hand. Rubbed his fingers over her knuckles. "Emerson, don't you dare walk away. You stay with me."

Her eyes widened.

Maybe that was a bit too intense. Screw it. Her taste was still on his tongue, and if his annoying visitor hadn't been there, he would be buried so deep in her that they'd both be lost to paradise. "Cass is my cousin."

"What the hell?" Cass exploded. "Look, man, there is her guessing, and then there is you *confessing.* Big difference."

He kept staring into Emerson's eyes. Those incredible eyes. Had he ever told her how bewitching he thought they were? "He's also a gang leader, so, yeah, just know that family or not, he's trouble. Dangerous to his core."

"Aw, thanks for that," Cass told him. "I'm flattered. Means the world coming from you." A brief pause. "Why are we over sharing with her? Want to explain that?"

He already had. Gray tugged Emerson closer. "Because she's my partner."

"Yeah, got that."

He angled his body a bit toward Cass. "She's going undercover with me on the case you insisted that I take."

"Again, got that. Still doesn't mean you give out secrets to her that you haven't shared with anyone else. I mean, the next thing I know, you'll be sharing with her about—" But he broke off. Because there were lines Cass would never cross, and Gray knew it.

So Gray crossed the lines for him. "Sharing with her about my bastard father? Been there, done that."

"Oh, shit." Cass's gaze swung to Emerson, and he was suddenly looking at her in a way different light. *"Partner."*

"Right," Gray told him grimly. "Now why the hell are you here? This meeting is unnecessary." And a bit reckless. Especially after the public showing outside of O'Sullivan's. "I told you already, I'm taking the case. I'll find out who killed Anzo and Kim. I will make the perp pay."

Cass was still staring at Emerson, though now he eyed her more like she was a bug under a microscope.

Gray waved his fingers in front of Cass. "Yo."

Cass slanted him a frown.

"There more intel you want to give me? That why you showed up tonight?"

"Wanted to meet tonight..." He rolled back his shoulders. "Because this bastard can't just go free, Gray."

Hell. He'd feared this. "Cass, I'm going to get him dead to rights. He won't be seeing the light of day again." But he worried that wouldn't be enough to satisfy Cass. Cass had been walking deeper and deeper into the darkness lately.

"You alert me when you have him in your sights. I can handle things after that. I just need his location." Cass smiled, all innocence. Except Cass had never done innocence particularly well.

Then again, neither had Gray.

"There's playing a role," Gray reminded him flatly, "and there is sinking straight into the dark and never surfacing again. Don't forget who you are."

Cass backed up a step. "You really are sharing all with her, aren't you?" He jerked a thumb toward Emerson. "You might trust her to keep your confidences, but I don't trust her with mine."

"You're working undercover. You're probably walking a very delicate balancing act." Emerson's statement was mild. "I'm not going to spill your secrets to anyone."

"I don't *know* you, lady, and you don't know me."

"Actually..." Gray couldn't help but smile as he delivered this taunt. Cass had it coming, after all. *Poor timing, cuz. Poor timing.* "Emerson's specialty is understanding killers. So she probably understands you perfectly."

Cass flipped him off. He also took another step away from them. "Psychopaths, huh? That's her thing? Totally makes sense then that she's sleeping with you."

Not yet, she wasn't. But it was on the agenda.

"I wouldn't say that psychopaths are my thing," Emerson's measured response. "But I do like profiling. By the way, not all psychopaths are killers, just as all killers are certainly not psychopaths."

"Great. Thanks for sharing that." Cass swung away and headed for the door. "I get enough of that psychological bullshit from him. And, FYI, I do not need you profiling me, too."

"You're highly protective," Emerson noted.

"Hell." Cass froze in his tracks. "She's profiling me. Didn't I just say I did not need this in my life?"

"You defend those that you believe belong to you. You're an eye-for-an-eye type. Someone hurt—someone *killed* an individual that you believe belongs to you. And whether you are just pretending to be some hardened criminal or if you've crossed the line and done things you regret, this Anzo was still one of yours. You won't rest until his killer has been punished."

He looked over his shoulder. "I'm not pretending to be a hardened criminal." His smile showed way too many teeth. "You don't get to be the leader without proving yourself. There are some sins that will never vanish."

Gray's fingers slid over Emerson's knuckles once more. Then he let her go. "I can get you out," he told Cass. It was an argument they'd had before. "You know I can. I can make it all go away."

"Sure. If I die. If I lose the life I have." He snapped his

fingers. "It will all go away, just like that, and what? I'll become some farmer in Wisconsin? Get a new life as a computer programmer in Denver? Nah. Not enough adrenaline for me, but thanks." His hand fell back to his side. "I'll just let you two get back to...business, shall I?" He took another step toward the door.

"Wait!"

He stilled at Gray's bark. "What, now?"

"Did you really see someone approaching us—a would-be mugger—when we were near O'Sullivan's?"

"You know that I don't lie to you, Gray." Cass turned toward him. "Just to the rest of the world."

Right. "Describe him."

"Hard to do. Only saw him for a second, and it was from the back. Probably a few inches shorter than us. Male. Dressed in black, probably because the dick wanted to hide in the dark." His lips pulled down. "Knife was gripped in his right hand. So, right-handed attacker."

A tremble slid over Emerson's body.

"He was intent on sneaking right up behind Gray. Gray, Gray, Gray." He clicked his tongue. "Try to be less distracted by your partner in the future, would you? I can't always save your ass from muggers."

He didn't think it had been a mugger. O'Sullivan's was well known as a cop and Fed hangout. Most muggers avoided the place because they were trying not to get their asses tossed in jail. He was surprised Cass had just ridden straight in with his crew. But then again, Cass was typically never afraid of anyone.

Another trait they shared.

He decided to lay a few more cards on the table because he was gonna need Cass's help. "Emerson had a break-in at her place tonight."

A slight hardening of Cass's jaw. "But you were there. No harm came to her."

"Not this time." *Not ever again.* "It's sure a very unlikely coincidence that we had a near mugging *and* a break-in all within such a short timeframe."

"You know I never believe in coincidences."

Gray typically thought they were BS, too. "Let me know if you or any of your members hear chatter focused on her. I want to know exactly who has too much attention centered on my partner."

"Done." That was all. Typically the way with Cass. His word was his vow. A reason he was respected in the more shadowy parts of the world—well, that and because Cass was one wicked and dirty fighter. Dude had always been way too into adrenaline.

And violence.

Following orders? Yeah, like Emerson, Cass couldn't follow orders for shit. That was the reason he'd never been a Marine. Gray had signed up, but his cousin had gone down a very different path.

Those paths were colliding now.

Gray trailed him to the door. He started to slam the door shut, but Cass's gloved hand flew up and pressed against the wood. "A word, Gray? Outside, away from the partner?"

Gray thought he'd made it clear that Emerson should hear everything.

"Go," Emerson urged from behind him. "It's okay."

Body tight, he crossed the threshold as Cass retreated a few steps. Gray pulled the door closed behind him.

"I don't want you ending up in a body bag," Cass muttered.

"Aw, you do care. So sweet." He put a hand to his heart.

A rough sigh broke from Cass right before he pointed at the closed door. "Do I need to be worried?"

"About what? My partner shooting you? Maybe, if you get on her bad side. She's a really good shot, just so you are aware. Tread carefully."

"Thanks for the tip about the shooting skills. I'll remember that. What I meant, though, was do I need to be worried about *you?*"

Gray did not change expression.

"You don't bring lovers home. You screw them in hotel rooms and don't call them back later."

"Ouch." Gray winced. "Pretty sure that's *your* style. I always try to properly thank a lady for a good time."

"You don't let lovers close. You know it. I know it. But you've got Ms. Gorgeous Eyes looking rumpled and recently sated—"

Hell, it had been *that* obvious.

"Even as you stare at her like you're dying to eat her alive."

He could go for another meal. He was feeling snacky.

"You let the woman know our secrets," Cass accused.

"Uh, for the record. I didn't let her know anything. She's observant. She picks things up."

"Because she's a mind fucker, just like you."

"I really don't like that particular term." Gray sniffed.

"Too bad, mind fucker. She plays head games. *Dr. Emerson Marlowe.* Yeah, frown at me all you want. I'm gonna dig deep on her because I want to make sure you aren't getting played. That prick with the knife was coming up way too intently on your back."

"Emerson had nothing to do with that attack."

"I've done some preliminary poking already," Cass revealed.

When He Defends

Like that was surprising. Emerson had dead-on pegged him when she said Cass was protective. That was one serious understatement. If you belonged to Cass, he would scorch the earth for you.

Sure, they might be cousins, but to both men, the link had always been deeper. *More like brothers. Even when the world said we should be enemies.* He would never, ever turn his back on Cass.

"Your lady has a thing for psychopaths."

Gray tilted his head to the side. "You heard her. Not all killers are psychopaths and not all—"

"Fine. Your lady has a thing for monsters. That better?"

Not really, no. He scraped a hand over his jaw.

"Oh, what? Come on, I knew that detail about your partner even before meeting her in person. Word travels in my circles. She likes to go into prisons. Interview killers. The more dangerous, the better."

"She's a psychiatrist. That's her job—interviewing killers. Understanding them. Trying to figure out how to stop them."

"Her current job is helping you, right? *Partner?*"

Yes, that was Emerson's current job.

"I just want to make sure none of her exes are out there, causing trouble. Getting possessive and deciding they don't want to share her with you. Because *maybe* that guy who was sneaking up on you in the dark is one of the monsters who took a liking to her."

"Emerson isn't what you think." *And I'm the monster who will fight to the death for her.*

"Do tell."

He did not, in fact, tell. *Because this is Emerson, and she is mine.*

After silence that stretched too long, Cass nodded. "Understood."

"There is one *ex* I wouldn't mind you and your guys keeping an eye on. A *covert* eye." Because Gray had his own suspicions about the things happening around Emerson.

Cass sent him a slow grin. "You know covert is my middle name."

No, it wasn't.

"Spill it," Cass added. "Tell me who I'm hunting."

"Dr. Nathaniel Hadaway," Gray said. "Her ex appeared in town right around the same time our mystery mugger did. *And* Nathaniel was close when her apartment had that unwelcome visitor who decided to smash up all her mirrors."

Cass nodded. "I can put a ghost on him."

A ghost. The term Cass used for an MC member who would not be seen or heard but would follow his prey to the ends of the earth. "Thanks. Report anything suspicious, would you?"

"And you'll report when you find my killer?"

No, he would not. Because Cass might eliminate the guy before Gray could get him locked away. "I'll take care of the situation. Justice will be served."

"Don't go getting your uptight ass killed," Cass warned. "The world is a bit more fun with you in it." He turned away. Seemed to immediately blend with the shadows near him.

Yeah, man, thanks. Love you, too. "Same," Gray tossed out. He waited, making sure Cass was gone, then Gray entered his house. He'd owned the home for years, and, no, he did not make a habit of bringing casual lovers to his place.

He shut the door. Locked it. Set the alarm.

Emerson wasn't in the den. He frowned. The gun was gone, too. Not on the table where she'd placed it. "Emerson?" Gray sprinted forward.

"In the bedroom."

He kept right on sprinting. Entered the bedroom. Froze just beyond the doorway.

Emerson was in bed. The covers were pulled up to her chin.

She looked incredibly good in his bed.

"Is he gone?" she asked.

Gray nodded. Her shoulders were bare. Did that mean the rest of her was, too? *Oh, yes, please, let the rest of her be bare.*

"Do you have any other secret family members who will be making an appearance tonight?" she inquired politely.

He shook his head. "Not that I'm aware of."

"Any other guests slated to pay you a visit?"

Again, Gray shook his head.

"Good." A long exhale. "Then how about we pick up where we left off?" She pushed down the covers to reveal that, hell, yes, she was completely bare.

And she was about to be completely his.

Chapter Twelve

"What do I think of my new partner? Agent Stone is intense, driven, and calculated. He would make for one very dangerous enemy." – Emerson Marlowe, on day one of her partnership with Gray Stone

HE SHOULD HAVE CONTROL.

He should seduce. He should tempt. He should caress every single inch of her. Treat her like a queen.

Not pounce on her like—

Like I want to do.

He was screwed. Gray shook his head.

Her hand tightened on the cover she'd just dropped. "Gray? Is there a problem?"

His dick shoved against the front of his pants. "Yeah."

"I-I thought you wanted me."

"That is not our problem. Will never be our problem." Not in a million years.

When He Defends

Her tongue skated across her lower lip. "Then what's the problem?"

"Trying not to pounce."

She leaned forward. Her beautiful breasts did the best jiggle in the entire world. "Why not? I would love for you to pounce. Consider this your pouncing all clear."

Fuck. "Be careful what you wish for."

"Why? I've been wishing for you since the first day we became partners. Seems to be working out so far."

He was her wish? Seriously? In what screwed-up universe? "Try to remember you said that." A nod. Then he began to unbutton his shirt.

Her gaze fell to his chest. Her eyes widened. That cute, little pink tongue of hers came out again. Her nipples were hard. Tight. He wanted them in his mouth. Wanted his mouth back between her legs as she cried out for him and pleasure made her whole body tremble.

He'd like more of that, hell, yes.

He popped a button off the shirt in his haste.

She gasped. Her eyes rose to lock with his. Her lips curved into the faintest grin. "Oh, no. Not your fancy shirt. You lost a button. However will you recover?"

He threw the shirt. Kicked out of his shoes and ditched his dress socks. "Emerson, don't make me spank you."

"Why not? Could be fun."

Everything stopped. Every fucking thing. She was teasing him. Flirting. Playing.

He wasn't. "You should...be careful." A gritted warning.

Only Emerson was not careful. She slipped from the bed. Naked. Her body driving him crazy. She crept toward him. Stopped right in front of Gray. "I'm always careful," she confessed. "All the time. With everyone." Her hands rose.

Went to the waistband of his pants. Undid his belt. Pulled it out from the loops. Let it fall. "With you, care and control aren't what I want. Like you told me, let's stop thinking." She unbuttoned his pants. Lowered the zipper. Shoved down the pants and his boxers, and she dropped to her knees with them. "Let's feel." Her fingers curled around his dick. She brought the thick head toward her mouth. Blew lightly over it.

His feet pressed harder against the floor. "*Emerson.*"

She opened her mouth and took his dick inside.

His hands clamped around her shoulders. She was hesitant. Careful, taking just the head. Licking him. Rubbing that sweet, sweet tongue against him, and then Emerson opened her mouth wider. She pumped the base of his dick with her hand and took more of him inside.

Yeah. I'm done.

His control ripped to shreds. He lifted her up even as he kicked away his pants and boxers.

"Gray? Did I—did I do something wrong?"

Hell, no. Too right.

He dropped her onto the bed. Yanked open the bottom drawer of his nightstand and had a condom out of that drawer and on in record time. Then he was climbing onto the bed. Pushing her legs apart.

He positioned the head of his cock at the entrance to her body.

Her breasts—those tight, tempting nipples—thrust up toward him.

He had to bend down. Had to lick. Suck. Had to taste. Had to use the edge of his teeth in a light, sensual bite.

"Fuck me, Gray. *Fuck me.*"

He drove into her. She'd been tight when he put a finger inside her before. Now, around his dick...*So tight that I am going to lose my mind.*

When He Defends

She gasped and moaned. Her legs flew up to curl around his hips. He gave her an instant to adjust to him.

So good. So insanely good.

He withdrew. Thrust into her. Again. Harder. Deeper. Her nails raked down his back. Her moans urged him on. His dick was thick and swollen. Hard as hell. He hammered into her. Pushed a hand between their bodies and stroked her clit, working her with his fingers even as he thrust his dick into her again and again.

Her body stiffened beneath him. Her head tipped back against the pillow. Her mouth widened, and she gasped out his name. He felt the contractions of her inner muscles around him, milking his dick.

Hell, yes. Hell, yes.

She came, crying out his name.

And that was fabulous. She felt *incredible*. But he wasn't done.

He pulled out of her.

"Gray!"

He flipped her on the bed. Brought her up to her knees. "Lock those hands around the headboard."

Trembling, uncertain, she did. She gave him one hell of a view of her ass.

And he remembered what she'd said about spanking...

Fuck, fuck, fuck.

His hand slid over the curve of her ass.

"Gray?"

"Hold tight, baby. I'm not close to done with you yet." He drove into her from behind, sinking into her hot, tight sex. One hand chained her hips against him. The other slid around her body. Eased between her folds. Worked her clit again and again because he needed her *wild*.

She arched back against him as he thrust into her. Her

hips rocked hard against his. She was thrusting and heaving desperately. He kept his hand on her clit. Thumb stroking. Fingers squeezing. Her hands whitened around the headboard as her grip became even stronger.

"Gray, I-I can't, I can't again—"

Oh, she could. He drove relentlessly into her. Felt her spiral into another release.

He poured into her. Her release had ignited his own. His hips slammed against her. That lush ass. That tempting body. Those soft moans. She drove him to the edge and beyond, and he poured hotter and longer into her than he ever had in his entire life.

By the time the orgasm ended, he felt emptied out. Sated.

Fucking mated.

No, no, wrong word. Too primitive. It had just been sex. Just sex.

Just—

She looked over her shoulder at him. Bright eyes. Trembling lips.

Fucking. Mated.

He kissed her.

Her lips parted beneath his. One hand still gripped her waist as he held her against him. Pleasure had poured through every cell of his body. The moment was tense. The air hummed with a dangerous, consuming charge around them.

He lifted his head and realized he was in trouble. *I don't want to let her go.* Not now. Not ever.

* * *

When He Defends

SHE STAYED the night with the FBI agent. Their lights finally turned off well after midnight.

He watched the house. A big house, one decked out with security cameras, so he hadn't been able to risk getting too close. He was used to Emerson's systems. Easy enough to bypass because he was always given access to her codes. But he didn't know what tricks Agent Stone might have at his place.

Better to wait.

To watch.

To learn his new enemy.

Emerson should have been afraid. She should have understood his message. She wasn't safe, not even with the FBI agent. The past could always come up and take her.

She didn't get to walk away. She didn't get to go off and start a life with someone else. He had plans for her. She would stay with him.

The house remained dark.

It was a big house.

Plenty of rooms.

Just because the house was dark, it didn't mean that Emerson was fucking the FBI agent.

They were kissing near O'Sullivan's. I saw them.

Just because the house was dark…

He reached for his knife.

I am going to kill the FBI agent.

Sooner or later, Gray Stone would die.

He'd always wondered what it would be like to kill someone. He thought it might be quite…fun.

Chapter Thirteen

"Sex doesn't change anything. Even great sex."
– Emerson Marlowe

"Yeah, it does." – Gray Stone

"Oh, look at that, Emerson." Gray's voice was hushed and falsely excited at the same time. An interesting combo. "A limo. One waiting right in front of the FBI office. Who could be inside?"

She'd spotted the limo just seconds ago, right after they'd rounded the corner as they advanced toward the FBI office. They were supposed to meet the others at 0600. A time that was less than fifteen minutes away. They'd stopped for coffee. She hadn't even batted an eyelash when Gray had rattled off her preferred—and somewhat convoluted—order. He'd been with her before for coffee pickups. So, of course, he'd memorized her order.

He'd just grinned when she'd rattled off his stark

When He Defends

request—black coffee. That was all he ever ordered, after all. Black coffee and a blueberry protein muffin.

They hadn't spoken about the sex. The mind-blowing, give-me-more sex. He'd slept in the bed with her. She knew because she'd woken up once, heart racing from a half-remembered nightmare, and he'd been there. Warm, strong body. An arm around her. She'd felt safe. Safer than she'd felt in years. She'd gone right back to sleep.

When she'd woken again, he'd been out of the bed. Showered and dressed already. Another crisp shirt—pale blue this time. Gray pants. Gray suit coat.

At first, he hadn't said anything as he stared down at her in the bed. But his eyes had blazed. Then he'd told her to take her time in the shower before he double-timed it out of the bedroom.

He'd made her an omelet. They hadn't spoken about the previous night. Just made small talk. He'd told her that his mother had taught him how to make omelets years ago. That he could also make some absolutely delicious grits and biscuits that were to die for.

She'd confessed to being a terrible cook. His omelet, by the way, had been heavenly.

The little kitchen routine had felt both foreign and oddly comfortable. Though that made zero sense.

And now...

The limo.

As she watched, the rear door opened. A tall, fit man with silver streaking through his dark hair rose from the back. "Emerson." His lips curled. A brief hint of warmth. Then, "Your mother would like a word."

Emerson stopped on the sidewalk. She'd known the confrontation would happen, sooner or later. "If she'd like to talk, then she should just call me, the way most mothers call their adult children. She doesn't have to show up in her limo, waiting outside of my work."

Owen Porter's head inclined toward her. "She does if she suspects you are dodging her."

"Emerson." Gray's delighted voice. "Have you been dodging the senator? How naughty. I approve."

She would have elbowed him, but Owen chose that moment to advance a step toward her. He motioned with one hand. "Just you, Emerson. We have to hurry, though. She has appointments in town today."

Of course, she did. Emerson had never thought that her mother had come all the way to Atlanta just to see her. That would be silly.

"Did he say, 'just you' right then?" Gray asked. "I'm hoping I misheard."

"You didn't mishear," Emerson replied.

"That's rather rude of him. Clearly, we are a package deal." Gray twined his fingers with hers.

She jerked at the movement.

"Partner..." His voice dipped lower. Just for her. "Remember when I said you needed to get used to me touching you? Consider our cover story activated now."

Only it wasn't really a cover, was it? Not if they were truly lovers? And they very much were. She still had some faint marks on her body to prove that fact. Plus, she was sore in places that she just wasn't going to mention to anyone.

But Gray advanced, strolling as casually as you please toward the limo, and his grip tugged her forward.

"An invitation wasn't extended to you," Owen informed him. His shoulders had stiffened.

"Owen Porter." Gray eyed him. "How many years are you going to keep guarding the senator? You've been her head of security ever since you left the Navy, yes? Former

SEAL. Decorated. I would have thought you'd be looking for a job with more adventure. More of a challenge. But a little digging on you last night showed that you'd been in this position ever since your discharge papers were approved...that would have been right after Emerson's father was laid to rest."

Emerson made sure to mask her surprise. *He'd been digging on Owen?* They'd collapsed together after the truly phenomenal sex. She'd assumed he'd stayed in bed with her all night. But, apparently, he hadn't been as tired as she had been, and Gray had...*investigated Owen?* Who else had he investigated? While she'd been dead to the world?

"Working with the senator is its own challenge, I can assure you of that." Owen's slightly mocking response.

Gray seemed to consider those words. "I can buy that. She's a pain in the ass, isn't she?"

"Gray!" Emerson couldn't believe he'd just said those words.

He winked at her. "Let's go see what she wants, shall we?" With that, Gray ducked into the limo, despite his very clear non-invitation, and he pulled her in after him.

Even as she got settled on the seat beside him, Owen was slamming the door and remaining outside. Emerson knew he'd stand guard and make sure no one else got close to the vehicle. That was his job, after all.

Standing guard. Making sure that Maxine didn't have to face any unwanted obstacles. To protect the senator from Maine at all costs.

"You shouldn't be here," Maxine began as she beetled her brows and glared at Gray.

Ah, well, she did have one unwanted obstacle who'd just blasted past Owen. Honestly, Emerson was surprised that Owen hadn't made more of an effort to block Gray.

He would have failed with more effort, though. She'd come to realize that pretty much nothing stopped Gray from getting what he wanted. Obviously, he'd wanted to chat with her mother.

"I was going to say the same thing to you. I mean, aren't several senators in town for a meeting with the CDC? You shouldn't be here. You should be getting ready for that meeting." He made himself comfortable on the seat. Sort of sprawled even as his fingers kept right on twining with Emerson's. "I don't mean to get in your business..."

Emerson was completely convinced that he did, in fact, want to get in her mother's business.

"But I think your driver made a few wrong turns," he finished. "The CDC building isn't anywhere close to this location."

Her mother raised her chin and let her icy gaze freeze Gray. "You do not want to play with me, Agent Stone."

"I don't. You are so right. I have things to do. Killers to stop."

Her mother's gaze shifted to his hand. The hand that gripped Emerson's. "Why are you holding my daughter's hand?"

"Because we're working on a case," Emerson said flatly. "Why are *you* in front of the FBI office?"

Her mother's stare rose. Pinned Emerson. Blue eyes. Not the exact shade of Emerson's. Her hair was blond. A blond applied every few weeks to make certain that no grays ever showed to the public. "You're not seriously going to do this undercover mission with him."

Gray sighed. "Figured you'd gotten the details from one of your spies. You have got to stop prying into FBI business. Get a new hobby."

Her mother sucked in a sharp breath. "I am not *prying.*"

When He Defends

She toyed lightly with the string of pearls that circled her neck. She always wore those pearls. Fancy rings. Glittering bracelets. "I am simply looking out for my daughter's well-being. It's what any loving mother would do." Then, "Emerson, you've trained with him for several weeks now. You've even managed to arrest a serial killer. Good job." Flat. "I think this exercise can now come to an end. I'd like for you to return to DC. You were offered the position at Georgetown, and I think it would be in your best interest to take it." She sent them a thin smile. Smugly satisfied. Certain. "Thanks for your cooperation, Agent Stone. But you are no longer needed in Emerson's life. This is where you say goodbye."

Chapter Fourteen

"What do I think of Emerson? I think she's danger wrapped in a beautiful package. I'll never underestimate her. That's a mistake other people make. Not me." – Gray Stone

EMERSON STIFFENED HER SPINE. SOFT, CLASSICAL music played in the back of the limo. Her mother's pale blue dress matched her emotionless eyes, and her mother seemed utterly certain that her decree would be followed. Then again, she was always certain. But by this point, Maxine Marlowe should be used to Emerson disappointing her.

I didn't take the career she wanted for me. I turned down law school for med school so I could be a psychiatrist.

I didn't keep dating the man she'd carefully selected for me. Told Nathaniel not to let the door hit him in the ass on his way out of my life.

And despite her telling me that I need to head to Georgetown, I will absolutely not leave Gray.

Emerson sent her mother a cool smile. The senator

wasn't the only one who'd perfected an icy grin over the years. "I have no interest in the position at Georgetown. I declined it. Twice. As you are well aware. I will not be leaving because I'm quite happy where I am."

"Emerson, you are meant to be in an academic setting! You're brilliant. You soared through college. Had top grades your whole life. You have opportunity after opportunity in front of you, but you are going to throw away these chances—for what? To play with criminals?" Disapproval dripped from her words.

Her mother had been horrified when she enrolled in med school. Emerson had been thrilled.

"You should be in a lecture hall," Maxine continued. "You have papers to publish. You can't still be angry that Nathaniel had the research breakthrough before you and released that paper—"

"Nathaniel wouldn't know a breakthrough if it slapped him in the face." She'd certainly been tempted to deliver that slap. "As I told you before, it was my work. That's why a retraction was published in the journal. He *stole* my work."

"And yet you're still trying to shove the jerk down her throat. Totally not a mother-of-the-year move there, Senator," Gray drawled.

Gray doesn't give a shit who my mother is. He's not intimidated by her power. By the contacts she has. In fact, I don't think he's intimidated by anything at all in this world.

And, damn, that was sexy. "I'm very happy with Gray."

Her mother's lashes—fake, they were also carefully applied, just like the hair coloring—flickered. Her gaze slid to Gray. "But are *you* happy, Agent Stone? You made it quite clear that you had zero interest in working with my daughter. She isn't actual FBI, as I believe you've pointed out on numerous occasions to numerous people. Surely you would like to get back to your original team. I'm certain that another agent—perhaps Trinity Coleman or Agnes Quinn—could work undercover on this case with you. You don't need my daughter."

"Oh, but I do." He brought Emerson's hand to his lips. Kissed her knuckles.

She didn't flinch. Or jerk. But she might have shivered the smallest bit.

He smiled. She caught the wicked grin from the corner of her eye. "You see, I need Emerson. Very, very much."

Emerson wet her lips.

"She's quite spectacular," Gray continued. "She can profile on the spot. Pick up small details. Analyze. Evaluate. Trinity and Agnes are good agents, yes, do not get me wrong, but I need a phenomenal profiler for this case. As I'm sure your, ah, FBI spies—I mean sources, your FBI *sources* have already told you, the perp we are after targets couples. I need someone who will pose as a believable romantic partner for me. A partner who can profile in her sleep. Emerson is perfect for me."

Maxine stopped toying with her pearls. She leaned forward. "On your last investigation, you let a twisted killer put his hands on my daughter." Icy fury. "He had an ice pick shoved beneath her chin."

"You've read the case report, hmmm?" Gray tightened his hold on Emerson's hand.

"I thought you would protect her. Now I see that isn't the case. You will use her as bait. That's what you did in that dingy garage with Jake Waller, isn't it? You used her to draw out the killer, to get his confessions. You think you'll use her again on this current hunt. Emerson is expendable to you." A hard, negative shake of her head. "She is not expendable to me. Emerson is done with her failed experiment. She's coming back to D.C. where she can be safe."

Gray let go of Emerson's hand. She immediately missed the warmth of his touch.

But his hand just rose and curled under her chin. Tenderly, he turned her head toward him. "Emerson," Gray said her name like a caress.

Her mother cursed. She did that often actually, behind closed doors. Sure, she might look like a lady, but when cameras and constituents weren't close, she talked like a, well, a former SEAL. Because she spent a great deal of time with Owen.

I know they've been a couple for years. I suspect they were together even before my father died. A tabloid story had hinted at their personal relationship once, only for the report to be immediately squashed by Maxine.

"Do you want to go back to D.C.?" Gray asked Emerson.

"No."

"Do you want to work this undercover case with me?"

"Yes."

His eyes narrowed. "Do you trust me to keep you safe?"

"Yes." No hesitation. If she hadn't trusted him, she wouldn't have fucked him. She'd learned from her mistake with Nathaniel. *Only take a lover if you trust him completely.* She did trust Gray, and because of that, she'd been able to lower her guard with him and get lost to the pleasure they created together.

He flashed her a smile. Warm. One that lit his eyes. *More gold, less darkness.* "Glad that's settled. After all, we have a meeting to attend." He turned his head toward Maxine. "Feel free to call next time. You don't have to pull out the limo just to impress us." He began to ease toward the door.

"*Stop.*" Maxine's voice. Shaking around the edges. "Do you think someone trying to kill my daughter is a joke?"

He focused on the senator. All traces of warmth left his face. "No, I think it's a lethal mistake."

Emerson remembered how he'd responded when Jake Waller had grabbed her. She swallowed. "I don't think you fully understand the situation, Mother."

"Oh, I *do* understand, Emerson. You don't. When we came up with the deal for you to work at the FBI, you were supposed to face no real danger. You were to hear about the cases, to stay in the office, to read the old files."

Emerson's brows rose. "Excuse me?" That had never been her plan.

"You were *not* supposed to be in the field. Not ever. As in, not even once. But Grayson Stone pushed and ignored the rules I'd set up. He risked your life because he thinks he can use you in order to bring down his prey. As I said, you're expendable to him. I won't allow this. Not happening. Your partnership is terminated." An inhale. "As of now. I will be contacting his supervisors at the FBI. He can take someone else out as his partner on this case."

She could feel the anger rising beneath her skin. Emerson was sure her cheeks had to be darkening. Her heart pounded, her body tensed, and she... "Gray, did you ignore rules?"

"Rules don't apply to me."

Such a Gray thing to say.

"And I don't really have supervisors any longer at the Bureau. Due to my track record, a whole helluva lot of closed cases, and a traitorous bastard in the upper echelon at the FBI that I helped to bring down...let's just say that I now get to make all the choices as to what happens with my team. And who is *on* my team." He winked at her. "Guess what, Emerson? I choose you."

Maxine slapped her hand down on the seat near her right thigh. "Because you want to use my daughter? Use her and fuck her?"

Shocked, Emerson turned and saw the flash of anger on her mother's face.

"I choose Emerson because I happen to respect the hell out of her." Gray's response came instantly. "She's brilliant. She keeps her head in the field when things go south, and she's also one incredible shot. She's the person I want at my side when there's danger. You're her mother, though, so I shouldn't have to tell you just how great she is. That's something you should already know. By the way, I don't like your tone when you talk to her. You need to watch that."

Both Emerson and her mother swung their heads toward him.

"Since we're having this little chat—and you are delaying Emerson and I from a very important meeting—it's my turn to interrogate."

Uh, oh. Emerson knew this was not going to be good. "Gray..."

"Why the hell have you let a stalker prey on her for *years* while you did nothing to stop him?"

Emerson's attention jumped back to the senator. Her mother seemed to stop breathing.

Then she grabbed for her pearls. Rubbed them with her index finger and thumb. "I have no idea what you're talking about."

"Liar, liar." A soft taunt and accusation from Gray. "You know exactly what—who—I'm talking about. But I'll clarify. I mean the bastard who broke into your home all those years ago. The one who left that scar on Emerson's throat."

Her mother's gaze darted to Emerson's throat. "You don't understand the situation." Maxine's guarded response. "I am sure Emerson doesn't want me getting into the specifics."

Gray grunted. "The specifics are that some creep terrorized a seventeen-year-old girl. And from what I can tell, he's been keeping tabs on her for years. The broken mirror bullshit? The breaking into her homes? Taking shit that belongs to her? Playing games with her? Oh, it's ending. So are the threats on her life."

Maxine stopped rubbing her pearls. "Excuse me?"

"When we were in Briar, someone broke into my motel room." Emerson was pleased that her voice held no emotion. She made sure to keep her hands flat against her thighs. No unnecessary movements. "A spray-painted message was left on my wall. The message said I would be dying."

Maxine leaned forward. "You need to stop working these FBI cases. *They are putting too much stress on you.* You are going to fracture, Emerson." A firm nod. "I didn't want to bring this up in front of an outsider, but you leave me no choice. Agent Stone, you've been misled." She rubbed the pearls. "Emerson is emotionally fragile—"

His laughter cut through her words. "You really need to watch your tells, Senator Marlowe. When you lie, you clutch those pearls way too much."

Her eyes widened. She immediately let go of the pearls.

"Emerson isn't emotionally fragile, and you damn well know it. But she does have a soft heart. I suspect she's let her feelings for you allow her to be manipulated for far too long. But that shit is ending."

When He Defends

"Oh, really?" Maxine's face flushed. "And I guess you are the one ending it?"

"Damn straight, I am. Unlike Emerson, I don't care at all about you. Have zero fucks to give, so there will be no manipulation of me. I'm her partner. That means I protect her from every threat. I'm sure you did your research on me before you decided I would be working with Emerson—"

"You didn't *want* to work with her! You fought it tooth and nail! You said she'd be a pain in the ass—"

"She's a pain in the ass that I happen to quite like. So understand me when I say that no one will threaten her. No one will manipulate her. And that stalker BS? You didn't put an end to it. I will."

"There was no proof of an intruder all of those years ago—"

"Sure, there was. She's got a scar on her neck."

Emerson could have sworn the scar burned.

"You don't understand—" Maxine began.

"I understand that Emerson didn't hurt herself. I understand that I *will* be hurting the person who hurt her. Now, if you'll excuse me..." He glanced at his watch. "Emerson and I are late for our own meeting. Very tacky, that. I don't like to be tacky. Got to keep it classy, am I right?"

Her mother's mouth opened. Closed. Opened another time.

"Great talk, Senator Marlowe. Super fun." He paused. "That was sarcasm. One of my tells. I get sarcastic when I lie."

No, he was sarcastic all the time. Gray was just playing games with her mother.

He slid toward the door. Opened it. "Emerson? Ladies first?"

"*I want to talk with you.*" Her mother's shaking voice. "Alone, Emerson."

"I have a meeting."

"Please."

Whoa. Stop. Had her mother just used the p-word? Emerson's head swung toward Gray. "Give us a moment?"

He nodded. "I'll wait outside. Been wanting to have myself a chat with Owen." But he frowned at Maxine. "Don't get Emerson upset. I will not be amused if you do." He slid out. Shut the door behind him.

The classical music kept playing. Emerson was sure the music was supposed to be soothing. She felt far from soothed.

"He's quite...protective of you," her mother noted.

That was one way of putting it.

"You didn't tell me about the threat in your motel room," Maxine added.

"I just did."

"No, Gray just did."

Right. Emerson glanced toward the tinted window on her side of the limo. Beyond the glass, she could see Gray talking with Owen. Gray's expression was very intent, but she couldn't hear the words he spoke.

"Why didn't you tell me?" Maxine wanted to know.

She rolled one shoulder in a shrug. "I'm the reverse girl who cried wolf."

"What?"

She kept watching Gray. He seemed pissed. Not good. "I've told you about the monster, over and over again. You never believed me, even though he was right there." She bit her lower lip. "In *The Boy Who Cried Wolf,* the boy was making up the story. No one believed him when he really needed help." Her head turned so that she could see her mother again. "Each time I cried out for help, the monster was actually there. No pretending. Only you never believed me. So I stopped crying out. What was the point? Help wasn't going to come, so there was no need to cry out."

* * *

"You're sleeping with the senator."

Owen cocked one eyebrow. "You're sleeping with Emerson."

Gray nodded. He also let out a brief sigh. "You and I are going to have a problem."

"Because you're an asshole?"

"Sure, that's one of the reasons." The street was quiet. They were about one hundred feet away from the entrance to the FBI office. "The other reason is that you didn't track down the sonofabitch who cut Emerson all those years ago. You left him loose."

Owen edged closer. "I tried to find him." His gaze darted around the street, seemingly searching for threats before he nodded and his sharp gaze swept back to Gray. "There was no trace of the bastard. No prints. No sign of forced entry. *Nothing.* We had a great security system. He got past it. Either he was freaking Houdini or—"

"Don't say Emerson made it up. I'm not in the mood for that crap. You don't believe it. I don't believe it. So spare me the BS story that her mother has fed you and her."

Owen's lips thinned.

"You must have looked for him since the initial attack. He's been breaking into her home. He's been following her. No way do you just ignore the continuing threat to her."

"She's had extra security over the years." Grudging. "Some of the security personnel...perhaps caught sight of someone once or twice. But he vanished before they could get close enough to apprehend him." The lines near his mouth deepened. "However, we have no reason to believe any *potential* attack from her youth—"

"Potential, my ass," Gray cut in.

"—may be tied to any other...incident in her life." Again, he surveyed the street. Always seeming to stay on guard like a good SEAL.

Gray wasn't impressed. "Really? You gonna say that bull right to my face?"

Owen centered his focus on Gray. "Emerson likes to study dangerous people. It makes sense that some of those people might develop an attachment to her. Case in point..." His stare raked over Gray.

"I'm definitely dangerous. And attached. Good for you to realize it."

"Does Emerson realize it?"

He wasn't going to touch that, not yet. "Your extra guards saw someone tailing her, but you just thought that was—what? Recent psychos? That's the story you're going with? The woman just collects psychos the way some people collect stamps?" Did anyone even still collect stamps these days? Was that a thing? Collecting psychos certainly was *not* a thing.

"Psychos." Owen laughed. The sound held little amusement. "Is that really an appropriate, technical term for an FBI agent to use?"

Gray shrugged. "It's a term that I use for some jackass who gets off on terrorizing Emerson. You got a problem with it? With me? Prepare to be shocked, but I don't really care."

Owen nodded. "I like you better than the weak-willed shrink she took up with a few years back."

"The one currently in town?"

Owen gave a slight start.

"Oh, didn't you realize Nathaniel had come to Atlanta? Surprise, surprise, he's here. Skulking around. The senator called him. Sent him running to do her bidding."

Owen's gaze darted to the limo.

"Your loyalties are with the senator," Gray said. "Mine are with Emerson. Understand that. I can't be bought. I can't be bullied. I can't be pressured. I'm not Nathaniel Hadaway."

"Duly noted." Owen rolled back his shoulders. "Navy?"

"Marines."

"Huh."

"Now that we're acquainted tell me this...who all was on the property the night that Emerson's father died?"

Surprise flashed on Owen's face. There one moment. Gone the next. "What?"

"Who all was on the property the night her father died?" The question had been perfectly clear the first time.

"Why the hell do you want to know that?" A definite edge.

And that tells me there is more to that night than meets the eye. "Because I'm a curious bastard. Also a tad bit obsessive. A character flaw. My new obsession is Emerson, and I want to learn everything about her. Particularly about the incidents that have left a mark on her over the years. So I'll repeat, third time being the charm and all of that, who all was on the property the night her father died?"

Owen crossed his arms over his chest. "Ask Emerson."

"She was seven. I figured someone who'd been an adult at the time might have a stronger recollection." He waited a beat. No answer was forthcoming. "So odd the way you won't answer such a basic question for me."

"Fine. I'll answer your question. But, in return, you have to answer one for me."

He caught sight of Rylan lingering near the entrance to the FBI office. Gray waved him on. After a brief hesitation, Rylan turned and entered the building. When Rylan was gone, Gray told Owen, "I'm feeling generous. Let's make the trade."

"Maxine was there. Both of Maxine's parents. Emerson. I was there. Two other guards."

"And no one tried to stop the man heading straight for the cliff's edge, eh?"

"You got one question. I didn't say anything about answering *two*."

"You're not even going to name the guards? That's hardly fair."

"My turn." Owen's arms remained crossed over his chest. "Why are you obsessed with Emerson?"

The limo door opened. Emerson appeared. Her face looked strained. Her eyes a bit sad. That was just unacceptable. Instantly, he was reaching for her. Taking her hand. Keeping hold of her. Time for them to get inside for their meeting.

But Owen moved into his path. "I answered your question, Agent Stone. You really the kind of asshole who doesn't keep his word?"

"Gray is *not* an asshole," Emerson hotly defended.

And that was cute and all. It really was. But they both knew she was lying. "Of course, I'm an asshole, sweetheart. Pretty sure that's one of the traits you secretly adore about me. But, in this instance, I am an asshole who intends to keep his word." He inclined his head toward Owen. "Why am I obsessed with Emerson? Easy. She's about to become my wife. What man isn't obsessed with his bride?"

Chapter Fifteen

"Everyone's a suspect. From the check-in clerk to the maids to the busy chefs at the on-site restaurants. Every person you see can be wearing a smiling mask but have a monster lurking on the inside. Stay on guard at all times." – Gray Stone, right before his "honeymoon" trip with Emerson Marlowe

"Our amenities include horseback riding, sailing, yoga at both sunrise and sunset, bicycle riding, skeet shooting, a world-class golf course, kayaking..." The concierge manager, Hannah McIntyre, stopped to clear her throat. "Although, as a honeymooning couple, you are certainly going to have as much privacy as you would like."

Emerson stood inside of the massive resort lobby. Marble floors. Gleaming chandeliers. And... "I'm sorry, but do I hear bagpipes playing?" They'd arrived at Sea Island, a private island off the southeastern coast of Georgia just thirty minutes ago. Right before they'd pulled in and Gray had handed off the car rental keys to a valet attendant, he'd slipped an engagement ring—with a mega diamond—and a wedding ring on her finger. The weight of the two rings was new, and it took considerable effort not to keep wiggling her finger.

The bagpipe music drifted through the massive, open doors that seemed to lead out onto a balcony.

Hannah beamed at her. "Yes, we have a nightly performance by our resident bagpiper."

A resident bagpiper?

"He serenades our guests to mark the end of the day."

"Lovely," Emerson murmured, and she meant it. The music was truly lovely, and if she and Gray weren't there to track down a killer, she could certainly enjoy the performance.

But...

They *were* there to find a killer. They were in the beautiful, posh setting because someone was killing couples, and it was their job to stop that perp. *My first undercover mission.* The day had been a frantic blur of activity. Her mother's unfortunate arrival. The meeting with the team. Packing and getting clothes to fit their new personas.

Gray had vanished for a while. She had her suspicions about what he'd been doing. *Maybe a meeting with Nathaniel?* A meeting in which he told her ex to stay the hell away? But she hadn't been able to question Gray about his disappearance because there had been files to read. Material to prepare. They'd had to get a rental car, get on the road and then...

They'd arrived at their honeymoon destination.

"I had a friend who stayed here about a year ago," Gray announced. He flashed a smile at Hannah.

Hannah's own grin stretched more even as she leaned

over the counter a bit toward him. Probably because Gray was using his meg-watt, extra charming grin.

Still...*He's married, Hannah.* Emerson wrapped her hand around Gray's arm. She let that lovely diamond catch the light and flash.

"My friend told me about another fun tradition that you have here," Gray continued. "He said that honeymooners sign your registry?"

"Oh, yes." A quick nod from Hannah. "Our honeymooning guests have been signing our registry since 1940. We've had celebrities, we've had royalty..." She gave a little hum. "Names are inscribed in the bound books, and couples come back again and again over the years to pull out those books and see their signatures. I had one couple who celebrated their fiftieth anniversary recently! They wanted to see the book to search out their signatures from their time honeymooning with us. Brought their grandchildren with them." A soft sigh. "This island is made for romance."

Well, if Gray's suspicions were true, it was made for the *deaths* of certain romantic couples.

"We have a book for each year," Hannah informed them. "You'll be in our current book, and who knows? Maybe fifty years from now, you'll come back, too!" She brushed back a lock of her hair. "Over forty thousand couples have signed our registry."

Forty thousand. Okay. That was quite extensive. Emerson realized Gray had probably asked about the registry because he'd wanted to see if there might be more victims out there for the FBI to discover. And a registry with a list of all the honeymooning couples who'd visited would certainly provide them with a great resource to search out potential victims. But...

Forty thousand? It would take some serious time to

check back through that many people. And, surely, the killer hadn't been attacking couples for *years*.

But the registry *would* be a good way for a perp to find his prey. Almost like a menu item for the killer. Open a book, pick a couple, plan for them to die. "What, exactly, is included in the registry?" Emerson wanted to know. "Just the names?"

"Names and towns." Hannah nodded. "I'm actually in charge of the registry." More than a hint of pride entered her voice.

Well, crap. That was definitely like a menu for the killer. He would know which city his prey would be returning to—all the better to make the hunt easier.

"You'll sign before you leave the island. And maybe love will bring you back one day," Hannah concluded brightly.

"Maybe so," Gray replied.

"You're in one of our best suites. Come, I'll take you to your room and give you a quick tour on your way."

Perfect. Emerson was sure that she and Gray could use that time to grill the helpful concierge manager.

"Justin?" Hannah waved toward a young man with black hair who waited nearby. "Bring their luggage up, will you?"

Justin hurried from behind the luggage desk. He wore a dark blue uniform, and his gold name tag was placed above his heart.

"They are our new honeymooners," Hannah said. "Mr. and Mrs. Anderson."

Gray had chosen Anderson as a fake last name. Way better than Smith, in Emerson's opinion, and there were still nearly eight hundred thousand people in the US with that last name.

"They are in the Crystal Harmony Suite." She pointed to the luggage.

The Crystal Harmony Suite had been a deliberate choice. It had been the same suite that Cass's friends, Anzo and Kim, had used on their anniversary trip.

"May their love be eternal," Hannah added as she beamed at them.

Justin grabbed their luggage. "Right this way."

* * *

GRAY LIFTED Emerson into his arms. Her sweet, sensual scent filled his nose even as she curled one arm around the back of his neck. Emerson laughed and smiled at him, and he tightened his grip on her because for one wild, crazy moment...

I want this to be real.

Hannah clapped. "Oh, how wonderful! I've got a fabulous feeling about you two! I know couples. I can always tell which ones have staying power, and you certainly have it. It's in the eyes, you know. You can *see* when two people are meant to be. After taking over the honeymoon registry, I've become quite an expert about this thing. You two are meant to be."

He carried Emerson over the threshold. Didn't let her go. Instead, with the door to their suite wide open and both Hannah and Justin watching, he lowered his head and kissed Emerson.

Not a light, soft kiss. Screw that. Gray figured that he and Emerson wouldn't have a light, soft kind of marriage. They would have the kind of marriage where he had to fight not to constantly rip off her clothes and fuck her everywhere. So he kissed her passionately. Mouths open. Tongue tasting.

"Oh, ahem. Yes, well, I bet you two would like to be alone. There is some champagne chilling and strawberries waiting, and I'll just close the door, shall I? Come along, Justin, let's give this couple their privacy. Ring if you need anything at all!" Justin and Hannah retreated. The door closed.

Click.

He kissed Emerson a bit longer. Mostly just because he enjoyed tasting her.

She kissed him back.

It could be real...It could be.

Then she pulled away.

But, fuck it, it's not real. Just an undercover mission that gave him a glimpse at a life he might be tempted to kill in order to possess. His head lifted. He did go right on holding Emerson.

"Did she just say there was champagne in here?" Emerson inquired, ever-so-politely.

"Um."

"Did you *order* the champagne?"

"Yeah. Kinda something I do."

She stared into his eyes.

He tried not to kiss her again. But her mouth was right there. Tempting. Perfect.

"Something you do..." Emerson prompted, her voice a careful whisper, "when you are with all of your fake wives?"

He smiled.

"That's lethal. You should be careful when you use that grin."

He carried her across the suite and sat her down right in the middle of the big, four-poster bed. "You're lethal." He

When He Defends

meant that. She was extremely dangerous to him. "Stay there a second, would you, sweetheart?"

Then he very thoroughly and methodically searched the room for any hidden surveillance material. Cameras. Bugs. Whatever. He was a suspicious sonofabitch. When he was certain the suite was clear, he returned to stand near the bed. And Emerson. "I've ordered champagne every time I've forced friends to go undercover. Always worked for them, so I figure, why the hell not?"

"Sure. Why not?"

"If you're honeymooning and you don't order champagne, it might look suspicious." The champagne chilled in a bucket near the bed. Two tall flutes waited beside the bucket. "But at least there are no rose petals in here. Heard those can be a pain when they stick to your ass."

"What?" Her brow scrunched.

He ran a finger down the bridge of his nose and remembered a particular conversation with his buddy Ronan. Ah, Ronan. A hitman turned devoted husband. That happened. A guy started playing pretend, and lines blurred. The next thing you knew...

Your wife is pregnant, and she and your kid are the only things that matter in the world. Mostly because they are your world.

Ronan had recently told Gray his good news about the baby. And maybe...hell, maybe...

Am I envious?

"Why are you looking at me that way?" Emerson asked. She scooted and sat on the edge of the bed. She crossed one leg over the other. Lazily kicked one high heel. Emerson and her heels. She truly had the sexiest shoes ever.

The next time he fucked her, the shoes were staying *on*.

"Just what way am I looking at you?"

Her lips pursed. "You're not doing it anymore. I shouldn't have said anything."

He shouldn't have been looking at her like she was his dream. This situation was about business. About victims. Not about him and his fantasies with Emerson. "Our second couple—Zac and River Turner—gave us an agenda to follow."

She nodded. "You mentioned in the briefing today that River posted her activities to her social media profiles."

"Right. So we're going to do exactly what River did. The sunrise yoga. The stand-up paddleboarding. You, not me. River's husband never got near the water. He just watched from the beach. I'll do the same."

Emerson winced. "Paddleboarding. I'm sure I won't wind up even a little soaked."

"Then there's the spa. River specifically mentioned a masseuse named Angel in one of her social media posts. But we can't start all this work until tomorrow. It's our honeymoon night. If we're suddenly hot and heavy on the activities, it might raise suspicions. After all, we are supposed to be deeply, deeply in love." He put his hands on the edge of the bed, on either side of her hips. He leaned in close to her. "I'm not supposed to be able to keep my hands off you."

She glanced down. "They are not touching me."

No, they were not. But he very much wanted them to be touching her.

"Rylan is on the grounds," Gray said because he hadn't given her this update yet. "He checked in an hour ago."

Her gaze was still on his hands.

"Agnes and Trinity will be arriving a bit later. Their

cover is that they are on a ladies' getaway. Rylan is here under the guise of participating in a golf tournament." Gray paused. "And Malik is holed up close by. Keeping out of sight, but he'll come forward if we need him. He'll be our primary tech support while we are at the resort." Made sense because Malik was a freaking tech genius. The guy wanted more field time, but his skills with computers were pretty damn priceless.

"You said none of the attacks actually happened *here*. The couples were all killed shortly after leaving the resort and returning home." She tucked a lock of hair behind one ear. "So we should be safe here. I mean, that's even provided that we attract the killer's attention."

"Sweetheart, you attract attention wherever you go." To be clear.

"Is that a compliment? Or a criticism?"

"You're fucking beautiful, and you know it."

She smiled at him. "That's really sweet of you to say."

No, it wasn't sweet. Maybe it would have been sweet if he'd left out the "fucking" part, but he hadn't. Because he was gruff and rude, and he felt too big as he towered over her. Too big, too...*wrong*. Everything in his life seemed to have been about violence and pain, and Emerson—she needed something good. Something to light the shadows that came so often to her eyes. But he wasn't light. He wasn't good.

He also damn well wasn't going to give her up. So, yeah, he was a bastard. He'd never claimed to be otherwise.

Emerson studied him. "Would you like for me to tell you that I think you're fucking handsome?"

Her words caught him by surprise.

"Because you are."

"*Emerson.*"

"Gray." Her hand rose. Pressed over his heart.

Back away. Back. Away. He started to retreat.

Her hand fisted in his shirtfront. "So we're going to stay here all night? Pretend to be newlyweds who can't keep their hands off each other as we wreck this suite?"

That was one option. But... "When things quiet down at the resort, probably after midnight, we're sneaking out. We'll investigate the entire property. We'll start by assessing all of the locations that River documented on her honeymoon trip."

"Oh, Gray, you have the best honeymoon ideas."

She wasn't mocking him. She was dead serious. Excitement gleamed in her eyes. That was the thing about Emerson. She loved the hunt just as much as he did.

And he loved that about her.

Fucking hell. Gray's breath hissed out. His hands clenched around the covers.

"Gray?" Worry crinkled her eyebrows. "What's wrong?"

He shot away from the bed. Away from her. "Time to review the case files." He backed up. Fast. A couple more extra steps.

"Now?"

"Now." A thousand times now. "You need to become more familiar with the couples. Their backgrounds. Their relationships. You heard our friendly concierge manager. Over forty thousand honeymooners have swept into this place over the years. Why were our victims chosen from among them? What made them stand out? I want your take on their lives. You profile the victims. See what's made them stand out." He glanced at his watch. "We have a good four hours for review before I want to start searching the grounds. We have a job to do. Time to do it." His head turned back toward her.

She sat straight up on the bed. "A job. Right. That's what we have."

Aw, hell. Now that was not what he'd meant. At least, not exactly. "Emerson..."

She rose. A whole lot slower than he had. "Something scared you."

Yeah, you scared me. Not what he would admit. Ever.

"Want to tell me about it?"

He did not. Time for distraction. "Want to tell me how the rest of the conversation went with the senator once I left the limo?"

She hesitated near the bed. "Pretty much how you'd imagine. She told me I was wasting my time. That you were using me. That I'd be in danger if I went into the field with you. That this was not the life I needed." A pause. "And that you were not the man I needed."

That was just annoying. "And why not?"

"You're too dangerous. Too unpredictable."

So a guy had a few character quirks. Was that the end of the world?

"I told her that you were exactly what I needed. But then again, I knew that before we met. It's why I worked so hard to get you to be my partner."

And damn if a warm, freaking, weird glow didn't start to spread through him because Emerson had just said he was exactly what she needed. Okay, okay, maybe he didn't have to be so hesitant with her. Maybe—

"You're a legend when it comes to profiling. I don't know if I've mentioned this before, but I actually came to a few of your lectures at Quantico over the years. Pulled some strings of my own, and I'd slip into some of the classes you conducted with the new recruits. You're really quite brilliant when it comes to entering a killer's mind. The last talk I saw of yours was actually a visiting lecture you did with grad students at Tulane. You were discussing why some serials don't actually have a cooling off period—because the rush from the kill is so comparable to the high of drugs and that they come to need it all the time after a certain point. Their tipping points. Interesting talk."

Emerson didn't want him for his body. She wanted him because he knew killers. Right. Check. "Sweetheart..." Gray let the endearment slide out because he could always claim it was just part of the cover. "Have you been stalking me?"

She remained by the edge of the bed.

"A little bit, you have, huh? Because you wanted to pick apart my mind." He turned away. "Well, let's see how *your* mind is spinning tonight. The files are on the laptop that the helpful bellhop delivered for us."

"I wanted to pick apart your mind. I also wanted to jump your body."

He stilled. "Your honesty can be surprising."

"Would you prefer I lie?"

"No. Too many other people already do that."

"Agree. So how about we both be honest with each other? You're retreating from me. Why?"

He didn't look back at her. "Because we have a job to do." He should say more. She'd given him honesty. He should do the same. But if he said he was trying not to fuck her senseless...nope, not real tactful. Time to change the conversation. "By the way, Nathaniel Hadaway swears that he only entered your condo when you opened the door for him."

"You went to have a talk with him. I *knew* it."

"Then you were correct. I went to have a talk with him,"

Gray confirmed. Like he would have left Atlanta without having an intent one-on-one with his new arch enemy. "Nathaniel said he didn't sneak in and break the mirrors. Claimed he had no idea that anything bad had happened at your place."

"And you believe him?"

"I believe that we understand each other." Nathaniel had been sweating bullets. "I think my reputation precedes me with Nathaniel. He was shaking in his loafers."

She rushed toward him. Her heels tapped on the hardwood floor. Her fingers lifted and curled around his shoulder.

As usual, that touch of hers swept through his whole body. *Yep, that's not gonna change. Fucking her did nothing to ease my attraction.* Quite the contrary. Fucking Emerson had only made him want her more. Because he knew how fantastic they would be together.

"What did you say to him?" Emerson asked.

"Oh, the usual." He angled his body toward her. Stared down at Emerson.

She waited. Didn't blink.

Fine. He'd give her a few more details. "Come near my lady, and I will destroy you."

Her lips parted.

"Don't worry. I didn't threaten physical violence, though, seriously, we both know I could take him."

"*Gray.*"

"I just mentioned that I didn't like cheaters. I really don't. He tried to cheat the academic world. He betrayed you. I simply said that if he'd done it once, then I suspect he's pulled that stunt before. I could dig. I'd find the truth, and whatever reputational clout he still has left in the academic world? I'd make it vanish. Along with that book deal he was bragging about." Simple. Done.

"You know exactly what he fears."

Sure. He turned toward her a little bit more. His hand rose. Cupped her chin. "That's the trick, isn't it? You have to find out what someone wants—what the individual truly wants above everything else." His thumb brushed lightly along her lower lip. He'd crushed that mouth beneath his own the previous night. And that mouth had been on his dick. Hesitant. So eager. So amazing. "You discover what a person wants the most. Then, threaten to take it away. Because what someone wants most? That thing is also the person's weakness. You want it so badly that not having it?" He dropped his hand. Took a step away. "Not having it can wreck you." His head inclined toward the laptop bag that waited near the door with their other luggage. "Time to review files. We've got a busy night ahead of us."

"What do you want most, Gray?"

You. His gaze remained on the laptop bag. "To put away as many killers as I can. So let's hunt this asshole before anyone else dies just because they have the misfortune of being in love."

Chapter Sixteen

"I don't remember much about the night my father died. It was storming. I could hear thunder rumbling over and over again. I-I was scared, so I went looking for my dad. I couldn't find him anywhere. Actually, I couldn't find anyone, not at first."
— *Emerson Marlowe*

For a honeymoon, there was a surprising amount of *no sex.*

Emerson crept behind Gray as they snuck around the sprawling resort property. They'd spent the last few hours reviewing the case files. Working silently. Not touching.

Okay, so fine. She'd expected sex on their pretend honeymoon. She got it was an undercover assignment. Understood. But after the previous night, after the way they'd burned up the bed together, she'd thought...

What did I think? That we would pick up where we left off?

Not happening. Clearly. Because Gray was...not interested? Because he'd only wanted one time with her? Because...

She'd disappointed him?

Emerson had a million questions swirling in her mind, but she kept her lips clamped shut as they maneuvered around the property. Gray had already given her schematics for the resort. They'd seen plenty of maps and layouts online. But he'd still insisted on walking the territory himself.

She wasn't even sure what he was looking for.

Three couples were dead. Three, out of over forty thousand.

The first couple, Kris and Wendy Prichard, had honeymooned on the island just a little over a year ago. They'd been high school sweethearts. Gone to college together. Got married shortly after graduation. Seemingly, they'd had an idyllic honeymoon. They'd gone home and, two days later, they'd died in a car accident.

Not some brutal murder. An *accident*. Or, so the police on scene had thought at the time.

But Gray had gotten access to a report that indicated the vehicle's brakes had been useless on the night of Kris and Wendy's deaths. Despite that revelation, a revelation their own investigation had uncovered, the local cops had clung tightly to the accident theory. Brakes went out. Tragic events happened. There'd been only a minimal investigation. Until now.

Couple number two on Gray's list—that would be Zac and River Turner. It had been Zac's second marriage. River's first. He'd been a doctor. She'd been an artist. They'd honeymooned at the island about four months prior. River's social media had been full of happy pictures from the resort. Sunrise yoga. Stand-up paddleboarding. Spa relaxation. Even a pic of River riding a horse on the beach as she grinned from ear to ear. Everything had seemed perfect.

Then they'd gone home. Two days later—*two days*—they'd been killed while they were on a morning jog together. Both attacked and brutally stabbed as they ran. Zac had died right there on the running trail. River had made it to the hospital. And only that far. She'd died in the ER.

The cops on that case had no leads. River and Zac had been running in a park right before six a.m. No witnesses. No leads.

Until now. Until Gray. Until he'd taken the case because of Cassius. And that led them to the third couple.

Anzo and Kim. Kim had been a cop. Anzo had been part of Cassius's MC. Kim and Anzo had first met when she'd been investigating the motorcycle club. Only instead of arresting the guy for anything, Kim had married Anzo. From the photos that Emerson had seen, the two had looked wildly in love.

Anzo had gotten out of the MC after his marriage. He'd stayed out, stayed busy opening up a series of restaurants, for five years. Then he and Kim had returned to Sea Island for their anniversary. If you looked at their photos, you would think they'd been deliriously happy. The perfect couple.

Sure, expressions could be faked. It was so easy to look happy in the two seconds that it took to snap a pic. But...

I saw the videos, too. Videos from their small wedding ceremony five years ago. Videos that had been taken on their honeymoon. Kim's father had paid for their honeymoon—their first trip to Sea Island.

For the anniversary trip, Anzo had proudly footed the bill. Had splurged hard on his wife and ordered all the bells and whistles for the trip. An adoring Anzo had followed his wife everywhere around the resort, always having his phone at the ready, and recorded videos had caught him telling her that he was "the luckiest bastard in the world."

After the weeklong trip, Anzo and Kim had gone home. Two days later—because it was always *two days* as Emerson had discovered when she studied the files—they'd been dead. Anzo had been shot with his wife's gun. One that she had then seemingly turned on herself.

Except...

There had been no gunshot residue on her fingers. And, in fact, two of her fingers had been broken. As if the person who'd shoved the gun into her hand had used far too much force. He'd snapped her pinky and ring finger. Plus, he'd put the gun in the wrong hand. It had been found in Kim's right hand.

She'd been a lefty.

All points that Emerson had learned Cassius had made to Gray in order to plead his case. Cassius had actually done the digging to find the previous two couples, as well. He'd put it all together because the deaths had occurred in different cities, with different cops investigating.

That was why it had been so easy to overlook the crimes. Different places, different types of kills. Especially the first, staged to look like an accident.

"Emerson, are you paying attention to anything I am saying?"

Her gaze had been on the stand-up paddleboard rental booths that waited down on the beach. She'd gotten lost for a moment, imagining Kim smiling at Anzo as she balanced

perfectly on the board. He'd filmed her doing that. And...
"I'm the luckiest bastard in the world.'"

He had been lucky. Until the end.

"I was thinking about the vics," she said, replying a bit too quickly. But she *had* been thinking about the victims and feeling so very sad for them all. Lives cut short just when they should have been at their happiest.

Gray grunted. "For the moment, how about you stay focused on us?"

She frowned at him. They'd already crept past two of the pool areas, then edged around the tennis court and the pickleball areas. Nothing out of the ordinary had jumped out at them. "What is it, exactly, that we're looking for in the middle of the night?" Everything was dead quiet. She hadn't even seen security guards patrolling the grounds.

"I'll know it when I see it," he muttered. He turned and stalked forward.

"Oh, that's clear." She advanced and plowed right into him when he spun around. His hands rose up and clamped around her shoulders.

She wasn't wearing her heels. Heels hardly went well with sand, so she'd traded them for flat sandals that strapped around her feet. A billowy skirt. A soft blouse. Meanwhile, Gray was clad all in black. He blended perfectly with the night.

"I don't *know* what we're looking for," he added, voice carrying just to her. "But that doesn't mean I won't search."

Okay. Again, not clear. "Is this going to be a gut-instinct type of situation?"

His hold tightened on her. "I had to fight for this case at the Bureau. The kills are too scattered. Victims in different states. Different methods of death. If Cass hadn't come to me, so very certain of his friend's murder, so certain that

Kim hadn't killed her husband, the perp would still be flying under the radar. I don't even know if there *are* more vics. No judge is gonna give me warrants to search here—the ties are too flimsy to order a full search of the resort. And the resort owner will lawyer up way too fast when he finds out what is happening. So you and I have to investigate as best we can. We have to look for something that doesn't belong. Something that might point us in the right direction."

Footsteps. Emerson heard them shuffling closer even as Gray swore. He pushed her back with his grip on her, turned quickly so that she would be the one spotted—easier to do in her brighter clothes—and he put his mouth on hers. Kissed her beneath a softly swaying palm tree.

The footsteps drew closer. She heard whistling.

Though it was pretty hard to concentrate on the footsteps and whistling when Gray was close and his mouth pressed to hers, tempting her to part her lips, to taste him, to—

"Oh, sorry, folks." A cheerful voice. "Almost didn't see you there."

Gray let her go. Her head turned toward the voice. She saw a flashlight hitting the ground nearby. She was glad the light hadn't been directed right at their eyes.

"Kinda late for a stroll, isn't it?" The voice belonged to a security guard. She could see the hotel's uniform. The star-shaped badge she'd noticed other security guards sporting at check-in.

"I wanted to take a walk under the stars with my new bride." Gray lifted her hand to his lips.

A shiver skated over Emerson when she swore she felt the lick of his tongue against her skin.

"Oh, the view out here is killer," the guard readily agreed.

Emerson stiffened at that particular word. *Killer.*

"A million lights shine in the sky. But to really see the stars best, you should head away from the resort. The darker it gets around you, the more incredible the view above is." He waved at them. "You stay safe out here." He strolled away, still whistling.

Gray kept right on holding Emerson's hand.

She watched the guard vanish. When he was gone, she slowly exhaled. Should she ask for her hand back? "So, that's our plan? Fake kiss if we're spotted?" Emerson nodded. "Got it."

He growled and let her go. "Just stay close."

"Right. Because you might need to grab me and kiss me to fool a guard. Check." Her heart was racing. Not from fright. From the kiss. Dammit, how could he be so unaffected? Did the previous night's activities truly mean nothing to him?

Emerson cleared her throat. Focused on the vics. "Look, we know two of the couples went paddleboarding. Or, at least, the wives did. The husbands watched. How about we head out on the beach and get a closer look at the rental booths? You can see if your spider senses start tingling there."

"Not funny, Emerson."

"I thought it was," she grumbled.

He took her hand once more.

She caught herself before stiffening. *It's for show. In case anyone else sees us.* They cut across the pathway, moving toward the beach and heading for the paddleboards. She noticed that Gray avoided the prominent, white security cameras that had been installed at various locations around the resort. Typically, the security cameras were perched up high so they could angle down and view foot traffic.

Gray was sneaky, she had to give him that. He knew precisely how to avoid being seen. Soon, the crash of waves teased her ears as they hurried across the sand and darted toward the rental booths. Three different white rental units had been set up on the beach and...

"Sonofabitch." Gray stopped mid-stride. He spun toward her.

There were no security guards around. No other people at all. A completely empty expanse of beach.

He pulled her into his arms. "Kiss me like you can't ever get enough of me." His head lowered. His lips took hers.

Sure, done. Her mouth opened beneath his. His tongue thrust into her mouth, and it was like going from zero to eighty in the blink of an eye. This wasn't the quick touch of lips they'd shared beneath the palm tree moments before. This was consuming. This was intense. This was *real*. She could feel the hunger in the hard press of his hands. In the heavy dick that shoved against her.

And her nipples were tight. Her sex yearning.

He lowered her onto the sand. It was soft, a cushion for her body. She was beneath him, surrounded by him. Gray's hands caught hers. Held them over her head against the soft sand. His legs slid between hers, and her skirt hiked up. She rubbed against his heavy cock, and her whole body yearned.

Gray's mouth pulled from hers. His lips skimmed over her jaw. Her cheek.

She looked up and a million stars glittered overhead. *Killer* view.

Gray let go of her hands. He caught the edge of her

earlobe with his teeth, and her eyes snapped closed as bliss and need whipped through her blood.

"Found it," he rasped.

Great. Wonderful. He could find what he needed with her all night long.

"I am tingling," he added, voice a hushed whisper.

Yes, so was she. Her hips rocked against him. Her hands slid over his arms, and she wondered if they were going to have mad, passionate sex right then and there. She'd never had sex on a beach. Actually, she'd only ever had sex in a bed. Was that too vanilla? Was Gray about to show her a whole new world? Because she was ready.

"I found what doesn't belong." The tip of his tongue skated over the shell of her ear.

She shuddered. But then his words registered. Emerson stiffened. She stopped grabbing at his arms. Her hands flew between them, and she proceeded to shove against him.

Only Gray didn't move. "Camera is on us, baby."

What?

He caught the lobe of her ear. Gave it a sensual tug with his teeth.

Her panties got very wet.

"The camera doesn't match the others. Wrong type. Different model. Different color. Small as hell, but I saw it. Someone else is viewing our couples, not just the security staff."

She hadn't seen a camera, but then again, she'd barely had time to look before he'd pounced on her.

All of this is for show?

Except you couldn't fake an erection. That part was very, very real. He was turned on. So was she. She was turned on because it was him. Was he just—was his arousal because of adrenaline? Because she was rubbing her body wildly against him and it was simply a physical response?

He'd wanted her to play his partner on this case because he wanted her. Because the attraction was there and scenes like this one would be easier to fake.

Ice slid over her skin.

"We're going back to the suite. Gonna pretend like we can't keep our hands off each other."

Pretend. That was the problem. She had to get her head in the game and stop acting as if everything they were doing was real.

"I'll try to spot more cameras on the way. Gonna contact Malik ASAP and see if we can figure out where the feed is being transmitted." He pulled back. Pressed his hands into the sand and levered up.

Before she could rise, he'd caught her hands, too. He lifted her up. Bent to kiss her again.

Her eyes closed. She kissed him back. The wind rolled in with the waves, and her skirt flew around her. A tear leaked from her right eye. She could feel it, but surely Gray couldn't see it.

A million stars overhead. And the waning moon. He saw the tiny camera, but you think he can't see a tear drop?

He let her go. Turned away.

She hurriedly brushed away the tear. Sand must have gotten in her eye.

He didn't comment so she hoped he hadn't seen the small movement. They rushed back through the resort area. Heading in a path that made no sense to her, but Gray moved unerringly. Every now and then, he'd pause. Either pull her into an embrace. Get her revved up and tense. Or he'd lean in close as if he were whispering some sort of sweet nothing to her. But in reality...

"There's another one, top of the dock house, pointed toward the area where they do morning yoga. Damn, would have missed it if I hadn't already known exactly what the secondary cameras looked like."

She still missed the camera. Wait, no, there it was. She'd been keeping track each time Gray stopped.

They hurried along and then... "Another," Gray told her. "Near the maintenance door in the pool area."

The pool glowed, a bright blue, courtesy of its underwater lights.

His arm settled around her shoulders. He brought her in close, nuzzling her neck. "The bastard watches everyone. He picks out his prey."

She let her hand rise, and Emerson curled her fingers around his. "What makes him pick certain people?"

His head turned. Again, he was in the shadows, but she was more easily seen. Her lighter skirt. The blouse. "I think it's the women. Something about them. They were the ones on the paddleboards. They were the ones at the yoga class. He chooses the couples based on the women."

And Emerson realized why Gray hadn't said a word when she'd come out in the light skirt and top, even though he'd dressed to blend with the darkness. He wanted her to be seen.

He wanted her to be the killer's prey.

"Then let's just hope he chooses me," she said. Deliberately, she pulled from his embrace. Went into the light cast by the pool. Even did a little twirl near the pool's edge.

"Emerson?" Anger roughed his voice. But maybe if anyone overheard him, they'd mistake the anger for lust.

She stopped her spin. Stayed near the edge of the pool. Not like she wanted to fall in, though that would certainly create a show for any watcher. Instead, she smiled at her "husband" as he waited in the darkness. "Come and get me." It sounded like a taunt for Gray. She even crooked her finger at him in sensual invitation.

But...

The taunt was for the killer. Whoever might be watching. Whoever might be looking for new prey.

Come and get me.

She'd catch his attention. One way or another.

Gray growled and burst from the darkness. He went right to her. In a blink, he'd picked her up. Tossed her over his shoulder. The reaction was *not* what she'd expected, and Emerson let out a surprised cry.

His hold tightened on her. "Got you." And with her over his shoulder, he carried her back through the dark and away from the gleaming water in the pool.

Chapter Seventeen

"What the actual fuck, Emerson?" – Gray Stone to his new partner, on any given day

He carried her over the threshold, with Emerson bouncing slightly over his shoulder. When she squirmed, he gave her a light tap on that phenomenal ass of hers.

Emerson stiffened. "Gray! You did *not* just spank me!"

Had he? Oh, right. He had, and he'd enjoyed the hell out of that too-brief tap.

She is driving me crazy.

His jaw was locked tight. He kicked the door closed. Marched for the bed. Dropped her on it, and that breezy skirt of hers flew up over her thighs. She looked sexy. Beautiful. *Delicate.* And she'd just taunted a serial killer. Even crooked her finger. She might as well have been wearing a neon sign that said, "Hey, come try to kill me!"

Since she'd been standing in the blue light cast from the pool, the woman *had* practically been glowing.

Sonofabitch.

His hands went to his hips as he glared down at her. "What the actual fuck, Emerson?" Gray snarled.

She tossed hair out of her eyes. "What the actual fuck, Gray? You can't just throw me over your shoulder and toss me onto the bed!"

His teeth snapped together. "What on earth possessed you...to say, 'Come and get me' to that prick?"

"I said it to you. Not him."

"Bullshit. And the finger-crooking bit?"

Her head tilted to the side. She played with a lock of hair. "Again, to you."

He surged forward until his legs hit the mattress. "Bullshit," he called a second time.

She stopped playing with the hair. "What's the problem, Gray? Isn't that what you wanted? For him to pick me?"

"No! I did not want you to taunt the killer!"

Her brows lowered. "You wanted him to come after me."

"I wanted his attention on me. Me." He slapped his chest. "I didn't want you waving yourself at him like a red flag!" Hell. Dammit. Hell. *Dammit.*

"Then why didn't you say something when I went out in my bright skirt and top? You were all dark and blending with the shadows, but I stuck out. I thought you *wanted* me to catch his attention. I thought that was the whole point of us parading out there."

He hadn't been parading. He'd been skulking. Gray kept glaring at her. "I didn't say anything because you looked—*look* pretty in the outfit. There was no sense in you changing."

She stared at him as if he had two heads.

"And *I* was going to blend with the dark—thus the dark clothes. But you were supposed to look normal. Touristy. Honeymoony. So your outfit was fine." He grabbed his phone. Dialed Malik.

She tried to sidle off the bed.

"Don't even think about it. We are not done." *Crooked her finger? Told the killer to come and get her?* His temples throbbed. Gray was surprised that smoke wasn't billowing from him.

"Someone is grumpy," she muttered. Then she brushed off her arms. Sand fell onto the bed. "Was the kiss in the sand really necessary?"

"Yes," he hissed.

"Yo," Malik said in his ear at the same time.

"We have a situation," Gray told him.

She brushed off more sand. Wrinkled her nose. "I probably need to shower," Emerson whispered.

He sucked in a breath and held onto his patience with all of his might. "Someone has their own video security system set up on the island. Tiny cameras. You have to know what you're looking for, but once you spot them..." He let the words trail off.

Emerson had just pulled her blouse a few inches away from her chest and was peering down her shirt.

Looking for sand.

Fuck.

"Emerson," he snapped.

She let the shirt fall back into place.

"How many cameras did you count?" Gray asked her.

A pause from her.

"Come on, Emerson, you count everything. How many did you see? I want to make sure I didn't miss any of them. After I pointed them out to you, I know you started keeping track."

"I don't count everything," she groused.

"Yeah, you do."

"Ahem." From Malik. "Should I call back?"

"No, you should use your tech skills—bring in any additional help you need—and let's figure out where the feeds are being transmitted." He put the phone on speaker.

"You're seriously telling me that the security guards at that place aren't aware that there are *extra* cameras watching guests?" Malik's voice had turned brisk.

"I'm seriously telling you that very thing. The cameras are tiny. No exaggeration. They are dark and they are attached to dark surfaces. If you don't know what you're looking for, you miss them. And the security guards I've met are all retired guys looking to chill and strolling around without any weapons and whistling to announce their approach long before they would ever surprise anyone. In other words, we are not dealing with the A Team here."

"How many cameras?" Malik pushed.

Gray stared at Emerson. She held up seven fingers. He nodded. He'd counted the same. "Seven. That we saw. Not like we could examine every inch of this place." But he rattled off the locations that they had checked.

"If the manager of the resort finds out about those cameras, he will insist on having them removed," Emerson warned.

Yeah. And a removal would mean that they couldn't track the signal but...

If we leave them up, the perp will have a chance to look for more prey.

"I want to attract his attention." Emerson swung her legs as they dangled over the edge of the bed. Sand dripped from her sandals.

"You *did* attract it," Gray snapped.

"Let's be sure of that." She thrust back her shoulders. "Malik can try to track down the signal for those cameras. See where they are transmitting. And I'll dramatically find one of the cameras when we are out hitting our list of must-do activities. I'll make sure and alert the security team with my grand discovery. That way, we'll stop our perp from watching anyone else *and* we'll make sure that he's extra angry with me."

Hell. That would catch the killer's eye. *Even more than it's already been caught.*

"That's why we're here, remember?" Emerson seemed to read his thoughts. "Besides, I have you to keep me safe. My protective, ever-so-attentive husband."

He nearly shattered the phone. "See what you can discover, Malik." After Emerson's "find" of the cameras, he'd get Rylan to covertly sneak in and get access to the equipment. Maybe the FBI techs would be able to learn more once they had the cameras in their possession. *Maybe the dumbass perp even left some prints for us to find.* In his experience, perps could screw up in the most basic of ways.

"On it." Malik ended the call after a short, terse exchange where Gray rattled off a few more orders. And then...

Gray tossed the phone onto the nightstand. Right next to the champagne that waited in the ice bucket. The bucket must have been helluva insulated because the ice had barely melted. He kept towering over Emerson because he knew a fight brewed between them. Her eyes practically shot fire at him.

He waved her on. Didn't crook his finger as she had done. *Waved. Her. On.* "Let me have it."

"How do you know I count things?"

That was her first shot? He sighed. "Emerson, sweetheart, sometimes, your mouth literally moves, and I can almost hear you saying the numbers."

The mouth in question dropped open in shock. "It does *not.*"

"Yeah, baby, it does so. You usually do it when you're super stressed. And even if you aren't silently mouthing the numbers, I can see your eyes ticking past objects as you count them." He shrugged. "I've seen you count steps when you enter a building. When you were in O'Sullivan's that night with the team, you counted to see how many tables were between you and the door."

"How do you *know* that?"

"Because I watched you. You know, when you were busy letting Rylan rub his arm all over yours."

She jumped off the bed. Bumped into him. "I did not!"

"Did not count the tables or did not let him rub his arm over yours? Because both things happened. I was there. Watching." Being a stalker. Doing his due diligence.

"You sound jealous," Emerson accused as she tipped back her head and glared at him.

"Probably because I am." Guilty as charged.

There was no fast, angry comeback from her. If anything, she appeared confused. When a bit too much time passed, she questioned, voice lower, "Why would you be jealous?"

"Because I don't want Rylan or any other jackass touching you." He'd thought that was pretty obvious. "Because you belong to me, Emerson."

Again, she sent him a look that suggested he had two heads. "Because I'm pretending to be your wife?"

Yes. Maybe. No. "Because you came harder for me last night than I'm sure you've ever come for anyone else." Savage truth.

"And that means...I belong to you?" Emerson shook her head. "I don't think so."

Fuck. Gray sucked in a breath. "I'm screwing this up."

"It seems that you are. Yes."

His hands clenched into fists at his sides.

"What else have I counted?" she asked, quiet.

"Windows when you're in a house. Pretty sure you counted the number of books on my shelves at home."

"I stopped because I got distracted." She wet her lips. "What other things have you noticed about me?"

Everything. He held that stalkerish retort back. Clearly, he'd made a mistake saying she belonged to him. He wanted to grab tightly to her, never let go, and she wanted...

To taunt a killer. "Wear a neon sign next time," he rasped.

"Excuse me? I never wear neon."

"No, you don't. You typically wear your heels because you like to be taller. You don't wear any jewelry at all—except for the rings I gave you. I suspect because your mother wears jewelry all the time, and you don't like anything that reminds you of her. You prefer casual settings to fancy events. You're shy, but you fight not to show it. You try to fit in with others and talk in crowds, but you would always choose to be in a one-on-one situation. You're on guard all the time with other people, you keep your feelings in desperate check, and you won't let your real self show... probably because you're afraid that you can't trust anyone to know the real you. The you that's kept prisoner beneath the careful surface you wear."

"That's a whole lot of profiling going on right there, Gray."

Yeah, it was. "I know a shit-ton about you. But I *never* expected you to just call out the killer and challenge him to come after you!"

"I thought that was what you wanted. You kissed me and pulled me down to the sand so we'd create a show if he was watching on the camera at the rental booth."

"Back the hell up," he barked.

She tried to take a step back, but the bed was right there.

Only he hadn't been talking about a literal step back.

"You think I kissed you on that beach to attract his attention?" Just so he understood.

Emerson nodded.

"No. *No*. I did that shit so I could hide the fact that I was telling you about the camera. *I* want him coming after me, not you."

"That's not possible. You know that with this killer, it's always a package deal."

And Emerson had just made them one very tempting package.

"What the hell am I supposed to do with you?" Gray spun away.

"Why didn't you tell me that I had disappointed you?"

Those words froze him. Gray shook his head because he must have misheard.

"I wondered why we didn't talk about what happened between us this morning. Or at all during the day. Don't worry, it's not like I'm going to pressure you for a repeat performance."

When He Defends

He spun around so fast that Gray was kinda surprised that he didn't give himself whiplash. "You can't be serious right now."

Those had better not be *tears* gleaming in her eyes.

She blinked, quickly, to try and bat them away.

Dammit, those *were* tears. His hands rose. He cupped her face. "There is nothing about you that could ever disappoint me. Not one single thing, do you understand me?"

"You don't have to lie—"

"Emerson, I have no tells when I lie. Unless I *want* to show someone a tell. Then I'll rub my nose or swipe a hand over my jaw. Toss out some shit to make people think they understand me." He used his fake tells in order to trick and manipulate others. "So you just have to take me at my word. I'm not lying. You were the best fuck of my life."

She...squeaked.

So freaking adorable.

Then she confessed, "You were the best of mine, too, though I didn't exactly have a lot to compare you against."

Yeah, just her two-minute wonder of an ex.

"You didn't mention what happened between us last night," she breathed.

"Because I was trying to be *tactful* and not say, 'Hey, Emerson, I want to fuck you up against the nearest wall at the earliest opportunity.'"

"Oh."

Uh, huh. *Oh.*

She licked her lips. "When we came in this room—the first time, you know, with Hannah—"

"Yeah, I know Hannah."

"You just dropped me on the bed. Then you backed away."

"The better not to fuck you because I was afraid I'd made you sore the night before. What with it being two years and all, and my dick being so big that I could feel you stretching around me with every inch that you took in that sweet, hot pussy."

Her eyes held his. "I was sore."

"I was trying to be a gentleman."

A pause. "I don't care about being sore."

His breath expelled. He kissed his control goodbye and told her, "And I am sick to death of being a gentleman."

Chapter Eighteen

"Touch my wife and I'll rip you apart. Does that sound good? Am I getting the possessive vibe down just right? Let me try again...No one fucking touches my wife. Better?" – Gray Stone, practicing for no reason in particular because he already has the possessive vibe down when it comes to Emerson Marlowe

HE GRABBED HER. THOSE BIG, WARM, STRONG HANDS curled around her waist, and he lifted her up. Their mouths crashed together. Open. Hot. Eager. She sank her fingers into his hair and loved the softness against her skin even as his powerful grip held her upright.

He was aroused. His heavy dick shoved against her.

She wanted him naked, and she wanted to see just how much of a non-gentleman he could be.

As they kissed, he lowered her back down on the bed. Followed her. Parted her legs and shoved up her skirt and pushed his hips against her, thrusting over and over. Her panties were in the way. His pants. Both needed to go. She didn't want some slow build up. She wanted to rip his clothes off him. Desire thundered through her blood.

Her hands grabbed for his black shirt. Not one of his fancy button-downs. A t-shirt. So very un-Gray-like. She twisted and heaved and tried to shove up that shirt. Hard when he was still kissing her.

Soft laughter came as his lips broke from hers. "I've got this," he assured her.

His t-shirt went flying. So did *her* blouse. Her bra. She sprawled beneath him on the bed as he levered up above her, and Gray reached out toward the nightstand with one hand.

What is he reaching for? Are there condoms in the nightstand? When in the world would he have stocked them there? Or was this one seriously well-prepared resort suite?

But when his hand came back, he wasn't holding a condom.

He had an ice cube in his fingers.

"Gray, what are you—" Emerson's question ended in a gasp because he'd just run the ice cube over one nipple.

"Cold," he said.

Yes, yes, it was freaking *cold*.

"Now hot," he growled, and his lips curled around the same nipple. He sucked and licked and his mouth was warm. No, *hot*, and the opposing sensations were wild and sent lust spiraling through her.

He treated the other nipple to the same sensual attention. Gray rubbed an ice cube over the tight peak, making Emerson gasp and shiver beneath him, right before that hot, hot mouth of his took possession of her. Sucking hard on her nipple. Making her push up against him even as her hips arched and a moan came from her lips.

Then he began to slide the ice cube—rapidly melting now—down her body. Over her stomach. Her belly button. Down, down to the top of her skirt.

Emerson realized she was holding her breath.

Would the ice cube melt completely before...?

He shifted his position, moving his legs from between hers. "You're sexy as fuck in the skirt, but it has to go." With one hand, he yanked away the skirt and the scrap of lace she'd been wearing as panties.

Her sandals were still on, and she should ditch them.

"Nope," Gray said, as if reading her mind. "They are almost as sexy as your heels. They can stay. Not in the way at all."

In the way...

Gray slid down. The ice slid down, heading straight for her core...straight for...

"All melted," Gray breathed. His breath blew against her clit. "Guess you'll just feel hot, sweetheart. Are you ready to be hot for me?"

Uh, she *was* hot for him. Done and done.

His mouth took her. Licked and sucked and kissed with no hesitation. Only with a primal sort of possession that had her bucking her hips against his mouth. His fingers joined his mouth, working her clit with a feverish intensity. His tongue knew exactly how to taste her. How to make her crave him, and she did, oh, she craved him so much.

Emerson knew she was going to come against his mouth. The orgasm built and built within her, and then, when his tongue thrust into her and his fingers stroked, stroked, *stroked* her clit, she cried out as she came on an endless surge against him.

He lapped her up all the more. Greedily. So possessively.

Then he left the bed. Even as her body still quivered, he left her.

Emerson blinked.

He'd stalked toward their bags. As she watched, Gray ditched the rest of his clothing. He pulled out a small packet from his luggage. He tore open the packet, rolled the condom onto his dick, and strode back to her.

She was still sprawled on the mattress, with her legs wide open. Uh, she should move, yes?

"On your knees, Emerson," Gray ordered.

She scrambled to her knees. The shoes were in the way, so she unstrapped them and kicked them aside.

"Ah, Emerson, I liked those. Gonna have to punish you for that."

Say again?

He climbed onto the bed. She hesitated beside him.

"On me, baby."

She jumped on him. His hands caught her. Positioned her with her knees on either side of his body. With her basically sitting right on his dick.

"Take me in," he said.

She pushed down hard and—

"No." His fierce grip stopped her. "Don't hurt yourself. Slow. Inch by inch."

"For someone who…um, said he wasn't going to be a gentleman…" Speech was hard. Way hard. She was too lost to feeling. The woman who—before—hadn't been able to shut off her thoughts now felt too much. "You sure are…being…" She stopped, mostly because Emerson just could not form more words. The head of his dick was in her. Her knees pressed into the bed. She rocked down on him, over and over again because she just liked that sensation.

When He Defends

He pushed up inside of her. Another inch. Two. "What am I being?"

Her mouth opened in a moan.

He pushed deeper. Gray's hold on her waist tightened. "Tell me what I'm being, Emerson."

She squirmed against him. She wanted *all* of him inside her. "Gray!"

"*Eyes on me, Emerson.*"

Her eyes flew open. He'd said something like that to her before. The words were familiar. Her gaze locked on his, and she didn't stare into a gentleman's eyes. His gaze blazed with a ferocious lust that seemed to scorch her.

"You want all of me?" he gritted.

Her inner muscles clamped hungrily around him. "Yes."

He yanked her down fully on his dick. Every single wonderful inch was inside of her. Her hands slammed onto his chest. Her fingers splayed as she gasped out his name.

"Ride me."

Her knees pressed into the mattress. She lifted up. His fierce grip brought her down. She rose up. He brought her down.

A moan choked from her. One of his hands slid to her clit.

"Up," Gray demanded. His fingers strummed her.

Emerson's body tightened. She pushed into his fingers, then went up.

Gray brought her surging back down. He did that move again and again, and each time she went *up*, his fingers strummed her clit.

Up.

Down.

She could not stand it.

"Up!"

Her knees pushed down on the mattress. Her body heaved up, until only the head of his cock was in her again, and then when those fingers of his raked over her clit, Emerson lost her control.

He didn't have to slam her down. She did that herself. She crashed onto him even as her climax exploded and sent waves and waves of pleasure pouring through her.

"You feel fucking fantastic. Yes, Emerson, yes, but...*eyes on me*. I need to see you. I need to see everything."

Her eyes opened. As the pleasure surged, her gaze collided with his.

His dick filled her. Her inner muscles trembled around him. And he tumbled her back. He rose onto the bed and sent her falling onto the mattress. He caught her legs, slid them over his shoulders, and Gray drove into her relentlessly. Over and over. Wild, deep thrusts that just made the pleasure she felt seem to last and echo through her body.

And for every single thrust, his eyes were on her. Hers were on him.

She saw the climax take him. The brutal satisfaction that flashed across his face as he drove into her one final time and let go.

Pleasure. Lust. So much need.

It was actually one heck of a pretend wedding night.

* * *

"Tell me about the night your father died."

Emerson had just been about to drift off to sleep. They'd showered together, which had been a whole new, fun, and amazing experience of its own, and she'd been

When He Defends

curled in the big bed with Gray. Sleep pulled at her because it was edging close to two a.m.

Emerson rolled to face Gray. They'd been spooning. She'd been enjoying that immensely, feeling oddly safe in his arms. Though maybe there wasn't anything odd about it. Maybe Gray made her feel safe.

Except...

She frowned at him. "You don't have the best after-sex talk."

"Sorry." He didn't sound sorry. "Character flaw." He shifted closer. "I'm curious."

A yawn came and went. One she tried valiantly to cover. "You're curious...now. About my dad."

He tucked a lock of hair behind her ear. His fingers lingered near her cheek. "When it comes to you, I want to know every detail."

Her head turned. Her lips brushed his palm. Were his words really so odd? Didn't she want to know everything about him? "I don't remember much."

"Tell me what you do remember."

Only one light remained on in the bedroom. A soft lamplight on the nightstand. Gray's side of the bed. He'd wanted to sleep on that side, probably so he'd be closer to the gun she'd seen him place in the drawer after their shower. "I remember thunder. A lot of thunder. It was raining that night."

"Your father was out walking in a storm?"

"Obviously, he wasn't thinking clearly." How many times had she heard her mother say words exactly like those? Emerson pressed her lips together. Then, "He just walked straight over the edge."

"How do you know? Did you see him?"

She blinked. "No, no, I was scared." This part, she

remembered. "Storms scared me when I was a kid. Especially the lightning. The thunder. My dad—he would usually come into my room. Sing to me." The memory made her ache. "But that had been before things started to happen." *Things.* "He saw things that weren't there. Got so paranoid. Thought someone was after him."

"Do you remember that happening? The paranoia? Him seeing things that others didn't? Or were you *told* those things happened?"

She stiffened. "What exactly are you suggesting?"

His hand stroked over her cheek. "Nothing." Soft. "I'm just asking."

No, he was not just asking. "Spit it out. Whatever you're thinking or suspecting, just say it." She tensed in the bed. Her heart drummed. *Say it.*

"Your mother is having an affair with Owen."

She nodded, moving her head against the pillow. "Yes."

"How long has it been going on?"

"As long as I can remember." Her mother and Owen had always been close. As a kid, she'd thought they were friends. When she'd grown older, she'd realized their relationship was a whole lot more complicated than just friendship.

"They've never gone public with the romance, though."

"No. My mother used to say it played better to be a grieving widow."

Silence.

"I know that sounds terrible. But she told me that she won her first election because everyone felt so sorry for her. She took my grandfather's senate seat when he retired. He had Parkinson's, my father had just died, and she used that opportunity to seize the goals she wanted. When she was elected, she swore that she would fulfill my grandfather's legacy. Only my mother has surpassed him over the years. Accomplished so much more. Gotten so much more power than he ever imagined."

Gray's hand slowly slid away from her cheek. "Your grandfather was at the house when your father died."

"Both of my grandparents were there. When I was scared..." This she did remember. "I finally found them. I searched the rooms upstairs for my mother and father, but they weren't there. I pounded on the doors downstairs until my grandfather opened one." She could still recall the way his hands had shaken as he'd held her.

She'd been shaking, too, but his embrace and his rumbling, worried voice had soothed her.

"My grandfather loved me," Emerson heard herself say. "He kept me safe in the storm."

"And you didn't see your mother that night?"

"A door slammed when my grandparents were taking me back up to bed. I-I remember my mother ran in the house. She was soaked, dripping water onto the floor. She said that Ethan—my father—she said he was gone. I didn't understand what that meant. I thought he'd driven to town. My grandmother started to cry, and I kept wondering why you would cry when someone just went away for a few hours." Only it hadn't been for a few hours. It had been forever.

"When did the police come?"

"Later that night. My grandparents had put me to bed by then, so I didn't really see the cops much. Didn't understand what was happening. Not until the next day. The storm had ended. When I looked out my window, I saw uniformed officers searching near the cliff."

"The storm would have washed away all evidence. Especially if it was a powerful storm. Sounds like it was.

Not like you're gonna have footprints or signs of a struggle left to see after that. And any bruising or broken bones on your father would have just been attributed to the fall."

Her heart seemed to squeeze in her chest. "Evidence? It wasn't a...crime scene, Gray." Such halting words.

"Emerson. Emerson, Emerson." Not mocking. Tender. Caring.

Since when did Gray care? They'd had sex, but it had *just* been sex. Not like emotions were involved. Not like he loved her.

"Emerson," he said her name once again. Still tenderly. "Why did you seek me out?"

"The lamp light is too bright," she heard herself say. "Turn it out?"

Without hesitation, he did.

The darkness closed around her, and Emerson could breathe again.

"Why did you seek me out?" Even softer. He wasn't touching her now, but she could feel him. His warmth, reaching out so temptingly toward her. "Why did you want to work with me so badly?" Gray asked her.

She'd told him this before. She blinked quickly. Tears wanted to fill her eyes. "You know killers."

"So do you."

Her lower lip trembled. "You know them better than anyone I've ever seen. You can hunt them, wherever they are." *Whoever they are.* "You don't stop. Nothing intimidates you."

"Nothing," he agreed. "No one."

Yes, yes, that was what she needed, that was what—

"I'll figure out who killed your dad, baby."

Thank you. She couldn't stop the tear drop. It rolled

from her eye. Fell into her hairline. She could feel the slow trek of the tear on its path. Such a slow path.

Like the path she'd taken to find justice for her father. Because the cops had never suspected anything but suicide. Her mother had told the world her father was schizophrenic. That he'd just walked right off the edge of that cliff.

No one had investigated. No one had helped.

But Emerson...

Gray knows killers.

"Any other secrets you want to tell me?" Gray asked her, voice very careful. "Anything else you want to say?"

Gray was going to help her. He'd understood what she'd wanted. Maybe he'd known the truth from the beginning. "No." A lie that came with a hard effort. Because what she wanted to say, another secret that she held so very, very tightly...

I love you, Gray.

She rolled away from him. Curled on the other side of the bed. Her eyes had adjusted to the dark. She could see the two windows. The faint starlight and moonlight that spilled inside. It let her see the outlines of the framed pictures on the walls. The pictures were of different shots on the island. She'd noted them earlier. Now, though, as she lay with her shoulders hunched, Emerson automatically began to count those outlined frames. *One, two, three, four—*

The mattress dipped. The covers rustled. Gray's warm body pressed to her own. His arm came around her, curled over her side, and his fingers brushed against her stomach. He pressed a kiss to the back of her head.

"One day you'll realize," a low rumble, "that you can tell me anything. I'm the one person you'll never have to lie to in this world. Because I can handle any truth you give to me."

The tension slid from her body. Eventually, she slept, safe in Gray's arms.

* * *

GRAY STONE HAD TO DIE. The FBI agent was an interfering pain in the ass. The jerk thought he was untouchable. That he could do anything he wanted. Take what he wanted.

He was pretending that Emerson was his. Touching her. Sharing a room with her. Probably fucking her.

The big, bad Man of Stone. But Gray wasn't invulnerable. He could be hurt. He had weaknesses.

The bastard was clueless. Gray had no idea that *this* would be his last case. That *this* would be the end of the line for him.

Gray had made a serious mistake by going to the isolated island off the Georgia coast. He didn't have his precious Marine friends as backup. They weren't guarding his six. No Semper Fi heroes to rush to the rescue.

For the FBI agent, there would be no rescue this time because...

Gray Stone had to die.

Chapter Nineteen

"I knew Gray could help me figure out the truth about my father's death. I've wanted the truth since I was seven years old. I was never particularly good at believing what I was told. Unlike the PIs and the cops, Gray won't be scared to investigate. I'm pretty sure nothing in this world scares him, and that is really, really hot."
– Emerson Marlowe

"OVER HERE, DARLING!" GRAY CALLED. HE MADE SURE to lift up his phone and film Emerson. Color him impressed because she was doing a pretty damn good job of balancing on the paddle-board. She also wore the sexiest bikini he'd ever seen in his life. One that drove him crazy with lust and had him glaring at any asshole who glanced her way a bit too long. *My wife, bastards. Move the hell along before I rip out your eyes.*

He held the phone with steady fingers, but the camera wasn't actually directed at Emerson. Instead, he'd hit the button on the screen so that the camera showed his own image—or rather, the images of everyone behind him. He surveyed the crowd near the paddleboard rental booth. Tried to see exactly who was lurking around. He'd already collected images of all the staff members who worked at the rental booth. Pretty soon, Emerson would be making her "dramatic" discovery of the hidden camera perched at the booth.

He'd be sure to get that discovery on video, too. He wanted to see the reactions of the employees.

He and Emerson had started the day with sunrise yoga. Fun fact, Emerson was exceedingly flexible.

Now they were on to the second agenda item of the day —paddleboarding. They were following the same agenda that River had shared online during her honeymoon trip.

He cut his stare away from the phone and back to Emerson just as she took a spectacular fall into the water. She slid right off the side of her board, splashed, and her laughter rang into the air.

He loved her laughter. Gray ran toward the shore, like any good, worried husband would do. He also still clutched his phone. The better to film all his suspects.

Emerson didn't remount the paddleboard. Instead, she grabbed it and began heading to shore. He waded out. Took the board from her. Kissed her.

It almost feels real. Almost felt like he was truly kissing his *wife*.

As they approached the shore together, he watched the water roll off her skin. Watched the bikini bottom cling to her phenomenal ass. Glared when the too-eager twenty-something attendant at the booth—*Theo, his name is Theo Spire*—bounded forward.

"It's easy to take a fall," Theo assured her. "Happens to everyone."

She smiled at him. "I just need a little break." She waved toward Gray. "Wanted to say hi to the hubby."

He lifted a brow.

"Hi, hubby," Emerson murmured.

Theo handed Emerson a towel. "We have bottled water at the booth," he told her. "Come this way..." He whirled.

Emerson followed, slowly, seemingly letting her gaze sweep over the beach and the three rental booths as a smile played at the edges of her full lips. But then, once she'd gotten the offered water bottle and was right next to Theo's booth, Emerson frowned. "What's that?" Her voice rose. She lifted a hand to shield her eyes and pointed with the water bottle. "Is that a video camera up there?"

Theo didn't even look in the direction she indicated. "There are no cameras on the beach area," Theo informed her as he bent behind the booth's desk. "But for the safety of our guests, there are security cameras installed in various locations at the actual resort."

"*That's* a camera." Emerson was adamant. "It's like one of those spy cameras you see in the movies. Super tiny."

Theo glanced over his shoulder. Finally peered at the top of the booth. "Sorry, ma'am, I don't see anything."

"*It's right there.*" Her voice had grown louder. And it was attracting attention. "OhmyGod, it's just like that little camera that was in that kid's dressing room that time at the mall. Honey, honey, you remember, don't you?" She spun to Gray. "It's so small. It's that little black square on the edge of the sloping roof. You see it, don't you?"

"Yeah, I see it, baby. Right there. Watching everyone who comes up." His gaze cut to Theo. "I mean, if you're recording for security, it's no big deal, man. You don't have to lie about it."

Theo crept out of the booth. A radio was attached to his waist. "But there isn't supposed to be a camera out here." He rose onto his toes and peered up at the small device. "That's not one of ours," he muttered.

No, it wasn't.

Theo yanked out his radio. "Gonna need security." A bark had entered his voice and suddenly, his thin body was tense. "*Now*."

* * *

"Are you absolutely certain of that fact?" Hannah asked as she held a phone gripped tightly to her right ear.

Gray and Emerson approached her desk with slow steps. Emerson had changed into regular clothes—another flowing skirt and a gauzy top—and Gray made certain he stayed at her side like the devoted husband he was.

Hannah's gaze rose and crashed into them as she spoke into her phone. "How do you know?"

Gray and Emerson were about two feet from her desk.

"I appreciate the information," Hannah assured the caller. "Thank you." She placed the phone back on its cradle. A bright smile spread across her face. "Mr. and Mrs. Anderson. I hope you are enjoying your honeymoon time on our lovely island."

"We're here about the cameras," Gray informed her grimly even as he watched closely for her response.

If anything, her smile grew bigger. "I have learned about the situation at the paddleboard rental booth. I can assure you that the unauthorized camera there has been removed."

Her eyelashes didn't so much as flicker. "I am grateful to you for bringing the device to our attention."

"Did you find more?" Emerson asked her. Just cutting right to the chase. "Because I heard some other guests talking about one being found near the dock."

"We have located a few more devices. It is nothing for you to be concerned about."

"Nothing for us to be concerned about?" Gray put his hands on her desk. "Lady, you are saying some random person put cameras all over the resort and was filming guests—filming us? Filming *my wife?* Hell, yes, I'm concerned." Damn but he truly loved the *my wife* bit. Felt natural to say. Maybe too natural.

Her smile finally faltered. Hannah swallowed. "Our security team is checking the resort fully. Every unauthorized device is being removed."

"How do you know that these *devices* aren't in the suites?" Emerson's hand pressed to her heart. "Oh, darling, what if someone was watching...?"

"I'll kill the sonofabitch."

"*Sir.*" Hannah sucked in a sharp breath. "There is no need for that sort of talk. The facility is secure, but out of an abundance of caution, guest rooms will be checked." A faint click as Hannah cleared her throat. "However, we have no reason to believe cameras are *inside.* The ones that we've located were all in public areas, easily accessed. All of our guest rooms are locked. Keys are *only* given to individuals who show photo IDs at check-in." The smile came again. It did not reach her eyes. "As I said before, I am grateful to you both for bringing this matter to our attention."

"It was my wife," Gray said. "She always notices the little things." His right hand lifted from the desk and moved to rest at the small of Emerson's back. *My wife.* He'd dropped the term again. It just rolled right off the tongue.

"Please allow me to thank you on behalf of the resort." Hannah tapped on the keyboard near her. "I see that you have a massage scheduled to start soon, Mrs. Anderson. A massage and then you're booked for a horseback riding session." Her lips pursed. "Know what? I will comp that massage for you. A sign of appreciation."

"That's awfully kind," Emerson murmured.

"We aim to please."

Yeah, about that... "We'd originally wanted a couple's massage," Gray said. Because that was what River had done with her husband. "With Angel, because we've heard exceptional things where Angel is concerned." River had raved about "touching heaven" with Angel as her masseuse. Gray didn't know who had been the second massage therapist in the session with River and her husband. He hoped to discover that info, stat.

"Sorry. That's just not possible." Hannah was firm. "Angel is our most popular masseuse, and his schedule often books weeks in advance."

Right. That had been why they couldn't get the couple's massage at the last minute. The longer, couple's massage hadn't been available, so they'd had to opt for the shorter, single "invigorating" massage. But, still, Emerson would have the chance to grill the masseuse who had been with River.

"But if there is any other way I can assist...?" Hannah stared at them with raised brows.

"When do we sign the honeymoon registry?" Emerson asked without missing a beat. "I've been wanting to sign, but no one has told me when we can add our names."

When He Defends

Hannah took a half-step back. "I'll be arranging the signing for you very soon. It's a special event. One for those who have promised to love each other forever." She cleared her throat. "As you can imagine, the, ah, discovery of those devices has caused a bit of a stir. Normal plans have altered." A brisk nod. "But you are a priority for me, I assure you." Her gaze darted to Gray, then back to Emerson. "You are both a top priority."

"Thank you." Emerson sent her a sunny smile.

"I'm afraid that I have to excuse myself for a few moments," Hannah added. "There is a group who will be checking in soon for a large family reunion, and I need to make certain that their bags are delivered to their connecting rooms as quickly as possible."

"Right," Gray drawled. "You have to keep all the guests happy."

She'd begun to turn away, but at his words, Hannah stopped. Her head angled toward him. "I began working here when I was eighteen years old. I'm twenty-eight now. I started by working as a waitress in the main restaurant. I learned this resort, inside and out. It is my home. The staff members who work here are my family. I love this place with all of my heart. Giving the guests what they need is always the most important item on my agenda. I assure you that I will do everything in my power to make certain that you and your partner have an unforgettable experience here."

Emerson curled her fingers around Gray's arm. "Thank you so much, Hannah." Warmth filled Emerson's voice. "I'd better get to that spa appointment. Don't want to have Angel waiting."

Hannah bustled away, heading straight for the luggage

desk. Justin hurried from behind the desk and met her midway. They leaned together, talking quickly.

"I think we have a problem," Emerson whispered to Gray.

Gray brought his head close to her, his mouth skimming over her cheek in what looked like a kiss, but he murmured in her ear, "She just called you my partner." Partner, not wife. He'd noticed that slip, too.

Could have been just semantics. Could have been just a way of saying a husband and wife *were* partners but...Gray's gut said no. His gut said she knew they were working undercover.

"We need to talk," Emerson breathed back to him.

One hundred percent, he agreed. Not there, in the middle of the lobby, with all eyes on them. They needed some place private. Secure. Luckily, he knew just the spot. "Angel's waiting," Gray reminded her.

Another person to interrogate. Another suspect. Everywhere they turned, there was another potential suspect. *Right now, Hannah is setting off every alarm bell in my head.* How in the hell had she learned that he and Emerson were partners?

At that moment, Agnes and Trinity appeared. They were holding tennis rackets. Laughing. Their gazes swept right past Emerson and Gray.

And Rylan came strolling into the lobby, hauling a golf bag with him. His sunglasses hung from the top of his open Polo.

Their backup was casing the resort. Their team was there. They were safe.

So why was tension growing heavily at the base of Gray's neck?

When He Defends

Because Hannah knows we aren't married. Someone told her the truth about us.

Someone betrayed us.

And Gray didn't fucking tolerate betrayal.

Chapter Twenty

"You think I'm gonna let anyone else put their hands on my wife? Hell, no. Those fingers will be broken long before they touch her. Count on it."
– Gray Stone

Soft, tranquil music filled the private room at the resort's spa. Water gurgled from a miniature fountain in the right corner of the room even as soft candlelight flickered nearby. *One, two, three, four...Four candles.*

Emerson, stop counting!

The massage table waited with its soft covers pulled down.

"Just undress to your level of comfort," Angel instructed her. "You can get on the table, and when you are ready, just call out to me."

She stood by the massage table, shifting slightly from foot to foot. "I had a friend who recommended your services."

Angel quirked a brow.

"River," Emerson offered the name in what she hoped was a casual tone. "She told me that you were phenomenal."

Angel frowned. "I don't recall a session with someone named River." Angel's smile came quickly, stretching across his face, flashing his dimples, and making his eyes twinkle. "But I have a whole lot of clients. Sometimes, people will come to see me each day of their stay. I tend to be pretty popular."

Yep. She could imagine that he was.

Angel looked like a Greek god. Tall, muscular, with features that could only be described as drop-dead gorgeous. If perfection had a form, it would be Angel's.

"Are there any particular areas of concern you have?" Angel inquired politely in his deep and warm voice. "Any areas of your body that you think I should focus upon?"

"Ah..." Emerson swallowed. "You know, feet. Feet work. My feet are tired. I do lots of walking in heels."

"Right. The feet. I'll be sure to give them attention." That perfect smile flashed once more. "Again, you undress to your level of comfort, and I'll be right back inside when you are ready for me." He headed for the door.

Before he could reach the door, it swung open. Gray stood there. A glaring Gray.

"Sir," Angel began as his body tensed. "This is a private session, and you can't—"

"That's *my* wife. I can. Trust me, *I can.*" His stare swept over Angel. Then, "Nope. Hell, no. This is not happening."

"Excuse me?" Angel backed up a step.

"You're not putting your hands on my wife. She's not undressing in front of you." Anger seethed in Gray's voice. "You're not rubbing her down with oil and giving her the fucking 'heavenly treatment' with Angel that I just heard about in the lobby. Screw that. She's skipping massage time with you. *I've* got her."

"Gray..." Emerson began.

His gaze collided with hers. "No." Flat. "Not happening. I'll pay for the time, but Angel can just take his ass on break."

"Well, someone is grumpy," Angel chimed.

"You do not want to go there," Gray warned him.

Angel peered back at Emerson. "What do *you* want?"

She hadn't exactly wanted to strip down and get rubbed up by a murder suspect. She and Gray had planned for this interruption. They'd planned for the whole scene. The jealous, overwrought husband persona was fake.

"She wants *me*," Gray snapped.

Angel waited.

Emerson let a soft sigh slip from her lips. "My husband is incredibly jealous. We're newlyweds." She wiggled her fingers. Made the big diamond flash. "It's fine, Angel. My feet feel better already."

Angel held his ground. "It's a massage, sir. And I am a professional, always."

"I'll give you two hundred bucks if you give us the room and you get your ass out right now."

Angel took the cash and got his ass out right then and there. The door closed behind him. But Gray reached over and flipped the lock to make the room extra secure.

The music kept playing. The water gurgled in the fountain.

"Checked his date book and his computer files," Gray told her.

Yes, that had been his job. While she distracted Angel, Gray had been doing a search.

"He did have an appointment with River."

When He Defends

They'd known that, thanks to River's social media posts about the "Divine Angel" session.

"But I don't think he ever saw Kim. The spa records are extremely thorough. I searched the database via his system, but Kim wasn't listed as a client at the spa. Neither was our first suspected vic, Wendy Prichard."

"He told me that he didn't remember River." Could have been a lie, of course. "And there is a chance that the records were altered."

"Yeah, but River's appointment was still listed in the system. Why leave her but take out Kim and Wendy?"

Good question.

Emerson exhaled. "Your timing was perfect."

"Tell me about it." His teeth snapped together.

"We were at the disrobing portion of the event."

"That was never supposed to happen." Real jealousy seemed to vibrate in his voice.

Emerson frowned. "Gray, it's a massage. Those happen every day, and they are one hundred percent normal, non-sexual events."

He began stalking toward her.

"I get that you're playing the jealous husband—the way-over-the-top, jealous husband—and Angel is now talking about you with the other staff members just like we planned. Everyone will think you are crazy when it comes to me."

He stopped in front of her. "I am crazy when it comes to you."

She swallowed. "That's the act."

"You've got to be a bit disheveled when we leave. I asked for the room and, with us in here alone, Angel and anyone else close by will think I wanted a place to fuck my new bride."

Her eyes widened. Fucking at the spa had *not* been on the agenda. "I...don't believe people will think that's what we're doing. Having sex, I mean."

"I'm fucking jealous." His hands curled around her waist. He lifted her up on the table. Her skirt fluttered around her legs. Yes, she had on another billowing skirt. What else did you bring to an island paradise? She wore a skirt, while Gray wore khakis and an unbuttoned, white dress shirt. His semi-casual look.

"Don't want some male-model-slash-bodybuilder rubbing his hands all over you." He actually *sounded* jealous. But they didn't have that kind of relationship. Did they?

His hands moved from her waist. Slid under her skirt. Pushed the gauzy material up until he hooked his fingers around her panties.

"*Gray.*" Her hands flew down. She slapped them on top of his. Her breath choked out. "There's *looking* disheveled and actually..." Her voice trailed away.

"Fucking?" Gray finished for her.

She nodded. Yes, yes, there was a difference between the two things.

"Don't worry. We won't fuck. But I am damn jealous." His words were gritted, and she realized...

Wow. "You aren't acting?"

A negative shake of his head. "No one else's hands get put on you, Emerson."

"Gray, I seriously don't think he was interested in me. Like at all."

"*No one*, Emerson. Because I am homicidal where you are concerned." A long exhale. "Yeah, I know that makes me seem deranged as hell. I'll work on it." Another hard exhale. "I'll work on it." He let her go. Moved back. "We should talk about the case. That's, ah, why I got us the room. So we could talk privately."

Her body *yearned* for him. "I think I'm homicidal where you're concerned." Didn't one bit of brutal honesty deserve another? "I don't want any other woman touching you. I get that we're supposed to be pretending, but I don't really care. With you, everything feels real." Done. "I'd be jealous if another woman touched your body."

He'd been sawing a hand over his jaw, but at her words, he stopped. The hand fell back to his side.

"I'd be jealous," Emerson repeated. Maybe lines were blurring. Maybe it had been a mistake to be partners and lovers at the same time or maybe...maybe it had been the best choice she'd ever made in her life. "I trust you, Gray. I want you. I trust you and..." *No, do not say it. Do not go there.*

A furrow appeared between his brows. "And...what?"

She wet her lips. There were some things that, once said, could not be taken back. It was time to focus before she went too far. "You were right. We need to talk about the case. You've just given us the perfect private spot."

"Um."

"It's partners."

He didn't change expression.

"You think that, too, don't you? We're not looking for just one killer. It's two. *Partners*. A team." Her words came faster. His gaze seemed so heated as it pinned her.

Her attention darted to the candles. The flames sputtered and flickered. "It's so hard to kill two people at one time. I mean, with the first couple—Kris and Wendy Prichard—it could have been done, of course, because it was their brakes that were sabotaged. Not like the perp had to *physically* overpower them. But with the others..." She looked away from the candles and found Gray eyeing her with predatory focus. "With the others, it was about being physically overpowered. I don't think one lone perp could do that. Especially with Zac and River. They were running. Zac was attacked, taken down, but if it was just by one attacker with a knife, then River might have been able to flee and get to safety. She didn't escape, though. They were both stabbed to death. When I read the case files, Zac's injuries were much deeper, harder, than River's." He'd been killed faster. "I think his killer was stronger. As for the person stabbing River—there were hesitation marks on her. As if the perp was uncertain. It took a lot more slices to kill River. I believe it's because there were two killers."

He didn't speak.

"Partners," Emerson repeated.

"Yes." Gray nodded. "I suspect the same thing."

Of course, he did. "You could have said something sooner."

"I wanted you to reach your own conclusions. I could have been wrong." He reached out. Picked up a bottle of massage oil.

"Are you often wrong?" Emerson asked.

He brought the massage oil toward the table. Toward her. "Occasionally," Gray confessed. "When I am wrong, it is a colossal screw up." He stopped in front of her.

She should probably hop off the table.

"Hannah knows that we're partners. Someone tipped her off," Emerson said.

He pushed up her skirt. One inch. Two.

"Who do we think t-told her the truth?" A little stutter because his fingers had skimmed the sensitive inside of her thighs.

"Has to be someone who knows that we're faking our marriage."

Yes, and that left their own FBI team. The team that was supposed to be watching their back. "The other agents," she murmured.

His hands moved away.

She could take a deep breath again.

"Yes." Flat. Cold. Gray opened the massage oil bottle. Poured a bit of oil into his palm.

"Uh, Gray?"

"Your mother knew we were going undercover."

She jerked.

"So did Owen Porter, her ever so loyal lover and guard."

He put the massage bottle down. Rubbed his palms together. Got them slick with the oil.

He had really big hands to go along with the rest of him.

"Owen wouldn't tip off anyone about who we are. I mean, why would he?"

"I notice that you said *Owen* wouldn't, but you didn't deny that your mother might commit such an act." His hands returned to her thighs.

She gave a little gasp because that must have been *warm* massage oil in the bottle. "My m-mother isn't happy with our partnership." Understatement.

"And if she isn't happy, she might get her guard dog to do her dirty work for her." His hands began to rub slow circles on her inner thighs.

Ohmygosh, that feels good.

He'd started those circles about two inches above her knees. But ever so carefully, he was inching up. Staying focused on the *inside* of her thighs.

"Then, of course, there is Nathaniel," Gray rumbled.

Her eyes had started to sag closed. "Who?"

He laughed softly. His thumbs pressed deeper into her inner thighs.

She moaned. *How can this feel so good?* Her hands flew behind her so she could balance on the table.

"Nathaniel Hadaway," Gray elaborated as his fingers kept working. "The idiot ex. He knew about the case, courtesy, no doubt, of your mother. He'd want you to fail here. Both so that he could make you look bad and thus hopefully get your job *and* so that he'd please the senator." His thumbs pressed ever deeper, and then his big hands slid up another inch. Up and up, smoothing carefully and rubbing, gliding over her skin thanks to the massage oil.

They should stop. They had a case to work but...

We are supposed to be playing the part of a couple that just can't keep their hands off each other. Gray already set the stage as the possessive and jealous lover.

But he'd confessed to truly being jealous. He'd said the feeling was real.

All of her feelings for him were real.

"Eyes on me, Emerson."

Her lashes lifted.

She found him staring at her with savage hunger. Burning lust. And... "Gray?"

His thumbs pushed into her thighs. Hit a spot that had been tight on her right thigh and sent a twisting blast of *almost* pain and ever-so-much pleasure pulsing through her.

"You can't trust anyone but me," he told her.

She nodded. She wanted those fingers of his to keep going. *Up, up, please.*

"I trust you," he added, voice low and thick and rasping with desire. "I'd trust you to have my six any day of the week."

"That's the..." She had to wet her lips. Suck in a deep

gasp of air. "That's one of the nicest things you've ever said to me."

His massaging hands rose higher, pushing up her skirt even more. If she'd looked down, she knew she would have seen her panties because the skirt was raised that high. But she didn't look down. Her eyes stayed on his.

"I'm not nice." One hand slid under the crotch of her panties. Slid between her folds. Over her clit. Rubbing. Rubbing...

She rocked against his hand.

He dipped a finger into her. First one. Then another.

His left hand kept massaging her. Kept rubbing her inner thigh.

"Gray."

"There's nothing nice about me." He stretched her with his fingers. His thumb pushed against her clit. "There's nothing *nice* about the way I hunt." He pulled his hand away from her sex.

No!

"There's nothing nice about the killers I track."

He dropped to his knees by the massage table. He caught her panties. Ripped them.

The ripping sound seemed overly loud.

He tossed the scrap of her panties and pushed her legs apart more. His fingers went right back to rubbing her thighs, but at this point, his hands were positioned very, very high up. And when his hands moved the slightest bit upward even more, he was almost touching her core. *Almost.*

"There's nothing *nice* about the way I feel for you. It's dark and it's savage, and I want to take and take when I'm with you." His breath blew against her clit. "And there's nothing *nice* about what I will do to *anyone* who ever hurts you." Then his mouth was on her. Licking and kissing. His tongue thrust against her. Then *into* her even as his hands kept stroking and rubbing along her inner thighs. Except those big fingers were so close to the center of her need, it felt like he was massaging her sex even as he licked her with his tongue.

His hands were relentless. The pleasure overwhelming, and she couldn't stop the orgasm that barreled through her. She barely had time to suck in a breath, to grab for his shoulders and hold on before the climax shattered through her. A careening release that pulsed and rocked and left her utterly wiped out as it seemed to go on and on.

"Eyes on me, Emerson."

Her eyes opened.

"You're fucking delicious."

He just went down on me in a spa room.

"And you're mine. Never, ever forget that." One more caress with his fingers over her quivering thighs. "Something else to never forget?"

The pounding of her heartbeat echoed in her ears.

He rose. Leaned in close, his mouth almost touching hers. "I'm happy to give you a massage any time you want. Angel isn't the only one who knows how to take you to heaven."

"I'm...pretty sure the man gives a *professional* massage."

"And I'm pretty sure you're the most delicious thing I've ever tasted in my life." He pulled her skirt back down her thighs. "I don't share, Emerson."

They were playing a role. This wasn't real.

Or was it? "When the case ends," she began.

"We don't." Flat. "We don't end."

Her eyes widened. "Gray?"

"I don't want to end with you. I *want* you." He backed

away. Pocketed her torn panties. "And, for the record, we both think Hannah is guilty as sin, right?"

She nodded. "Absolutely. Guilty as sin." The woman had access to all of the victims, their locations—not just because of the honeymoon registry, but because she had the power to find their addresses, their credit cards, their *lives* all with a few clicks on her keyboard. Hannah could learn everything about the honeymooning guests at the resort.

"Good. Glad we're in agreement. Now let's go find the evidence to nail one of our killers...and then we'll drag her partner out of the dark and send them both to rot in prison." A pause. "Case closed."

Chapter Twenty-One

"What happens if there is a choice between saving myself or saving my partner? Dumb question. There is no choice. Emerson will always come first. Always." – Gray Stone

He had a colossal hard-on. His dick ached, he wanted to drive balls-deep into Emerson, but he had a killer—correction, a freaking *pair* of killers to hunt down—a traitor to root out, and, oh, yeah...

He was in love.

Emerson's panties were in Gray's pocket. He hadn't meant to take them as a souvenir. Not like they were a trophy. He wasn't one of the serials that he hunted. Truly, he wasn't. No matter what the gossip might claim. But after he'd accidentally ripped her panties, it hadn't been like she could put them back on, and he certainly hadn't been in the mood to leave her panties for that overly muscled jerk Angel to find.

Angel is on my suspect list, too. He'd already texted

Malik a list of individuals to investigate. Hannah, naturally, was at the top of the list. But then there was the bellhop, Justin. The friendly paddleboard guy, Theo. The freaking too attractive Angel. Everywhere he turned, a new suspect walked into his path.

He and Emerson were in agreement that they were after partners. Hannah set off every alarm bell he had, so he knew she was one of the potential killers. He'd bet her partner was a male, and that was why all of the other suspects he'd sent to Malik had been men. Hannah and her partner were probably sleeping together. So the next step was figuring out who seemed particularly interested in Hannah.

Back at the spa, Gray had intended to *play* the role of the jealous lover. Only when Gray had actually entered that small room and seen the other guy so close to Emerson, when he'd thought of Angel putting his hands on her...

Emerson belongs to me.

A savage thought, totally not rational given the situation, he got that. *A freaking massage.* But...

Maybe he wasn't a rational guy. Maybe he was too savage. Especially when his emotions were involved.

I love Emerson. He'd realized that fact, well, to be honest, he'd been dancing around the truth since Emerson had taken him down in the training room.

She'd knocked him off his feet, literally. Figuratively. Every single way imaginable. And the tangle of emotion that he felt for her just got stronger with every moment that passed.

Was he still trying to understand her?

Hell, yes.

Still trying to unwrap the many mysteries that made her into the person she was?

Again, hell, yes.

But he *was* figuring her out.

Emerson wasn't emotionally fragile as Nathaniel Hadaway had claimed. Quite the opposite. She was fierce. Determined.

She was loyal and strong and when he was with her, Gray could imagine a future for himself. One that wasn't just focused on monsters and killers. He could imagine a future with a little girl on his shoulders. A girl with her mother's unforgettable eyes.

He wanted it all. A marriage. A home. A family. *Emerson.*

If he worked hard enough, maybe he could convince her that dream was something she could want, too. He could prove himself to her.

After they stopped the current killers they were after, of course.

"When did you start suspecting Hannah?" Emerson asked. They were on their way to the stables. Horseback riding. The next item that had been posted on River's social media account during her honeymoon trip.

Gray glanced over his shoulder as they walked along the narrow trail. No one was close by. They could speak freely. Actually, when they'd left the spa room, no one had been around there, either. No sign of Angel.

Not even a person at the spa's check-in desk.

His senses were on high alert. He had a gun tucked in a holster on his ankle, one hidden beneath the khaki pants he wore. A gun on the right ankle. A knife strapped to the left.

"Gray?"

He stopped in the middle of the trail and angled his head toward her. "I thought that, in order to get the home addresses of the vics, we would be looking for a perp who had full access to the information on all the guests. With her position, I knew Hannah would have that access. The woman is really good at controlling her tells, I noticed that the first time we talked."

Emerson hummed. "I noticed that, too."

"She did a half-step retreat today," Gray remembered. Something that had immediately fired alarm bells in his head. "When you asked about signing the registry."

"She knew we weren't a real married couple. She didn't want us to sign."

He nodded, agreeing. He could have sworn that he heard some kind of...thunder in the distance. Weird, when the sky was perfectly clear. "It was like she was so physically against the idea of us being in the precious book that she couldn't handle it. She retreated. An absolute denial. A physical reaction."

"We don't have proof, Gray. We have suspicions, and we have—do you *hear* that?"

Yes, yes, he damn well did. "Emerson..." His head whipped to the left.

Horses raced straight toward him. Toward Emerson. A tight pack of horses galloped hard and fast. Horses that should have been secured in the stables but were running straight at them. Barreling with wild eyes and desperate hooves.

The horses were coming so quickly that if he and Emerson didn't haul ass, they'd be crushed beneath the stampede. In a flash, he imagined what those pounding hooves would do to Emerson's body.

Fuck, no. Without hesitation, he grabbed Emerson. He wrapped his body around hers even as he tried to hurtle them out of the way. They didn't make it. Or, he didn't. At the last moment, he shoved Emerson hard, pushing her off that path and thrusting her to safety.

He could feel the breath of the horses on his neck. Then Gray went down. A hoof slammed into his shoulder. Another rushed over the back of his thigh.

He tasted dirt in his mouth. He could hear the wild cries of the horses. The screeches.

And...

"Gray! Gray!" Emerson's screams. He could hear Emerson's screams.

* * *

No, no, no, no. Emerson watched in horror as the horses galloped away. They'd stirred up dirt and dust or who the hell knew what in their wake. They'd come from the stables, rushing furiously, and shouldn't attendants have been chasing them? Shouldn't someone be there?

"Gray!" He'd shoved her to safety. Damn the man. He should have gotten himself to safety. But one minute, he'd been covering her, shielding her, and then he'd been *throwing* her out of the way.

Only for him to go down beneath the hooves.

The thunder of the hoofbeats echoed in her ears. It pounded over and over, like thunder that just wouldn't stop.

"Dad, Dad, where are you?" A child's voice—her voice—echoing in her mind. Because there had been thunder that terrible night, too, so much thunder.

Emerson climbed to her feet. Her knees were bleeding, scratched, as she ran back to Gray. He was face down on the ground, with his right leg drawn up close to his body. His right arm was beneath him. His head turned toward where she'd been moments before.

His eyes are closed.

She reached out. Her first instinct was to touch him, to make sure he was okay.

How can he be okay? He was just caught in a stampede with thundering horses. Seven horses. Eight?

Was his spine injured? His neck? He couldn't be moved until he was stabilized. She had to call for help. Dammit, where were the other FBI agents? The others were their backup. They were—

A twig snapped.

Emerson leapt back to her feet and whirled toward the sound.

"Does it hurt?" Hannah asked as she walked from beneath a nearby tree.

"I-I'm not injured." The blood on her legs was nothing. "Gray is. We have to get Gray help!"

Hannah's arm lifted. She held a gun in her right hand. "He's not going to get help. He's already dead."

No, no, she'd seen his body moving. Hadn't she? Her fingers hadn't touched him, not yet, but Emerson was sure Gray was alive. There was just no other option for her.

"Come here, Emerson," Hannah ordered her.

She stayed exactly where she was. "Why are you holding a gun on me?"

"Don't play dumb." Hannah took another step forward. "I know what you are."

"My husband is hurt! We have to get help!"

"He's not your husband. Don't waste my time with more lies." Her left hand came up from behind her body. The right hand gripped the gun. The left held a syringe.

Emerson maintained her position between Gray's sprawled form and Hannah.

"Even before I got the phone call today," Hannah

continued, voice grim, "I knew. I met up with your buddy Rylan late last night. Guy probably thought he'd give me some drinks, my tongue would get loose, and I'd say something to help with the big investigation you seem to have going on here at *my* resort."

"Gray needs help," Emerson whispered.

"But Rylan never noticed when I slipped a few special drops in *his* drink. Suddenly, he couldn't stop talking to me. Telling me how important he was. Telling me that he was hunting a serial killer. That he was part of an undercover team."

Rylan.

"Then a helpful phone call came right when you approached my desk today. An anonymous, Good Samaritan who wanted to speak with someone in charge. Of course, I am the person in charge at the resort. Suddenly, there was a rasping voice telling me that I needed to know individuals at my resort were using fake identities. Maybe even fake credit cards. That I had to check you out. Investigate. Even gave me a full, physical description of you and your *partner*." Mocking laughter. "As if I didn't get suspicious when you magically found the cameras. I already know about your nosy night walk last night. Harris told me."

"Harris?"

"The night guard you encountered." Hannah surged forward.

Emerson held her ground. That woman was not getting near Gray.

"Harris saw you. He reported to me. Everyone reports to me. *I am the resort.*"

"Pretty sure the owner of the place might disagree."

"Hold out your fucking arm!"

Emerson kept her arms by her sides. "I'm guessing you

sent the horses on that stampede? Where are the attendants? Shouldn't someone have noticed that horses just galloped wildly through the area?"

"I snuck into the vet's area. Gave the horses a little something extra that set them off. Made sure the stables were deserted first. Easy to divert workers when you're the boss."

"Uh, those horses could be out hurting other guests..."

"Like I give a shit?"

Right.

"Hold out your fucking arm."

Emerson's gaze locked on the syringe. "Why? So you can make killing me easier?"

"I can shoot you in the knee cap. Take you down and make you *hurt*. Or I can give you a little shot. No pain. No blood. You'll be out before your body ever hits the ground. You can die beside your fake husband."

Emerson swallowed. "What's in the syringe?"

"Horse tranq. Enough to send you racing straight to hell."

"I don't think I'm going to hell." She wanted to look back at Gray. So badly. "I haven't killed anyone. You can't say the same."

"They deserved it!" Spittle flew from Hannah's mouth. "Men say they will love you forever. They say that you're the only one they want. The one they will spend eternity with—only they *lie*. They break your heart. They shatter it. They *fucking have sex with their massage clients!* And you're supposed to just move on? Act like it never happened? Love doesn't last. Not unless we *make* it last. I made sure those couples were together just like they vowed...until death."

Emerson nodded. "Someone broke your heart. Guessing that someone was Angel?"

"He's the devil!"

"Angel cheated, and, in response, you decided to go on a killing spree? Hate to be the one to point this out..." Where in the sweet hell was her backup? "But that's going overboard, don't you think?"

"Hold out your fucking arm!"

"Who's the partner for you in this little drama? Not Angel. You two are *clearly* on the outs. So who helped you with the killings?"

Hannah gave a quick start of surprise.

"After your breakup, you found a rebound guy, am I right? Someone who went along with your deadly new agenda?"

"Screw you, bitch," Hannah spat. "I'm shooting you in the kneecap and when you're bleeding on the ground, I'll drive the needle in your throat."

"You're not going to shoot me." Emerson spoke with utter certainty even as fear froze her heart. *Gray is okay. Gray is going to be fine.* "If you were going to shoot, you would have done it already. But me having bullet holes in my body isn't on the to-do list. You set this scene up with the horses because you thought it would look like an accident. You probably thought both Gray and I would get trampled. At the most, we'd both be dead. And if not dead, then injured enough that you could sneak up on us and drive your tranq into our veins. Either way, we'd be dead by the time help arrived, and it would look like some tragic accident."

Hannah had a smug smile on her face.

"But Gray saved me." He'd sacrificed himself, for her. Gotten taken down beneath the pounding hooves, for her.

"If you shoot me now, that whole *accident* narrative vanishes. So you can't shoot me. All you can do is come at me with that needle, and if you do come at me, you'd better hope to hell that you can take me down, because as soon as I get my hands on you...you are done," Emerson swore.

That smug smile of Hannah's slipped.

"Something you should know," Emerson added. "I'm not nearly as *delicate* as I might look."

Gray needs help. He needs help now. There is no time to waste.

An animalistic growl tore from Emerson as she lunged for Hannah.

Hannah's eyes widened in horror. She gaped at Emerson.

"Emerson, *down!*" Gray roared.

He'd always told her that she couldn't follow orders for shit but...

Emerson dropped. Right there. She fell. Sank like a stone to the ground. Gunfire erupted. A hard blast. One bullet slammed into Hannah. It hit her high in the right shoulder. She dropped the gun and syringe and screamed as blood spattered. Then, when Hannah collapsed on the ground—

Justin.

The bellhop was there. He'd been rushing up behind Hannah. His wild eyes took in the scene. He lunged for Emerson with his hands outstretched. One of his hands clutched a wickedly sharp blade. A blade that he was slashing toward her.

"*Stop!*" Gray bellowed.

Justin didn't stop.

Gray fired again. The bullet slammed into Justin's chest. Justin's eyes flared wide with surprise, and then he swayed. His knees hit the ground first. Then he fell forward, smashing into the ground with a thudding impact even as the knife clattered from his hand.

Emerson scrambled up. She grabbed the discarded gun. Stomped the syringe into pieces. She kept her gaze on a writhing, cursing Hannah. "Gray?" Emerson called. "Tell me you're all right!"

"I'm all right."

Footsteps rushed toward them. Emerson tensed, but Trinity burst up the path.

"Emerson!" Trinity yelled. She had her own gun out. "Agnes and Rylan are having to control freaking *wild* horses!" She raced to the scene. Stopped. Gaped.

Gray had rolled onto his back. He still had his weapon gripped in his right hand.

"What happened?" Trinity demanded.

"Those wild horses..." Gray groaned. "Trampled over my ass."

"Jeez." Trinity dropped to her knees beside him. "I don't think you should be moving."

"Tell me about it," he muttered. "Emerson?"

Her breath shuddered in and out. Blood covered Justin's chest. She knew that shot might be killing him. *Too much blood. Acute bleeding. Could be myocardial damage, rupture, could be valve damage, could be—*She snapped to attention. "Trinity! I need you to guard Hannah!" Hannah was down, but her injury didn't appear life threatening. Emerson was pretty sure the bullet had gone in and straight out of Hannah's shoulder. There was blood loss, but nothing that would indicate substantial damage.

Trinity immediately appeared at Emerson's side. Emerson turned, and she went straight to Gray. *He* was her priority.

Her hands fluttered over him. "Don't move. Not anymore, you understand me? You could have spinal injuries. I need to get your head and neck stabilized. I need—"

"You followed orders."

Her gaze jumped to his.

"I knew you would," he said. "Because when it's life and death, you trust me."

"*You should stay still.* You shouldn't have fired. Shouldn't have moved at all! Gray, dammit, if you have a spinal injury, you could be hurting yourself more. Paralyzing yourself! You have to look after *yourself*—"

"Not when your life is on the line. *I look after you.* Don't care what risk I have to take, I'll always fight for you."

She wanted to crush her mouth to his. Wanted to hold him desperately. But...

He has to get stabilized. No more movements.

"I've had worse," Gray told her. "I'm gonna be *fine*."

"You'd better be," Emerson replied as she blinked away tears. "Because I love you."

His eyes widened.

"Love isn't real!" Hannah yelled. "It doesn't last. They swear they'll love you forever, but they don't. It's. Not. Real!"

Emerson did not look away from Gray. "Yes, it is." The way she felt for Gray was the most real thing in her life.

More footsteps. Rylan appeared. Followed immediately by guards wearing the resort's uniform.

"Thank goodness!" Hannah called out. "These people are crazy! Martin, Fletcher!" she rattled off the names of the guards—names clearly displayed on the badges near their hearts. "Take them into custody. Take their weapons away!"

Martin and Fletcher didn't move. Rylan rushed

forward, with his gun out. "They know we're FBI," he said flatly. "And *I* know you drugged me last night."

Gray sat up fully. Winced.

Emerson's fingers fluttered over his shoulders. "*Gray. Stay still!*"

"I'm okay. Do what you need to do."

What she needed to do was get him secured.

"Go, Emerson," he urged. "I'm not the one dying." Grim.

She looked over her shoulder.

Justin's body bucked. Shuddered.

"He doesn't have long," Gray rasped.

Her shoulders squared. "We need a transport out here!" Emerson's voice rang out even as she jumped toward Justin. She had to stop the blood flow. Assess the damage. "Need transport for our vics, and Rylan, you make sure Gray does *not* get off that ground, understand me? He's getting secured and his spine checked out, stat."

From the corner of her eye, she saw Gray begin to rise.

"If you love me," she snarled at him, "you will follow orders and keep that ass *down*."

Gray...kept that ass down.

Her head whipped toward him.

"Yes, ma'am," he told her.

Yes...as in...*he loved her?*

But she didn't get to dive deep into that revelation because Justin the bellhop—and serial killer—began to shudder and heave.

"Dammit!" Emerson cried out. Her fingers slid into the open wound on his chest.

Chapter Twenty-Two

"Believe me when I say...even wild horses wouldn't be able to drag me away from Emerson.
Been there, done that shit. One star. Do not recommend."
– Gray Stone

"I HAVE NOTHING TO SAY TO YOU," HANNAH MCINTYRE snarled. She sat at the interrogation table in the FBI's Atlanta office. Oh, yeah, he'd had her brought in, complete with ankle and wrist shackles and with an FBI escort in the form of a currently glowering Malik Jones. "I know my rights," Hannah huffed. "I want a lawyer! I want bail! I want *out of these damn things!*" She tried to lift her wrists, but they couldn't raise too high, not with the way the shackles connected to her ankles.

"Relax," Gray advised.

She did not, in fact, relax. Instead, Hannah emitted a guttural scream.

Right. Gray quirked a brow toward Emerson. "She's not relaxing," he noted.

"Nope," Emerson agreed. Her hand rose to tuck a lock of hair behind her ear.

Her fingers weren't covered in blood any longer. They had been, back on Sea Island when she'd literally had to shove those fingers into Justin McClintock's wounds in order to stop his blood flow and keep the bastard alive. Emerson had stayed with the wounded perp while he was airlifted and flown for treatment. She'd been in the ER with him. Been there when the guy finally opened his eyes.

Of course, Gray had been there, too. Justin had been damn grateful to be alive. Grateful people tended to be very, very chatty.

Gray settled more comfortably in the stiff chair as his attention shifted back to his prey. "I thought you might want to know that your latest boyfriend turned on you. Instantly." Mostly because the guy knew Emerson was the only reason he had survived. "Said everything was your idea. You were the mastermind. Justin was just following orders because he was in love with you. Wanted to make you happy." Sure, why not kill people to make your girlfriend happy? Like that crap was rational. "He's going to cooperate fully with our investigation."

Hannah wasn't screaming any longer. Good, his ears could use a break.

"You said you want a lawyer. Stellar idea. You're going to need one." Gray inclined his head toward her. "If you were my client, I'd advise you not to speak, and, hey, you know your rights...You totally have the right to remain silent. Anything you say can be held against you and all that. By this point, I'm sure you've heard this spiel a few times."

When He Defends

Rage swirled in Hannah's eyes.

"So you should probably just listen," Gray continued. He was highly conscious of Emerson standing near the one-way mirror that was positioned on the wall to the right.

Emerson. She said she loved me.

She had said that, hadn't she? He had been suffering a concussion at the time. One of the horse's hooves had clipped him on the side of the head at some point.

He'd gotten trampled in the back, luckily *away* from his spine. Gotten hit in the leg. Once on the shoulder, too. Plus, the head snap. Not his best of days, but, honestly, it could have been one hell of a lot worse. All things considered, he'd been really lucky. He'd had to fake being knocked out for a moment while Hannah made her confession and while he waited to catch her unaware so he could attack.

But there had been *no way* he would let the woman shove horse tranq into Emerson's veins. So he'd fired.

Emerson followed orders for once. She'd dropped. He'd gotten the shots off at Hannah and at Justin. The bad guys had been captured.

Now it was time to make sure neither one got out anytime soon.

"Listen to what?" Hannah snapped. "You ramble? You two make me sick! You think you love each other? You think you're going to walk away from this and live happily ever after?"

Sounded like a plan to Gray. "What do you think, Emerson? You in the mood for a happily ever after with me?" She wasn't wearing her wedding ring any longer. Maybe he could change that...

"I—" Emerson began.

"There *is* no happily ever after!" Spittle flew from Hannah's mouth. "It's a lie. No one gets that."

"Your father was a mechanic," Gray said. His fingers tapped on the edge of the narrow table. "Justin told me that your father trained you in his garage when you were a kid. That was how you knew how to sabotage the brake lines. You were the one who came up with the method of murder for Kris and Wendy Prichard."

Hannah's lashes flickered.

"And you were the one who had the idea of attacking Zac and River Turner while they were running. Zac was a big guy, so I'm thinking that Justin took him out." He slanted a glance toward a watchful Emerson.

"Makes sense to me," she murmured. "And Hannah went after River." Her gaze was on the killer. "Harder to stab someone than you realized, wasn't it? I don't think you were prepared for her to fight back. Or maybe you didn't like all the blood flying all over you."

Hannah licked her lips.

"Then there was the third couple. Anzo and Kim." Gray exhaled. "You really fucked up with them. The others—honestly, no one was even connecting them. You should have been more careful with your prey."

"They were *nobody!*" Hannah leaned forward. "A chef and a low-rent cop. There was nothing special about them! Why the hell should they get *five years* of a happy marriage when I couldn't even get a year with Angel? I never even got marriage! And Justin—he was just convenient. I never gave a damn about him. He was only in it for the sex, but man, he was so easy to manipulate." Her smile stretched nearly from ear to ear. "I had him wrapped around my finger."

Emerson took a step forward. "He was younger than you, more moldable, and willing to do anything to make you happy. Even if that anything included murder."

Hannah's head jerked toward her. "Your precious fake husband was ready to kill for you. He shot Justin in the *heart*. It's quite the feeling, isn't it? When you know you have someone so obsessed with you that they'd willingly kill for you in an instant."

"Gray was fighting to keep me alive. He wasn't killing innocent people because I had some twisted vendetta against the world. A vendetta that just started because I'd been dumped before."

Hannah's mouth dropped open.

"You're going to be in for a world of pain," Gray warned.

Her head swung back to him.

"The chef and the low-rent cop were very much *important*."

"No, they weren't. They had no family. They had a damn boring life, and they had—"

"They had safety," Gray corrected. "They had love. And while they may have possessed no biological relatives, they have a whole army who wants vengeance for them."

"What are you talking about?"

He'd gotten the confession that he needed. Hell, he'd gotten that back at the island. But Hannah had just chosen to overshare again, even when he'd reminded her that she should keep quiet. She had the right to do that, after all. To remain silent. But Hannah hadn't kept quiet.

And the interrogation was being recorded. A very obvious camera in the upper right corner of the room. Not like the tiny devices Hannah and Justin had used to find prey and watch them on the island.

Speaking of watching them... "What were all the cameras about? You had access to all of the victims' addresses. Why did you and Justin put up the cameras? Seems like an unnecessary risk."

Hannah lifted her chin and didn't answer. Oh, so *now* she got quiet? Fine with him. Gray pushed to his feet. His back ached, his thigh ached, and he still had a headache throbbing behind his temple.

It had been *two days* since they'd left Sea Island. Two days of case files and investigative reports and trying to figure out all the moving pieces. This meeting was the final nail in Hannah's coffin.

"I know why you did it." Emerson's voice was certain. "You told us already."

"I have *not*."

"Sure, you did. It was the first day we met. When you said that you could tell which couples had staying power. You specifically said you could *see* it when two people were meant to be. You watched the couples interacting. You saw which ones seemed to be the most connected. 'It's in the eyes.' That's what you told us before. You watched the couples because you were looking for your perfect targets. When you found them, you went to your computer, and you got their addresses. You waited for them to leave the resort, and you followed them home."

She didn't deny the words. In fact, Hannah hunched in on herself a bit.

Gray eyed her in disgust. "One of my agents discovered that Justin used a credit card in the same town where Zac and River Turner were murdered. Pretty sloppy." Gray grimaced. "But I guess it's just hard to find a good partner these days, isn't it?"

Or, it was hard for some people.

His gaze cut to Emerson.

He had the perfect partner, and there was no way he'd let her go. No. Way. Slowly, his stare returned to the perp.

"I want a lawyer." Hannah nodded. A tear leaked from her eye. "*Now.*"

Gray walked away from the table. Malik stood at attention near the door. He'd silently watched the entire scene unfold. "Of course." He raised a brow at Emerson. Was she ready to leave?

Emerson nodded. She advanced toward Gray.

"How did they have an army?" Hannah asked.

Gray looked back at her.

"The chef. The cop. What army did they possibly have?"

Gray smiled at her. "You ever hear of the Night Strikers Motorcycle Club?"

Hannah's eyes widened. "Wh-what do they have to do with anything?"

"Oh, you'll be finding out, and it will not be pretty."

* * *

Cassius "Cass" Striker glared through the one-way glass. Hannah McIntyre rose to her feet. She stumbled a bit, thanks to the ankle shackles, and the FBI agent with her, Malik Jones, put a steadying hand on her shoulder.

The door to the observation room opened, but Cass didn't take his gaze off his prey. Footsteps entered the room. The heavy tread of Gray's steps. The tap-tap-tap of Emerson's heels.

The door closed softly behind them.

Hannah had tears on her cheeks.

"I'm pretty sure that I told you I would handle Anzo's killer." Cass's hands fisted at his sides.

"Pretty sure I told you that I wasn't just going to stand there and let you kill someone," Gray retorted.

Cass finally turned his head away from the glass. He glared at Gray. "You got to shoot her accomplice in the chest."

"He was going after Emerson at the time. Not like I would *ever* let anyone hurt her."

Cass's gaze shifted to Emerson. "Why the hell did you save him? Heard you fucking had his veins in your fingers or some shit like that in order to stop the blood flow."

"That's not *exactly* what I did."

His eyes narrowed.

"But I saved him, yes." A nod from Emerson. "Justin McClintock is the reason we now know so much about the murders. He's cooperating fully, and he *will* be spending the rest of his life in a cell."

He'd wanted the bastard in the ground. Cass advanced on Emerson.

Surprise, surprise, Gray stepped into his path. "What the hell else did you expect her to do? Emerson isn't a killer."

Cass's hands moved fast. A blur as he signed, *I am. You are.* Signing was almost second nature to him, especially when he was with Gray. Sign language had come in damn handy as a way for him and Gray to communicate when they didn't want the people around them—often enemies—to know what the hell they were saying.

"She *isn't*." There were dark shadows under Gray's eyes. His cousin's skin was a bit paler than normal, and Cass thought about the story he'd gotten...how Gray had been *trampled* beneath horses. His cousin could have died on the case. A case that Cass had insisted Gray take.

Then what would I have done? Because he had the MC. Yes. But Gray...

Gray was more like a brother than a cousin. After Cass's mother had died, Gray had been the person there for him. Always, Gray was there. Whenever he needed anything. No matter the risk.

"Hannah and Justin will both go to jail for a very long time." Emerson edged closer. *Tap, tap, tap.* "With Justin's cooperation, we will be able to determine if there were any other victims. We will give all of the families the justice that they need."

"Justice. Right." He nodded. "That's what you're after." He slanted her a glance. "Meanwhile, I personally just like some good, old-fashioned revenge. You know, the eye-for-an-eye type of vengeance. You fuck with me, and I fucking put you in the ground. That type."

Gray shifted slightly, putting himself in a position where he shielded Emerson. As if Cass would ever hurt her. He knew how Gray felt about the woman. *He was willing to give up his life for her.*

"You wanted to know who killed Anzo and Kim. I got confessions for you. You know now." Gray nodded. "The rest...I can't control the rest."

No, you can't. I can. If they get locked away, I have reach behind bars. I know how to make problems vanish. So he really should just calm the hell down. This was a win. Except... "I'm pissed that you were hurt." That hadn't been the plan. "Thought you were always prepared for dangerous situations. You slipping?" Maybe Gray was slipping because he was too tied up in his partner.

"Didn't expect charging *horses* to come at me," Gray threw back. "Sorry. They caught me by surprise. I'll be looking for a stampede next time."

There wouldn't be a next time. Cass had thought that the other Feds would have Gray's back. That team of his had certainly disappointed Cass.

He didn't like disappointments.

"I held up my end of the deal," Gray told him.

Ah, right. "And you wonder if I did you the favor that you requested?" Cass inclined his head. "I am a man of my word." His word was law in his world. "Followed her ex. Might have tapped into his phone lines. Traced his calls. Did all my illegal due diligence."

Emerson tapped closer. "You traced Nathaniel's calls?"

Hell, yes, he had. "Want to guess who called the island and spilled all about you two not being a couple to Hannah?" Because, yeah, he'd been briefed on that bit already. But he *hadn't* been given the opportunity to share what he knew. Until now.

"That sonofabitch," Gray snarled.

"Good guess." Cass rocked back on his heels. "Nathaniel made the call, but considering he also made an early morning visit to have coffee with the senator and her always-present guard Owen, I'm pretty sure he was following their orders." He studied Emerson. As much of her as he could see with Gray in his way. "The senator doesn't like you playing FBI agent, Emerson. She was ready to blow up your world in order to get you back home."

"Emerson could have died when our covers were blown." Rage rumbled in Gray's voice.

"You almost did die." Emerson stepped to his side. Her hand curled around his arm. "I can't believe she did that. It's so—"

But Gray's head had turned toward Emerson. The two stared at each other. Long and intense and, yeah, Cass started to feel uncomfortable. Like he hadn't *already* been uncomfortable standing around in the FBI office. The place was hardly his cup of tea.

Then again, he didn't drink tea. He preferred whiskey.

"You can believe it," Gray said, voice soft. "You've been denying the truth for a long time. It's why you came to me. Time to shine a light in the dark, baby. But when the light hits, what you see isn't going to be pretty."

"Yeah." Cass scraped a hand over his jaw. "You two are talking in code, I'm feeling left out, and I'm damn pissed that I didn't get to kill anyone today. Time for me to make my exit before I wind up shoved in an interrogation room." But, one more thing first... "Thank you," he said, the words gruff.

Gray's head swung back toward him.

"I'll pay back what I owe." He always paid his debts.

"You already did. You kept tabs on her ex."

Nah. He owed his cousin more. Especially considering Gray could have gotten his spine crushed by those stampeding horses.

Hannah McIntyre would pay for the attack on Gray. Her accomplice would pay. The MC's reach was far. Deep. Gray had been right on that score. Gray had warned the woman what would be coming.

When the punishment hit, Hannah would only have herself to blame.

Cass sidestepped around Gray. Headed for the door. He slipped into the hallway, more than aware of a few stares slanting his way. But even the Feds weren't bold enough to actually approach him. They knew he was off-limits.

"You're Cass Striker."

He stilled.

He'd never even seen the woman coming. She thrust her hand toward him. "I'm Agnes Quinn."

He was not going to shake her hand. An MC leader did not shake hands with a Fed in an FBI office. That was like, Underworld Crime Management 101.

Her fingers wiggled. "Are you really as bad as they say?"

Now he had to smile. "Just wait and see."

Chapter Twenty-Three

"The past isn't pretty. It's twisted and bloody and, sometimes, you just might be better off leaving the secrets buried. Before you go digging up a grave, make sure you can handle the ghosts that you're going to wake up." – Gray Stone

"Emerson, you know it's going to be bad."

Emerson pulled in a deep breath. She tried to control the rage that made her fingers want to shake. She hadn't expected Cass's bombshell. No, dammit, she *had* expected it. Feared it. But actually getting confirmation… "We both could have died when she blew our cover." Her own mother, putting her in danger. Worse, *putting Gray in danger.* There were some sins that could never be forgiven.

"Technically, that prick ex of yours blew it." His eyes never left her face. "I already have an agent digging into his records because I figured he'd been the one to sell us out.

Thought he wanted to have the case blow up so he could try and replace you."

"Instead, he was just following orders. The way he's always done." Her mother said jump, and Nathaniel obeyed.

"I think he's been tied to the attacks on you."

She could not move. There were buttons on the wall near the observation mirror. *One, two, three—*

A light knock rapped against the observation room door. The door opened a second later, and Agnes popped her head inside. "They made contact, Agent Stone. Just like you said they would." Her lips pulled down. "Rylan was always a bit of a jerk, but I didn't know he was a traitor, too."

Gray advanced toward Agnes. "What did you learn?"

"Rylan just called Nathaniel Hadaway. They plan to meet outside of O'Sullivan's tonight. Honestly, it's not the smartest place to meet. I mean, come on, tons of cops and agents hang out there. If you're gonna have a clandestine meeting with someone, *be* more clandestine." She rolled her eyes.

"Does Rylan realize you're aware of the meeting?" Gray asked.

"I don't think so. I can be very sneaky when the occasion calls for it." A pause. "The occasion called for it."

"Thanks."

Emerson felt a heavy weight settle in her stomach. "Guessing we just found out which person at the FBI has been feeding intel to Nathaniel."

"And to your mother." Gray was grim. Pissed. "I already peeked into Rylan's bank records. Some large deposits were made recently. Deposits that traced back to one of her donor accounts."

Right. Of course. A donor account. Not her mother's *own* account. She would try to hide her paper trail.

"You want me to be your backup?" Agnes remained in the doorway. "Because I know you're planning to make that meeting tonight."

"Damn straight, I am. But I have other plans for backup."

"I want to help." Agnes lingered. "What can I do?"

"Get me the exact location for Senator Maxine Marlowe and Owen Porter."

Agnes bobbed her head. "Done." She bustled off down the hallway.

Emerson realized that she'd twisted her hands together. Slowly, she let them fall.

Gray eliminated the distance between them. His hand rose. Cupped her cheek. "Before this night is over, you'll get all the answers that you want. No more fear, Emerson. No more broken mirrors. No more always looking for a shadow to sweep out and attack you."

She swallowed. "You think Nathaniel has been stalking me."

"Don't you?"

The idea that a man she'd been involved with intimately might be tormenting her, playing sick games with her... "He's a psychiatrist. He's supposed to help people." Nathaniel? No, no. Emerson shook her head. "I've already *looked* into this. Into him. You think I didn't suspect Nathaniel, too? The way he steamrolled into my life? The way he wouldn't let go when I tried to break things off? But he *can't* be the one who first attacked me all of those years ago. When I was seventeen, he was studying in Oxford. He was an ocean away. There is no world in which he was the man who broke into my home back then."

"Maybe not then," Gray agreed. "But I sure as hell suspect the bastard *now*." His fingers slid down her cheek. Down her neck. Rested over the faint scar that marked her.

His touch was warm and strong and so careful, all at the same time.

"You said you loved me, Emerson."

Her chest ached. "I did. I do." She wasn't going to pretend or hold back. With Gray, she wanted to be all in. No hesitation and no fear. "But *you* haven't said—"

"I love you, Dr. Emerson Marlowe. I would fight like hell for you. Any day of the week."

Two days. *Two days* had passed since she'd watched Gray fall beneath the pounding hooves of horses. Two days since he'd fired his gun to save her. Two days since she'd told him that she loved him.

Two days of chaos. Of case work. Investigations. Getting transported back to Atlanta. Two days of not being alone with him. Of aching to just throw her arms around Gray and make certain he was safe. Alive. To be certain that they'd made it out and everything would be fine.

But things weren't fine, not yet.

"Cass wanted revenge." His gaze never left hers. "What do you want, Emerson? What do you want me to do for you?"

"I want to find out what really happened. When I was seventeen. Now. I want to find out what happened to my father when I was a kid." So many secrets. Way too much pain in her life. "And I want to bury that part of my life. I want it deep in the ground."

"You want me to kill for you." A nod. "Done."

"Wait, no!" She grabbed his shoulders. He'd way misunderstood. "No. No, I want the answers. I want *proof*. I need proof because I have to know that—" Emerson caught herself. Held the words back. But, thought...*screw it*. "I have to know that I'm not crazy. That I'm not slipping away in the darkness the same way that my father did."

His features softened. He bent his head, and his lips brushed over hers. "Sweetheart, I'm so sorry but..."

Why was he sorry?

"I don't think he ever went into the darkness at all."

Her brow furrowed. "Gray?" A fist seemed to squeeze her heart.

"But I'll get you the truth." Another soft kiss. "I'll get you any damn thing that you want in this world. Always. Know it. Believe it. Believe *me*."

* * *

"We shouldn't be meeting," Rylan Tate groused, as he glanced over his shoulder toward the busy road near the entrance of O'Sullivan's. He was huddled on the side street. The same street where a perp with a knife had once nearly attacked Emerson and Gray. "This is bullshit, and there is zero need for us to interact like this. You owe me money, but you could have sent it to me via an app like everyone else does, dumbass."

Nathaniel Hadaway stepped from the shadows. The sun had already set. Darkness slithered from the corners of the nearby buildings. "I need more information."

"I have nothing else to give you! Look, I know you said that if you took Emerson's place, I'd be the agent featured most in your new book, but I can't help you any longer." Rylan made a slashing motion with his right hand. "Can't. Won't. This shit ends now. I'm done with the sneaking around and the reporting, and I don't even care if the senator is involved or not. Gray Stone fucking scares me, and if he finds out that I've been feeding you information—"

"Spoiler alert, he's found out," Gray announced as he pushed away from the brick wall. He'd been there the whole time. Watching. Waiting. He'd arrived before Rylan. Before Nathaniel.

It had been easy to hide in the dark.

At his words, both men spun toward him.

"Oh, hell." Rylan's shoulders slumped. "I'm about to be demoted so hard."

"You're about to be in a world of pain." Gray smiled at him. He walked forward, his suit coat covering the gun he had holstered beneath his arm. "You sold me out because you thought you'd be the hero in his book? Seriously? That's why you did it? For five minutes of fame?"

"All I did was tell him a few details about what you and Emerson were investigating. Senator Marlowe asked me to do it. Personally ordered me to cooperate with him. Said he'd be taking over Emerson's spot." Rylan backed up a step. "The senator swore that if I didn't help her, then she'd make sure I never advanced in the FBI."

"Advancing is going to be highly problematic for you," Gray assured Rylan. *"Highly."* But he turned his attention to Emerson's ex. Nathaniel who had gone eerily still. "What was the plan?" Gray asked him. "Why lure Rylan here?"

"Lure?" Rylan repeated the word, turning a bit toward Nathaniel.

"Were you hoping to make *him* look guilty?" Gray asked, curious. "He already had deposits that could tie back to the senator in his bank account. Maybe you thought you could pin Emerson's attacks on him. Maybe you thought you could kill him and make yourself look like a hero. Bet that seemed like a fun storyline for your book, huh? Psychiatrist unmasks rogue FBI agent."

"Rogue agent?" Rylan seemed to be repeating a lot of things. He shook his head. *"Kill me?"*

But Nathaniel didn't speak. Just stood there, with his hands buried in the pockets of his oversize coat.

Gray pulled out his own weapon. He aimed it straight at Nathaniel. "It's over."

Nathaniel still didn't speak.

"Lift your hands out of your pockets. Put them in the air."

Rylan whipped out his own weapon. Pointed it at Nathaniel and then...then he pivoted and pointed the weapon right at Gray. Laughter poured from Rylan. "You really thought I was being led around by this prick?" More laughter. Coming harder. Faster.

Nathaniel kept his hands in his pockets.

"I knew you were watching me, Agent Stone. Always believing you were two steps ahead. Screw that. Nathaniel here, he didn't have the balls to take you out. Oh, he wanted to. I caught him stalking you and Emerson. Realized he was the prick who was in this very alley the first night you were making out with Emerson." Anger roughened his voice. "I wanted to fuck her, but you swept in. And the Man of Stone always gets what he wants."

"Not always," Gray returned as he shifted his gun to point at Rylan. "Drop your weapon. *Now.*"

Rylan didn't drop his weapon. "I told Nathaniel we could work together. He wanted to see what it was like to kill. He wanted it so badly I could practically see him drooling. But the guy has performance anxiety. So I told him, said...'I'll help you out.' And here I am, helping. Threw out just enough of a trail for you to find me. But you came alone, didn't you? Big, bad agent. I don't see Emerson. I don't see other agents. I damn well don't see your *Semper Fi buddies.* You're on your own. You're gonna die right here, on your—"

Gray fired. So did Rylan. Gray's bullet slammed into his target, ripping into Rylan's shoulder and sending the other man staggering back. As for Rylan's bullet, it found its mark, too.

It hit Gray in the chest. In his bulletproof vest. A good two inches to the side of his heart. It was like being pounded with a hammer, but it was a pain that Gray could easily handle. *I didn't aim for your heart, jerk, because you don't get to die and escape punishment. Your ass is getting locked away.* He shifted his weapon. Fired twice more. One shot to the hand that still clutched Rylan's weapon. Rylan screamed as blood flew, and the gun fell from his nerveless fingers. The next bullet Gray fired went into Rylan's knee. It took him down. No way would Rylan be getting away.

Then Gray shifted his weapon once more and locked its aim on Nathaniel.

Nathaniel's hands were still in his pockets. He looked over at Rylan. "I think," Nathaniel spoke softly, "that he's useless now." His head turned. He stared at Gray. "I wanted to kill you."

"Fair. I *want* to kill you, too." It took all of his will power not to pull that trigger.

Rylan was crying and moaning and being a general pain in the ass.

Nathaniel backed up. "I was going to stab you right here. I was so close that first night, and then I heard the roar of motorcycles."

And right then, as if on cue, the growl of motorcycles

When He Defends

vibrated in the night. A growl that grew stronger and stronger, and Nathaniel flinched.

Gray didn't move. "Did the roar sound just like that?"

Headlights flashed.

"Rylan was right," Gray allowed. A Rylan who still was moaning and bleeding all over the place. Gray marched toward him and shoved his foot over Rylan's left hand. The right hand was totally out of commission, but Gray wanted to make sure the prick didn't try to grab for the weapon Rylan had lost with his non-dominant hand. "My *Semper Fi buddies* aren't here tonight."

Motorcycles swept into that narrow street, right on the side of O'Sullivan's. Even more motorcycles than had been there the first time. The motorcycles circled them.

Nathaniel spun around, but there was nowhere for him to go. He was trapped.

"But who needs friends, when you have a whole army at your beck and call?" Gray could see Cass. And behind Cass, Emerson.

She had not been down with the plan to ride with Cass. Not at first. She'd wanted to be in that alley with Gray.

But he'd been afraid of the way Nathaniel might react to her.

Even now...

Nathaniel scuttled toward her like a rat.

"*She's not for you,*" Gray roared at him.

Nathaniel froze.

"You terrorized her. You tricked her. And you're going to pay for what you've done."

Nathaniel's fingers finally jerked out of his coat pocket. In his right hand, he gripped a knife. "I did what I was supposed to do! I followed orders! I did what I was told!" He weaved a bit. "Emerson, I-I did it at first so I could understand. Get in a predator's mindset. See what it was like to hunt...to stalk..."

She climbed off the motorcycle. So did Cass.

"You were afraid." Nathaniel raised the knife and pointed at her. "When we were together, your fear made you turn to me all the more. You needed me. And I didn't know how much I needed your fear. Not until you were gone."

So the sick fuck had kept terrorizing her. The headlights illuminated the scene perfectly. "*Who* told you to break her mirrors? To threaten her? Who gave you the orders?" Each question was snarled out. Gray wanted to attack, but Emerson needed her answers. Her proof.

Nathaniel looked down at the knife. "I wanted to see what it would feel like to kill."

"*Who gave you the orders?*"

"I'll be okay in prison," Nathaniel mused. "So many criminals. I can talk to them for hours and hours. Just think of all the books I can write."

Emerson surged forward. Cass grabbed her. Pulled her back.

"*Who gave you orders?*" Emerson yelled at him. "Who told you to screw with my life?"

His head lifted. He stared straight at her. Then his shoulders sagged. "I really wanted to see what it was like to kill." Nathaniel sighed as he looked away from Emerson. Focused on Gray. "And I wanted to kill you." Then he smiled and he—he ran at Gray. With the knife up. With a yell bursting from his lips.

Gray waited. He waited. And then...

He fired at the bastard's right kneecap. Just as he'd done with Rylan. And, just as with Rylan, Nathaniel went down with a howl. With his left hand, Gray ripped the knife from

Nathaniel's grip, and, in a blink, he spun the knife around to shove it against the SOB's throat. "We don't always get what we want."

Nathaniel screamed.

Gray let the knife cut deeper. That stopped the screams.

Emerson had noticed the giant pool of blood spreading beneath Rylan. He heard her heaving gasp. "Don't worry, sweetheart," Gray reassured her. "I didn't hit anything too vital. He's bleeding and moaning like a sonofabitch, but he'll survive." Not like he wanted her shoving her fingers in Rylan's wounds the way she'd done with Justin.

I'm damn good at taking out my targets. And Emerson was also good when it came to saving people. A talent she had.

Even as he was aware of the gang members spreading out near him, Gray's main focus remained on the piece of shit who'd tormented his Emerson.

"Who gave the order?" Gray asked him.

When he confessed, Nathaniel didn't scream. He whispered...

Chapter Twenty-Four

"Monsters can be everywhere. Sometimes, they can even be right in front of you. And you don't even see them because they're wearing the masks of loved ones. I think those might just be the worst monsters of all."
– *Emerson Marlowe*

"Hello, Mother."

"Emerson, darling!" Her mother came across the luxury suite on a quick glide. Effortless. Graceful. After all, she'd once been a prima ballerina. She air-kissed Emerson's right cheek. Then her left. "How wonderful to see you! I was planning to leave town tomorrow, heading up to D.C., and your timing is perfect." She beamed at Emerson even as she pulled her forward into the hotel suite. "You've come to your senses? Decided to leave this awful experiment behind?"

"Not exactly." She'd been standing in the open doorway of the presidential suite. Her mother's eager pull had taken her over the threshold and allowed Gray to move in behind her. "I didn't come alone."

Her mother immediately dropped her hold on Emerson. Her head jerked toward Gray. "*Agent Stone.*" An arctic greeting.

"Hello, Senator Marlowe. Mind if we have a moment of your time?" he drawled.

"I'm never too busy for my daughter." She sniffed. Turned away from the door. Motioned for them to follow her.

She was on the top floor of the ritzy hotel. A high-rise in downtown Atlanta. Gray had needed to flash his FBI credentials in order to get access to her secure floor. Emerson had gone to the door first once they actually arrived at the suite because she'd known her mother would look through the peephole before allowing anyone inside.

Emerson had understood that her mother would open the door for her. No hesitation.

"Where's Owen?" Emerson asked as they entered the glamorous sitting room. She'd expected him to be there, waiting.

"Oh, he's out taking care of some business. Running a few errands." A wave of her hand. Casual. Her fingers skimmed over her pearl necklace before Maxine sat on the plush, white couch. "What is this meeting about?" She patted the cushion next to her. "Emerson, sit."

She did not. Emerson remained standing. Her gaze swept the room. To the right, a white door was closed. The bedroom door? Slowly, her stare returned to her mother. "Nathaniel Hadaway was arrested tonight."

Surprise flashed on Maxine's face. Surprise and a hint of worry. "For what?"

"Breaking into my condo. Destroying property. Turns out, he's been stalking me for quite some time."

Maxine's hand covered her mouth. A brief expression of deliberate shock before her fingers dropped. "I am stunned. Horrified. Your own lover...?"

Yes, like that didn't make her stomach churn.

But her mother seemed to rally quickly as she noted, "Well, you did pick him. We all make mistakes with our partners." A telling glance at Gray and a bit too much emphasis on *partners*.

"Yes," Emerson agreed. "We do."

Gray was right at her side. "We know who ordered Nathaniel to terrorize Emerson."

"Ordered?" Maxine frowned.

"Nathaniel was on your payroll," Gray continued in a voice that seethed with tension and fury. "You funded his research. You wanted him to keep tabs on Emerson and report back to you. Just like you wanted Rylan Tate to tell you everything that's happening at the Bureau."

Maxine reached for her pearls. "Rylan? The name doesn't ring a bell."

"It should. Right before he was hauled away in an ambulance tonight, he was talking plenty about you and how you paid him to give every secret he could discover to *you*," Gray snapped.

Her hand fisted around the pearls. "What ambulance?"

"It was a big night," Emerson revealed. Big and exhausting, and it wasn't even close to being over. "Rylan was shot." Multiple times. "Nathaniel tried to attack Gray with a knife. Nathaniel confessed that he really enjoyed the stalking job he'd been hired to do on me..."

Maxine paled.

"And he liked it so much, in fact, that he was planning

to kill Gray. Then I suspect he would have killed me. He loved being immersed in the criminal world. Wanted to see what it was like to actually take a life."

"Emerson!" Maxine leapt to her feet. "I had no idea—*he planned to kill you?*" She seemed genuinely shocked. And her hand still fisted around the pearls.

"He was told how to terrify me." Emerson was surprised her voice came out so steady. "He was given the alarm code to my home—an alarm system that Owen installed. Nathaniel was told to break mirrors. To write messages. He was told my schedule, so he'd know when to follow me. Exactly where to go."

Maxine shook her head. "Emerson..."

"Nathaniel was intent on hurting me, but he *couldn't* have been the person who sliced my neck when I was seventeen. He wasn't even in the country back then. That attacker had to be someone else. And, the more I thought about it, I realized that Nathaniel couldn't have been the one who broke into my dorm in college. Or who terrorized me in med school. He was far away in those instances. Gray checked. We *double-checked*. Nathaniel is making my life hell now, but someone else had to do it before." Just saying the words hurt so much.

She'd been terrorized for so long.

Gray's arm brushed against her. She pulled in a breath. Steadied herself.

"Someone else had to do it before." Emerson was amazed that her voice came out so level. "Someone who wanted me to be afraid. Someone who wanted me controlled. Someone who wanted me always looking for threats. Being paranoid. Telling others that I was being hunted...*hunted*." She nodded. "That's what you told me that my father used to say, remember? That he felt *hunted*."

"Your father was a-a disturbed individual, Emerson. Deeply disturbed."

Her hands curled into fists. Her nails bit into her palms. "But what if he wasn't?"

Maxine's lips quivered. "What?"

"She said..." Gray's voice. Angry. *"What if he wasn't? What if someone was playing fucking mind games with him? Making her father believe he was seeing things that weren't there? Pushing him to the edge? Making his own family members doubt him? So that when he died, there wouldn't be so many questions. So that a murder could look just like a suicide."*

Maxine's hand jerked. The strand of pearls snapped. Some flew into the air. Some hit the floor. Rolled. Maxine shook her head. Over and over and over. "No, no, no. That's not what happened." Then her head whipped toward the door on the right. The closed, white door. The bedroom door. "Tell them!" Maxine's voice rose. *"Tell them that's not what happened!"*

Gray tensed, and from the corner of her eye, Emerson saw him pull out his gun.

The bedroom door opened. Slowly. Creaking.

Owen Porter stood there, clad in a white robe. Hair wet. Face grim. Sad. He stared straight at Maxine. "I'm sorry."

Maxine fell. Her knees seemed to give way, and she hit the floor.

Emerson and Gray had known that Owen was in the suite. After all, her mother's lover was always close.

"He was in the way." Owen remained in the open doorway. "You said a divorce wasn't possible back then, that it would cause a scandal if our affair was discovered. It was an easy way out for you. I planned it all perfectly."

This man had killed her father. "He never had schizophrenia, did he?"

Owen's head slowly angled toward her, like a snake, following prey. "You saw the files on him. Read reports from shrinks."

Yes, she'd read them. Over and over. Always, with terror in her heart. *What if I'm like him?* That fear had haunted her for so many years. And all along, Owen had known the truth. *I never needed to fear that fate.* But she had needed to fear the man pretending to be a protector for her and her mother. "With the right pressure, those files can be faked. I'm sure you knew how to apply the right pressure."

The lines on Owen's face deepened.

"You kept me afraid all of these years. You knew I feared turning out just like him...and you had someone terrorize me. You set the scene so I would question my own sanity." She shook her head. *"How many times? How many people?"*

"Emerson..."

Maxine began to cry.

"Your mother wanted you close," Owen explained with a voice that cracked. "I was just trying to—to *control* the situation."

Rage built inside of Emerson. Battling with her grief. "You wanted to control me."

Once more, Gray's arm brushed against her. "Who the fuck cut Emerson's throat when she was seventeen?"

A gasp escaped her mother. Her tear-streaked face turned to Emerson, then back to Owen.

"He's long dead," Owen assured them. "Some crazed protestor who wanted Maxine to change her vote in the senate. I eliminated him the day after the attack. No one will ever find his remains."

Nausea rolled inside of her. *All of these years...*Owen had pretended to care. To be—to be family. And he'd made her doubt her own sanity. Made her so afraid.

"Emerson..." Her mother's weak whisper. "I didn't know. *I didn't know!*"

Owen advanced. His attention was on the senator. "I love you," he told Maxine. "I did *all* of this for you. You wanted your husband gone. I made him go. You wanted your daughter close, so I kept her controlled. You wanted—"

"Hey, asshole!" Gray called out.

Owen jerked. His head snapped toward Gray.

"You don't control shit," Gray informed him. "Now put your fucking hands up because you're under arrest for murder. Multiple damn murders."

That was when the rest of the FBI agents swarmed. They rushed into the suite because Emerson and Gray had been wearing wires. They'd just caught every bit of the former SEAL's confession.

Owen was shoved to the floor. Cuffed.

Her mother kept crying. Begging Emerson to forgive her. Saying that she hadn't known. That she couldn't have known. And Emerson...

Owen looked up at her.

"Go to hell," she told him because that bastard had killed her father.

He would *pay*.

Chapter Twenty-Five

"There has to be more to the world than just monsters. I want that more. I'll fucking have more. I'll have Emerson."
— Gray Stone

She wasn't a ticking time bomb.

Or...maybe she was.

Her father's schizophrenia had been faked. He'd been tricked. Manipulated. Murdered. And all in the name of love.

Love wasn't supposed to make you into a monster. It wasn't supposed to twist you and make you kill people. It was supposed to make you a better person. Supposed to enrich you.

Except...

Love could be dark. Or maybe for some people, love brought out the darkness already in them.

Emerson knew darkness lived in her. So maybe there *was* a ticking time bomb inside of her, after all. Tick, tick, ticking, and one day, it would explode. One day, she might explode. One day—

"Darling, if you think any harder, I will literally hear your thoughts."

Her head swung to the right.

Gray had entered his office. She'd been waiting for him. After avoiding him for thirty-six hours straight, she'd forced herself to head to the FBI building. To stride right inside and march to his inner sanctum.

Only the office had been empty. Sort of anticlimactic. So she'd sat in the chair across from his desk. Waited.

And she'd been so deep in her thoughts that Emerson hadn't heard him glide into the room.

He offered her a half-smile. "Decided to stop running, did you?"

"I wasn't running, I—" Emerson heaved out a breath. "Avoiding. I was avoiding, not running."

He strolled around her and leaned his hip against the desk. His arms crossed over his chest as he stared down at her.

"I knew you had a lot of work to do, what with closing all the cases." Cases that had all centered around her. The mess of her life.

"Your mother held a press conference yesterday."

Emerson nodded. "Yes, I saw it. She's apologetic. She's the victim. She never saw the monster beneath Owen's mask."

"You don't sound like you believe any of that."

Her hands gripped the armrests of her chair. "My mother never believed me. No matter how many times I told her what was happening."

"I'm sorry."

"Why?" Her chin lifted. "You believed me. From the very first moment. You never doubted anything I told you."

"Of course, I didn't."

She shot out of the chair. Reached out for him. Stopped herself at the last minute. "Why not?"

"Because you're my partner."

"A partner you didn't want."

"Oh, Emerson, you know there is no one I want more in the entire world than you."

His words made her ache. "I brought so much danger to you."

"I don't mind danger. It keeps life interesting."

It did *not*. "Why didn't you ever doubt anything I said to you?"

He smiled at her. A soft smile. Not his megawatt, manipulative smile. "Want to hear a secret, Emerson?"

"I don't know." Blunt. Truthful. "I've heard a lot of secrets recently, and they have not been very good."

His right hand extended. Skimmed over her cheek. "This one is good. It's one of *my* secrets. I have a lot of secrets, you see. And I've decided, well, you're my partner, so you get to know all of them."

She exhaled. "How many secrets do you have?" *A lot* wasn't a specific number.

"Oh, tons." Breezy. "Like...did you know I was a member of the Night Strikers MC?"

"*What?*"

"Yep, that's why I didn't sweat the scene outside of O'Sullivan's. I knew that the Strikers were all around me. Not just the ones who came roaring up on the bikes, either. Others were hiding in the shadows of O'Sullivan's the whole time. Some were on the rooftops of nearby buildings. Cass had my six."

"How is an FBI agent also a former member of one of the most notorious motorcycle clubs out there?"

He winked. "Did I say that I 'was' a member? My bad. Probably should have said that I *am* a member."

Emerson felt her eyes widen.

"But that's really not the secret I wanted to share with you. The secret I wanted you to know, the reason I believed you from the beginning, it's because I loved you from the beginning."

She could feel every hard beat of her heart.

"I didn't want you as a partner at first because I knew I would cross lines with you. It was inevitable. I looked at you, I talked to you, and I fell for you. I knew I would always want for you to be far, far more than just an associate working cases with me. I would want you to be my whole world."

She swayed toward him. Caught herself. "What if…if I'd been wrong? About it all? What if I'd been…" Her words trailed away.

"Emerson." A shake of his head. "I could see the truth about you every single time I looked into your eyes. You weren't weak. You were battle scarred and soul strong. *That's* why I loved you. But I knew I couldn't rush you. You had to tell me your secrets in your own time and in your own way." A pause. "Just like I had to tell you mine."

"It's been thirty-six hours," she whispered. Yes, she'd counted every single hour that she'd been away from him. "You didn't…you didn't come rushing after me."

"No." A shake of his head. "Because I will never try to control you. Because I know when you need your time. Your space. I want you to choose me, Emerson. A partner not just here at the Bureau, but in life. All your days—I want you to choose to be with me."

"There is no one else I could ever want this much." Truth. "I love you, Gray. I want to be with you forever. You understand me like no one else ever could." He'd given her justice for her father. Stood by her. Protected her.

Loved her.

She loved him so much that it scared her.

"What do you say, sweetheart? Want to keep hunting monsters with me?"

Emerson nodded.

"Want to keep profiling, bringing those dark deeds into the light?"

Another nod.

"Want to stay with me always, marry me, maybe have us a daughter with your gorgeous eyes?"

"Yes." She couldn't stay away any longer. Emerson leapt at Gray. He caught her, wrapping his arms around her, and hauling her close. And it was there, in his arms, with his warmth around her, that Emerson finally realized the truth...

I am safe.

No ticking time bomb. No deadly whispers in her mind.

Gray was safety. Gray was her anchor. Gray was the man who'd fight the world for her.

He was everything she needed. There was no one she could want more.

He was her perfect partner.

Because she'd fight the world for him, too. She'd keep his secrets. She'd watch his back. She'd be a pain in the ass when he tried to get too arrogant with her, but...

She'd love him until she died. Love him and be happy with him, and Hannah McIntyre and all the other killers out there could just go screw off.

Because sometimes, love was real. Sometimes, people

did get happy endings. Endings that you bled for, that you fought for, and that you won.

A love that you treasured more than anything else. A love that—

"We are *not* honeymooning at Sea Island," Gray told her, his lips right above her own.

She laughed. For the first time in thirty-six hours, the heavy weight that Emerson had carried lifted. She could breathe again. She could be free of the past. She could focus on her present. Her future. The life that waited. And they would definitely not, one hundred percent *not* be honeymooning with the stampeding horses. "Let's go somewhere cold," she decided. "Let's get a tiny cabin in the woods, be naked in front of a fireplace for days, and let's lock out the rest of the world."

"Done."

She laughed again.

I love this man so much.

The perfect partner.

Her partner. Always.

Epilogue

*"Do I have a dark side? Yes. You have no idea how dark. But mess with my Emerson, and
you'll find out."*
– Gray Stone

GRAY OPENED THE CELL DOOR. HE MARCHED INSIDE, grabbed the prisoner from the bed, and threw the bastard up against the bars.

Nathaniel Hadaway cried out, his whole body shaking, and damn if the little asshole didn't piss himself.

Gray shoved him away in disgust. "I can see prison life is treating you well."

Nathaniel collapsed on the floor. "Get me out! Get me out! I can't stay here—the other inmates terrify me! *Please, get me out! I have to get out! Please!*"

"You were stalking Emerson. *My* Emerson. And you wanted to kill me. Bastard, you will never see the light of day again. Just got orders, you're being transferred to maximum security. Hope you enjoy the ride." Then, hands fisted, he turned away.

"No, *please!* Don't—"

He exited the cell. The door clanged shut. Gray didn't look back. Rage had been riding him hard all day, and he'd needed to make sure certain loose ends were tied up.

Nathaniel Hadaway was finally being transferred. The shrink had already been targeted by gang members. He was going to be meeting a world of pain at his new home in max security.

As for Rylan, the FBI agent had recovered from his gunshot wound, he'd pled guilty to the charges against him, and, oh, yes, he was certainly going to have to watch his back for the next twenty years in prison. Former Feds never fared well in general pop.

Gray marched down the narrow hallway. No guards appeared, per his commands. He'd ordered the place emptied out. The better for him to hunt. He turned to the right. Stopped in surprise.

Cass was waiting. Blocking his damn path.

Gray frowned at him. "What in the hell are you doing here?"

"You know I have connections." Cass quirked a brow. "And forget the fake outrage at seeing me. I should be the one who is pissed. I mean, come on. I don't get to have fun, but you do? That hardly seems fair."

"Who said life was fair?" He sidestepped.

Cass moved with him. "You going to terrorize Owen Porter? That the next stop on this exciting, post-midnight tour that you have going on?"

Hell, yes, he was paying a visit to Owen Porter. "Just want to make sure that he and I understand each other."

When He Defends

"Uh, the guy is going to get life without parole. He'll die in prison. I think he understands plenty."

Not yet, he didn't. *"He made Emerson afraid for years."*

"And if she finds out that you're sneaking into prisons, twisting the law and maybe killing people, what will that do?"

Gray's breath sawed out. He wasn't going to *kill* Owen Porter. Just make the guy wish for death. Those were two totally different things.

Tap, tap, tap.

Both men turned around at the faint sound. *No, no, it can't be—*

But it was.

Emerson walked down the corridor with her heels tapping.

"I'm back from my honeymoon for one month. *One month.* And my husband is already taking up new hobbies." She sighed. "Are you bored with me already?"

"I could live a thousand years and never be bored with you." He turned to fully face her. Of course, she'd realized what he'd planned. Even though he'd tried to be so very careful. Arranging for the prisoners to temporarily be in the same facility, making sure he'd have access to them, pulling all the strings, getting the security cameras turned off...

Tap, tap, tap.

Emerson stopped in front of him. "You don't have to hurt them for me."

He was hurting them for *him.* Because he hated what those bastards had done to her. Because the beast inside called for vengeance. Sometimes, he was far too much like Cass. *Eye for an eye. Pain for pain.*

"We have a life waiting. The darkness doesn't get to drag us down." She caught his hand. Pressed it to her stomach. "The baby wants us to leave these particular monsters alone. They have their punishments coming. We won't have to do anything else."

The baby?

She smiled at him.

Cass whistled.

The prison was too dark. The sins there too great.

"We started trying before the honeymoon. Told you, it wouldn't take long." She smiled at him.

Of course, he'd been trying for a baby before the honeymoon. As soon as Emerson had suggested they ditch the condoms, he'd been game on. In her bare? Making her pregnant? Having a little Emerson 2.0?

That's what I want. That's my future.

She was telling him that future lived beneath his hand. Their future.

The baby can't be here. Not in this darkness. He nodded. Pulled Emerson close. Held her.

Cass slapped him on the shoulder. "Get the hell out of here. Go celebrate."

The baby.

"I'll have fun for us both," Cass added.

Gray slowly turned his head toward his cousin.

Cass winked at him. "I got this. Let someone else do the dirty work for you."

No, Cass shouldn't be there, either. Cass...

Cass was already too close to the dark.

"The baby's godfather needs to haul his ass out of here with us," Emerson instructed in a tone that brooked no argument. "You two have to set positive examples. You can't be terrorizing criminals. It's just not done."

But, wasn't it done? Especially when they deserved some terror?

When He Defends

She pulled away. Turned. *Tap, tap, tap.* "Leave them." Emerson's voice drifted back to Gray and Cass. "They are in their own hell."

"Great," Cass groused. "Now your wife isn't letting *me* have any fun."

Gray smiled at him. "I'm going to be a dad."

Cass glowered and then he grinned, too. "You're gonna be an awesome dad."

Gray threw an arm around Cass's shoulders. "You're gonna be an awesome uncle."

His grin slipped. "I'm...your cousin, not your—"

"Awesome uncle." Gray tightened his grip on Cass's shoulders. "Now start reforming your ass so my baby girl can be proud of you."

"Uh, you don't even know that you're having a baby girl."

True. And it really didn't matter what he had. He was just delighted by the idea of Emerson's *baby*. His and Emerson's *baby*.

He had to call his friends. They'd all been at the wedding, and he knew they'd be thrilled with this news. *Tyler, Ronan, and Kane are going to flip.*

His Semper Fi buddies would celebrate hard with him.

He walked out of that prison, with Cass at his side, with Emerson and his baby in front of him, and Gray knew that...

This is what a dream feels like.

He'd had plenty of nightmares in his time. He'd *been* a nightmare to plenty of people. But finally, there was more out there. More for him.

Joy. Hope.

Emerson glanced over her shoulder.

His partner.

His wife.

His life.

He'd protect her with every breath in his body. Always.

THE END

Know what I really love? Cold case solving...and a bit of Christmas fun at the same time.

She's coming home for the holidays...and there's gonna be hell to pay.

Last Christmas, Melody Mage vanished without a trace. The wealthy socialite was presumed dead by her loved ones. But on the anniversary of her disappearance, Melody appears on the doorstep of her family's estate. Her memories are fractured, her past shrouded in fog and confusion, but she knows one thing—someone attacked her. Left her for dead. She just has to figure out *who* the guilty culprit is. Then she'll make the person pay.

In other words, Melody has to solve her own cold case mystery. And she's going to do it—no matter what it takes. No matter how many skeletons she has to drag out of her wealthy family's closet. And no one will get in her way. Not even her father's intense—and dangerously attractive—protégé, Victor Alexander. Victor has just taken over as the company's new CEO. He's driven, powerful, and he stares at her with eyes that glitter with far too much...longing?

He ripped apart the world looking for her, and the love of his life just casually knocked on the front door.

Except Melody doesn't know that Victor had his heart carved out of his chest when she vanished. Their relationship had been secret. On the outside, he and Melody had appeared to barely tolerate each other. In private, they'd touched—and ignited. She'd been his obsession. He'd been her personal attack dog. Now she's back, saying she's looking for justice, and he's going to give it to her. He will give her *anything*. Unfortunately, Melody has no idea that she once promised to love him forever—or that when she vanished, she was wearing the engagement ring he'd given to her.

He never stopped loving her. Too bad she believes he's the enemy.

Up Next From Cynthia

Victor has been working with the Ice Breakers, a cold-case solving crew, and he suspects that Melody's attacker is someone in the family's inner circle. He also knows that there is no way on earth he will ever let Melody vanish again. He'll protect her, he'll win her heart once more, and he will see to it that the person who hurt *his* Melody is buried in an icy grave before the new year dawns.

Author's Note: It's Christmas *and* cold-case solving time...only for this book, the heroine is the case. Melody can't fully remember her past. She doesn't know if she can trust Victor—or if he might just be a villain she should fear. No worries on that score. While Victor may have a dark side, he's only a villain to the rest of the world. Never to her. Let's deck the halls, solve a cold case, and fall in love this ICE COLD CHRISTMAS.

Author's Note

Thank you so much for reading Gray's book! I had been wanting to write a story for Gray ever since he first slipped onto the page in WHEN HE PROTECTS. The challenge was coming up with a heroine who would match him. I hope that you thought Emerson was the right match for Gray—and I very much hope that you enjoyed their romance.

It has been an absolute delight to write the Protector & Defender books...and I have another one coming your way soon! There is no way I could leave Cass out in the cold. He'll have his story told in WHEN HE GUARDS.

Thank you, again. I've been addicted to romance books ever since I picked up my first Harlequin years and years ago. I love reading romances, and writing them is truly a dream come true for me.

If you have time, please consider leaving a review for WHEN HE DEFENDS. Reviews help readers to discover

Author's Note

new books—and authors are definitely grateful for them! (Believe me—we are super, super grateful!)

If you'd like to stay updated on my releases and sales, please join <u>my newsletter list</u>. Did I mention that when you sign up, you get a FREE Cynthia Eden book? Because you do!

By the way, I'm also active on social media. You can find me chatting away on <u>Instagram</u> and <u>Facebook</u>.

Until next time…may your life be filled with happy days and may your books be filled with happy endings.

Best,

Cynthia Eden

<u>cynthiaeden.com</u>

More Books By Cynthia Eden

Protector & Defender Romance
- When He Protects
- When He Hunts
- When He Fights

Ice Breaker Cold Case Romance
- Frozen In Ice (Book 1)
- Falling For The Ice Queen (Book 2)
- Ice Cold Saint (Book 3)
- Touched By Ice (Book 4)
- Trapped In Ice (Book 5)
- Forged From Ice (Book 6)
- Buried Under Ice (Book 7)
- Ice Cold Kiss (Book 8)
- Locked In Ice (Book 9)
- Savage Ice (Book 10)
- Brutal Ice (Book 11)
- Cruel Ice (Book 12)
- Forbidden Ice (Book 13)
- Ice Cold Liar (Book 14)

Wilde Ways
- Protecting Piper (Book 1)
- Guarding Gwen (Book 2)
- Before Ben (Book 3)
- The Heart You Break (Book 4)
- Fighting For Her (Book 5)
- Ghost Of A Chance (Book 6)
- Crossing The Line (Book 7)
- Counting On Cole (Book 8)
- Chase After Me (Book 9)
- Say I Do (Book 10)
- Roman Will Fall (Book 11)
- The One Who Got Away (Book 12)
- Pretend You Want Me (Book 13)
- Cross My Heart (Book 14)
- The Bodyguard Next Door (Book 15)
- Ex Marks The Perfect Spot (Book 16)
- The Thief Who Loved Me (Book 17)

The Fallen Series
- Angel Of Darkness (Book 1)
- Angel Betrayed (Book 2)
- Angel In Chains (Book 3)
- Avenging Angel (Book 4)

Wilde Ways: Gone Rogue
- How To Protect A Princess (Book 1)
- How To Heal A Heartbreak (Book 2)
- How To Con A Crime Boss (Book 3)

Night Watch Paranormal Romance
- Hunt Me Down (Book 1)
- Slay My Name (Book 2)

- Face Your Demon (Book 3)

Trouble For Hire
- No Escape From War (Book 1)
- Don't Play With Odin (Book 2)
- Jinx, You're It (Book 3)
- Remember Ramsey (Book 4)

Death and Moonlight Mystery
- Step Into My Web (Book 1)
- Save Me From The Dark (Book 2)

Phoenix Fury
- Hot Enough To Burn (Book 1)
- Slow Burn (Book 2)
- Burn It Down (Book 3)

Dark Sins
- Don't Trust A Killer (Book 1)
- Don't Love A Liar (Book 2)

Lazarus Rising
- Never Let Go (Book One)
- Keep Me Close (Book Two)
- Stay With Me (Book Three)
- Run To Me (Book Four)
- Lie Close To Me (Book Five)
- Hold On Tight (Book Six)

Bad Things
- The Devil In Disguise (Book 1)
- On The Prowl (Book 2)
- Undead Or Alive (Book 3)

- Broken Angel (Book 4)
- Heart Of Stone (Book 5)
- Tempted By Fate (Book 6)
- Wicked And Wild (Book 7)
- Saint Or Sinner (Book 8)

Bite Series
- Forbidden Bite (Bite Book 1)
- Mating Bite (Bite Book 2)

Blood and Moonlight Series
- Bite The Dust (Book 1)
- Better Off Undead (Book 2)
- Bitter Blood (Book 3)

Mine Series
- Mine To Take (Book 1)
- Mine To Keep (Book 2)
- Mine To Hold (Book 3)
- Mine To Crave (Book 4)
- Mine To Have (Book 5)
- Mine To Protect (Book 6)

Dark Obsession Series
- Watch Me (Book 1)
- Want Me (Book 2)
- Need Me (Book 3)
- Beware Of Me (Book 4)

Purgatory Series
- The Wolf Within (Book 1)
- Marked By The Vampire (Book 2)
- Charming The Beast (Book 3)

- Deal with the Devil (Book 4)

Bound Series
- Bound By Blood (Book 1)
- Bound In Darkness (Book 2)
- Bound In Sin (Book 3)
- Bound By The Night (Book 4)
- Bound in Death (Book 5)

Stand-Alone Romantic Suspense
- Waiting For Christmas
- Monster Without Mercy
- Kiss Me This Christmas
- It's A Wonderful Werewolf
- Never Cry Werewolf
- Immortal Danger
- Deck The Halls
- Come Back To Me
- Put A Spell On Me
- Never Gonna Happen
- One Hot Holiday
- Slay All Day
- Midnight Bite
- Secret Admirer
- Christmas With A Spy
- Femme Fatale
- Until Death
- Sinful Secrets
- First Taste of Darkness
- A Vampire's Christmas Carol

About the Author

Cynthia Eden loves romance books, chocolate, and going on semi-lazy adventures. She is a *New York Times*, *USA Today*, *Digital Book World*, and *IndieReader* best-seller. She writes romantic suspense, paranormal romance, and fun contemporary novels. You can find out more about her work at www.cynthiaeden.com.

If you want to stay updated on her new releases and books deals, be sure to join her newsletter group: cynthiaeden.com/newsletter. When new readers sign up for her newsletter, they are automatically given a free Cynthia Eden ebook.

Made in United States
North Haven, CT
21 September 2025

73121234R00183